DOTMEME

Also by Mike A. Lancaster

Human.4
The Future We Left Behind
dotwav

DOTMEME

MIKE A.LANCASTER

SKY PONY PRESS
NEW YORK

First Edition

This is a work of fiction. Names, characters, places, and incidents are from the authors' imaginations, and used fictitiously.

Sky Pony Press books may be purchased in bulk at special discounts for sales promotion, corporate gifts, fund-raising, or educational purposes. Special editions can also be created to specifications. For details, contact the Special Sales Department, Sky Pony Press, 307 West 36th Street, 11th Floor, New York, NY 10018 or info@ skyhorsepublishing.com.

Sky Pony® is a registered trademark of Skyhorse Publishing, Inc.®, a Delaware corporation.

Visit our website at www.skyponypress.com.

www.themindfeather.com

10 9 8 7 6 5 4 3 2 1

Library of Congress Cataloging-in-Publication Data available upon file.

Cover photo: iStockphoto
Cover design by Sammy Yuen

Hardcover ISBN: 978-1-5107-0807-5
Ebook ISBN: 978-1-5107-0808-2

Printed in the United States of America

Interior design by Joshua Barnaby

This one is for the resistance:
the people who refuse to let greed, bigotry, and hatred
overwrite their common human decency.

Contents

You want to get a look at the true soul of humanity?
Look at what it does on the Internet when it thinks no one is
watching, or it thinks that the only ones watching are its ap-
proving peers. Watch the time it wastes, the flame wars it starts,
the bullying it engages in, the gossip it spreads, the lies it tells.

95% of the world's data was created in the last two years.
Ask yourself: How much of it do you think is worth the
memory space it takes up?

Then despair.

R.K.O. Dubrovna
The Internet You Deserve

no2sjws

evolution is past STUPID. things ca'nt just appear out of chaos

Theresa Madoff-Wood
+ no2sjws

Things not only can, but they DO just appear out of chaos. It's called *emergence*. Put enough energy into small systems, give them enough time, and complexity emerges. Larger systems—which often seem impossible to account for without ascribing them to miracles—are really just products of information, energy and lots and lots of time.

no2sjws
+Theresa Madoff-Wood

ha ha ha ha ha I put energy into my horse two years ago and it just became a unicorn

YouTube Comments

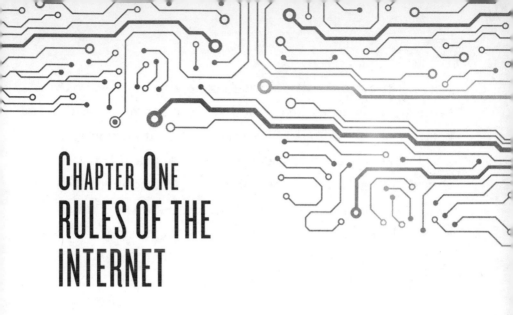

Chapter One
RULES OF THE
INTERNET

When the kid with the Nike cap and wispy sideburns took his seat in front of the computer, he had no way of knowing that he was completing a complex circuit that had been a full five weeks in the making. Although he often posted about conspiracy theories on message boards and comments sections—from the Illuminati plan for a *new world order*, to mind controlling chemicals in airplane contrails—as far as he was concerned, today he was just having a bad day.

Sure, his laptop had gone down in spectacular—and, indeed, fatal—fashion; and his parent's broadband, which had been getting flaky for a while now, had decided to crash and burn, meaning he couldn't even use his dad's computer. But he hadn't seen the pattern that was hidden beneath recent events, just as he hadn't seen the reason behind that pattern, or the people responsible for making it a reality.

So he was oblivious to the fact that it had been five

3

weeks, almost to the day, since a single, careless keystroke had leaked his unmasked IP address to a computer terminal in London, leading to his immediate identification.

Or that he had been under four weeks of near-constant surveillance from members of the Youth Enforcement Task Initiative, a secret branch of law enforcement that recruited and used teenage operatives to carry out its missions.

He certainly wouldn't have believed that it was three weeks since a section of YETI moved to the West Country, took up the lease on an abandoned shop on Yeovil's South Street, and opened up its own cyber cafe a few hundred meters from the kid's house, purely with the intention of luring him inside.

Nor had he noticed the two weeks of careful social engineering and manipulation that had not only made him aware of that cyber cafe, but had worked to associate it in his mind with the keywords *discretion* and *safety*.

The week YETI had spent remotely mucking with the kid's computer and home network to loosen his trust and faith in both computer and network had been discounted as a string of bad luck, nothing more.

The hour since a remote logic board burnout turned his laptop into an expensive paperweight had not been a continuation of that "bad luck," as he thought, but rather the final part of the plan.

Everything had been leading to this precise moment.

The moment the trap was finally sprung.

The moment his addiction to online hijinks led him to the new cybercafé on the high street. The one that—for reasons he would never be able to parse—felt safe enough for him to engage in some digital mischief.

Ani Lee was already in position—the digital spider at the heart of this very special corner of the web—three screens down and running software that would make Sideburns think he'd woken up in a science fiction movie if he got even a sniff of its code. Hell, it made Ani feel that way, too, and she'd been using it for months.

She watched as the target took off his cap and suppressed the urge to roll her eyes when he linked his fingers together and cracked his knuckles before lowering his hands down to the keyboard like a maestro sitting down at the piano.

The kid's name was Eddie Wells, and he was seventeen years old.

He certainly wasn't a maestro.

If truth were told, he barely knew his scales.

To his school friends, he was generally quiet and unremarkable—monosyllabic mostly. His teachers thought he was treading water, capable of doing better in pretty much all his subjects, just too lazy, or disinterested to bother.

Online, however, he was far from quiet. With a list of aliases including *chimpotle*, *e-boy*, *sux2bu* and *c@fish*, Eddie missed few opportunities to troll, abuse, insult, and punk. Of course, there was no law against being obnoxious online, but he didn't stop there. As part of the online group *victorious*—activists and hactivists from one of the dark hive minds that thrived on the Internet—he was responsible for acts of mischief and mayhem that had quickly attracted YETI's attention.

He was also the first *victorious* member they'd managed to put a meatspace name to.

Eddie took a thumb drive from his pocket and slid it into the computer's USB port.

Showtime, Ani thought. *Let's see what you've got.*

She opened up the window that mirrored Eddie's screen and watched as he pulled a browser off the thumb drive and opened it up. It was a custom job, set to a home page that was a *victorious* message board called dot2me. Bookmarks for warez sites and pirate torrent sites sat on his menu bar, mute testament to Eddie's browsing habits. As good as a written confession if it fell into the wrong hands, at least offering probable cause to give his whole computer a good going over.

Ani had been logging on to dot2me often enough to know that ninety-something percent of the site was a waste of bandwidth and time: terabytes of offensive images and movies; bad Photoshopping; juvenile jokes, stories and fantasies; memes and absurdities; all mixed up with a whole heap of tedious profanity.

Eddie clicked through a few threads with the listless casualness of someone with a limited attention span. He made sure to stay away from threads labeled NSFW, and that seemed to limit his browsing options. To just about zero. He frowned, closed the browser, took what he thought was an innocent look around the cafe, then went back to the thumb drive and opened up another program.

Ani was underwhelmed with the software. Although it was a custom implementation of the ForceCrack password cracking utility, it was one that had been floating around the net for months, and was hardly state-of-the-art. Eddie got ForceCrack monitoring the traffic in the room over Wi-Fi, then started pulling data from the other users in the area, looking for something he could mess with, steal from, or exploit. Just another kid looking for mischief, given bigger scope for said mischief by his software's knowledge of Wi-Fi protocols.

"Looking for trouble? Here's something I made earlier," Ani muttered to herself, as she pulled up another window and set her own skills loose.

She started up by brute-forcing her way into an ad hoc network that YETI had set up to look like the back end of the biotech company, Instanto, whose genetically modified crop agenda was back in the news after cross-contamination from an experimental site had spread to fields in the USA that were supposed to be safe from such accidents.

Which was just the kind of target that would get Eddie excited, based on some of his recent posts and boasts. He was one part bored teen, searching for trending videos and giggles; two parts malicious troll, flaming anyone who disagreed with his poorly formed opinions and—when it suited him—one part S.J.W.: social justice warrior.

Ani checked on Eddie's screen to make sure he was keeping up. Sure enough, he'd turned his attention to her tantalizingly encrypted data. She got her own software to fight him off, just not too well, leaving him some gaps to slither through, which he'd peg as good luck or great skills depending on the composition of his ego.

Ani made the whole process look legit, and YETI's fake Instanto network did its part, appearing to rebuff her digital advances, and allowing her to show off madder and madder skills. With one eye on Eddie's computer screen, she saw the precise moment when he noticed what she was up to. He suddenly ignored everything else in the room and focused in on her activity.

She let him watch the ease with which she cut through layer after layer of—albeit compliant—security, and she ended up in a convincing simulation of an executive's mailbox.

When she thought he'd seen enough to whet his curiosity, she triggered an alert, shut down all her activity, acted panicked, grabbed all her stuff, and headed for the door.

She got ten yards down the road before she felt the tap on her shoulder.

Hook, line, and sinker, she thought before turning around.

<*))))><

"I saw what you did." Eddie Wells said with an air of vain arrogance that he really hadn't earned. The only thing he'd achieved, in truth, was walking into a baited trap—and that was what a lot of mice got broken necks for. And it had been a trap devised and baited by Ani, who was still only fifteen years old (if only for a few more weeks), two whole years younger than he was.

Still, Ani had to make him think he had the upper hand. And the only way that was going to happen was through the employment of skill that intelligence field operatives the world overused every day of their lives: acting. She made her face look as shocked as she could.

"I-I don't know what you're talking about," she said, weakly, turning to leave.

They were standing on the pavement outside a Chinese restaurant and were the only people on the street as far as Ani could see. Which just went to show how good YETI's surveillance was; she *knew* it was there, and *still* couldn't see it.

"It's okay." Eddie said. "I'm not a nark."

Nark? Ani thought. *Someone needs to watch less TV.*

"I'm not the police, either," Eddie felt the need to add.

Well, duh, Ani thought, but what she said was, "Then why were you watching me back there?"

"Curiosity, I guess. But that was some righteous skillage."

Skillage? Really?

"I'm sorry, but you're mistaking me for someone else. Look, I'm going to just go . . ."

"Wait up. I'm serious about your skills. Don't see many people like you in this town . . ."

"I'm not *from* here," Ani said. "My parents brought me here. They call it a holiday, but it's more like a punishment. Don't like it. Not staying. So I'm not going to be around to join your Secret Squirrel club, or whatever. Nice meeting you, though. Except it wasn't."

Eddie laughed.

"Instanto?" He said, incredulously.

Ani feigned surprise.

"You saw that?" she asked. "I knew someone was trying to spy on what I was doing, but I had no idea . . ."

Eddie puffed up with some weird kind of personal pride. Pride for something that YETI had drawn him into, and that Ani had pretty much spoon-fed to him. She'd even added the word *spy* to her sentence to fake-flatter him more. Sometimes, she despaired about the human race. People rarely painted self-portraits when they described themselves—even when they were describing themselves *to* themselves—and whoever Eddie Wells saw when he looked in the mirror, Ani bet it wasn't the clumsy e-clown who, if YETI played its cards right, was going to bring down the collection of hackers, activists, and digital pranksters that called themselves *victorious*.

<*))))><

"Have you heard of *'victorious'*?" Abernathy had asked her, five weeks before.

They were in the briefing room at YETI HQ. Ani had been called in from a combat training day on very short notice, which seemed to suggest some urgency, although it had taken Abernathy eight minutes of small talk to reach the question: How she was settling in, finding the training, liking the salary package, enjoying the London life?

Then, when he'd run out of those kind of questions, he'd asked her about *victorious*.

"Are things so quiet around here that you're watching old reruns on Nickelodeon?" Ani asked back. "Because that way lies madness. Believe me, I know."

"Nickel-what?" Abernathy muttered.

"The cable channel?" She received a blank look from Abernathy. "*Victorious* was a sitcom. For tweens. With music . . ." Another blank look. "Then you must mean *victorious*, the hactivists, a new group with random targets, sort of like *anonymous*, but with longer attention spans."

Abernathy knitted his brows together in what was either thought or a frown. Ani still couldn't read the guy. She guessed that was sort of the point.

"*victorious* has been on our radar for a few months," he said. "But then groups of hackers teaming up for coopera-tive mayhem tend to have that effect on us. I don't know if you've been following their exploits . . . Except, silly me, I do know, because that's the business I'm in . . . So perhaps you can give me your observations before I waste my breath explaining things you already know."

He settled back in his seat and watched her.

Expectantly.

Ani nodded.

"Just as the 4chan image board gave birth to *anonymous*, *victorious* leapt from another Internet hive mind: this time called dot2me. dot2me was always seen as an inferior copy of chan, with less emphasis put on grotesque and offensive content, and more on memes and bad Photoshop. So, with a lot less nudey pictures and bad language, 2me was seen as a lot less cool than 4chan, but lately it has gained some web cred by spawning its own cyber-activism arm, modeled on *anonymous*. It appears to be by invitation only, the mischief arm of 2me, and I can't figure out how to get an invite.

"One thing, though: they're getting bolder, more auda-cious, with every exploit. They started off by hacking into, and then exposing, some of the big charities for the donations they're wasting on salaries and SUVs, and not putting into the hands of those who need the money. Then they started obtaining and leaking confidential data from big companies, bringing some of their darker secrets into the light. Word is that they've been working on world government systems recently, trying to destabilize entire countries with secrets that the individual governments would prefer stayed secret.

"Web chatter says that they're gearing up for something big, but chatter on the Internet is as likely to be as wrong as it is to be accurate."

"Every fifth or sixth word of that made sense to me," Abernathy said, "But it pretty much matches the answer I have on the card, so would you like to gamble for tonight's grand prize?"

"Oh gosh, dare I?" Ani said. "Well, I came here with nothing. . . . I'll gamble."

"Excellent. And here is the big money question: Which fledgling member of YETI is going to be helping infiltrate *victorious* with a view to discovering just what lies behind their seemingly random reign of digital terror?"

Ani feigned the excitement of a game show contestant, hand up in the air and shifting from foot to foot as if she needed to visit the toilet: "Oh me! Pick me! Please, pick me!"

"And tonight's lucky winner is: Ani Lee." Abernathy said, grinning in spite of himself.

"I never win the bloody holiday." Ani said, gloomily.

"Not so fast, there." Abernathy said. "There is a holiday that comes along with this prize. Think of a romantic location."

"Rome? Venice? No, Paris."

"Close." Abernathy said. "Try Yeovil."

"Where?" Ani asked.

Abernathy's grin told her everything she needed to know.

<*))))><

They grabbed a coffee in Starbucks and stared at each other over the table, somewhat awkwardly. Of course the awkwardness was, she guessed, pretty much a constant feature of Eddie's life; hers, on the other hand, was carefully cultivated. Again with the acting.

Since joining YETI, and moving to London from Cambridge, she'd found most of her teenage awkwardness had pretty much disappeared. Being a handpicked member of a teen spy ring had that effect on a person. Lodging with Gretchen—who was, quite simply, the coolest, cleverest person that she had ever met—and finding herself treated and listened to as an equal, had sanded off the last few corners of her self-consciousness.

It had been the kind of self-consciousness that Eddie was twitchy with now. It was as if his heart were pumping it around his blood stream.

He'd make a terrible operative. He was far too jumpy. His demeanor pretty much screamed, "I HAVE SOMETHING TO HIDE!" In the privacy of their bedrooms, at the launch pad of their laptops, these kinds of misfits saw themselves as kings of all they surveyed. In life, they tended toward socially dysfunctional.

"I have a boyfriend," Ani said. "I mean, I'm flattered and everything . . ."

It was a nice, awkward opener for a conversation that had stalled as soon as they'd sat down. It made her seem naïve, but also put the idea of her as a *girl* rather than just a *hacker* front and center in his mind. It also put him slightly on the defensive, which was always handy.

"Oh," he said, following it up with a swift trip around the more common sounds of hesitation. "Um. Well. Er."

Ani waited. Sense would issue from that mouth at some point, she was sure of it.

"Look," he said, "I think you've got the wrong idea. I'm not interested in you that way . . ."

Wickedly, and for no other reason than the sheer heck of it, Ani pretended to be insulted. She frowned, narrowed her eyes, looked downward—and thus, downcast—as if his dismissal had wounded her.

"I-I mean, of course I'm . . ." Eddie's attempt at freeing himself from his tangled feelings tailed off, presumably to prevent causing more offense than he already hadn't.

Eddie tried again. "I, er, belong to a group."

Of all the ways she'd been expecting to get him to reveal *that*, pretending to be slighted hadn't even been on the list. Perhaps she was even better at this than she thought. Or Eddie was just lousy at keeping his mouth shut.

She looked up again, but still played dumb. "I don't have much time for music," she said. "Would I have heard of you?"

Eddie laughed. "Not that kind of group. Have you heard of *victorious*?"

Ani did a measured double take.

"The hacking group?" she asked, making sure her tone contained enough awe and surprise to sell it. "Freedom fighters of the information superhighway. What about them?"

"*Them* is a dataset that contains *me*," he said. "And judging by your skills, it could include you, too."

"Me?"

"Don't be modest. You killed it back there. You were in an Instanto email server. Goodness only knows what havoc you'd have caused if I'd have left you to it."

Ani looked coy.

"I can get into places," she said. "I just never know what to do when I *am* in."

"We can help you with that."

"You can? But I'm going back to London tomorrow . . ."

Eddie grinned.

"You're from London? All the better. *victorious* has cells all over, you know, but down here, we're thin on the ground. Plenty more of us in London. Give me your deets, and I'll pass them on."

"Do I have to take some kind of test?"

"I'd say you just passed," Eddie said. "With an A+."

<*))))><

When they were finished, and Eddie had left the coffee shop, Ani took out her phone and speed-dialed Abernathy.

He answered before she even heard it ring.

"Ms. Lee," he said, "how delightful to hear from you.

I'm told the weather is lovely in the West Country this time of the year. Do I take it we were successful in our endeavor?"

"Mission accomplished," Ani said. "I'm in."

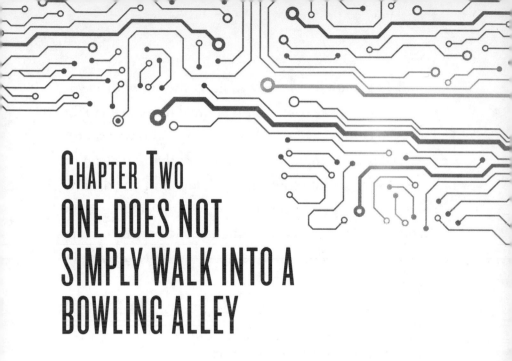

Chapter Two
ONE DOES NOT SIMPLY WALK INTO A BOWLING ALLEY

Joe Dyson stopped in front of the building and his mouth twisted downward into a frown. He thought two things in rapid succession. First up was: *Bowling?* And then: *I must be in the wrong place.*

Even though the address matched the one he'd been given by the shifty-looking guy with the thatched eyebrows, he was still sure he'd made a mistake.

He thought, again: *BOWLING?*

The alley was on the edge of a set of sinister industrial units on the dark side of Luton, and it was rundown and badly in need of a new coat of paint. Like the rest of Luton he'd seen, actually.

It was called *Midwest Lanes*, although "*Midwest of what?*" was a pretty valid question. It had a vague 1950s American vibe, but like something you would come up with if you were trying to capture that feeling but had never been to the U.S. (Joe, of course, had. He'd been born and raised there), or seen pictures of the 1950s, and were relying instead on half-memories of shows like *Happy Days*, but you'd never actually seen the shows and were reduced to listening to the descriptions of a slightly crazy uncle. So, in order to really commit to this ludicrous project, you decide to deliver the final absurdity:

You put the resulting folly down on an industrial park in Luton.

And left it to rot, by the look of it.

Cracked pavement set up trip hazards that—anywhere else—would be magnets for litigious chancers. There was a lot of malfunctioning neon lighting and bad paintwork that had been bad even *before* it had started to peel.

Joe approached the front, pushed hard and the IN door squeaked open. He waited a couple of seconds, preparing himself, and then stepped through.

Inside, the lighting was poor, the carpet was worn and caught his shoe soles, and the air was full of cleaning chemicals that failed, somehow, to cover unpleasant odors from the distant past: beer, tobacco, and dead dreams, presumably. Off to Joe's left were the bathrooms, to his immediate right was the reception desk. Straight ahead was a café that had seen better days: a greasy spoon, heavy on the grease, and you probably needed to bring your own spoon. A group of youths sat on chairs and tables in the café, and they watched him with suspicion from the moment he entered the place.

Seven of them. Not good odds if things turned bad, but better odds that one of them knew the answer to the question that had brought Joe here in the first place.

Better not get into a fight, then, he thought, then crossed the foyer toward them.

<*))))><

Sometimes, YETI missions weren't about saving the world or even putting bad guys behind bars; they were about doing something small, just to help someone out.

Abernathy was funny like that.

For every few officially sanctioned missions, there was one like this: off book, unauthorized, more to do with righting a wrong than impressing his bosses in Whitehall.

Abernathy had come around to Joe's place on Mortimer Street when Joe was grabbing some down time. Playing on one of his pinball tables and racking up a score that—at long last—stood a chance of overtaking Ellie's from a few weeks back.

Joe had celebrated the bump in salary he'd gotten in the aftermath of the Palgrave affair by investing in a Stern *Walking Dead* table, the one with zombie heads and a crossbow. It turned out that Ellie—another definite plus in the wake of the .wav business—was a natural when it came to pinball. She'd been ribbing him about it for a while now, and Joe thought it was about time to play catch-up.

Abernathy had let himself in, and Joe quit the table—and the multiball he'd just triggered—nodding a greeting.

"I assume we have Ms. Butcher to thank for the sudden attention to cleaning." Abernathy said. "How is everything going?"

"Not bad," Joe said, gesturing at the oversized sofas that Abernathy had footed the bill for. "Is this a social call, or have the YETI headquarters been compromised again?"

"Ha ha." Abernathy sat down, still ramrod straight and surely not taking full advantage of the plush upholstery. "I have a little job for you, but it's not quite YETI."

"A charitable cause?" Joe asked. "Where and why?"

"A friend of a friend threw this my way. I tried to get the official stamp for it, but even though it didn't make so much as a ripple in Whitehall, I still believe it to be worthy of our attention. Condensed version: a concerned social worker in Luton, of all places, is worried that a few of the teenage runaways that they have sleeping on the streets there have dropped off the radar."

"Maybe they're just trying out a new town? Or a new city? Or a friend's couch . . ."

Abernathy tilted his head and raised an eyebrow.

"I guess that's the question you need to answer, isn't it?" he said. "The Luton train leaves from St. Pancras in"—he consulted his wristwatch— "thirty-five minutes. You'll need an overnight bag."

<*))))><

You could tell a lot about a group dynamic by observing it as you approached. If you watched carefully, watched the group's initial movements, saw them operating under primal pack rules, you could usually figure out the pecking order of the individuals within the system. You got to see who was the muscle, who was the brains, and who was its heart.

The "muscles" flexed, because their first reaction to a new-comer was always protective. They would change their body language to reflect their defensive instinct—often subtly— telegraphing which way they'd go if it looked like trouble was coming. Their bodies would shift in one of two directions: either toward the newcomer, or away from him, depending on the kind of leader that beat at the heart of the pack.

If their alpha was made of intellect and strategy—if his control over them was primarily cerebral—then the mus-cles, move would be forward, so when push came to shove, they'd be ready to put themselves between the interloper and the alpha of their particular pack, primed to act as a buffer for any violence that ensued. If the alpha was, on the other hand, defined by his own violent tendencies—if his control over the pack was one of physical threat—then the move would be backward, to flank the alpha and offer support in the teeth of the oncoming threat while maintaining silent deference to his alpha status.

The "brains" of the group would remain still, analyzing the situation, but not committing to pack behavior yet. They would run scenarios, study the intruder, work out his weaknesses and strengths, and only then would they start to move to support the outcome of the best simulation they had played out in their heads.

The "heart" was always the alpha, the nucleus around which the other electrons circulated. If he was a thinker, then he would usually relax, safe behind the physical screen that the rest of his pack would provide. If he was a fighter, then there was a high probability that he would tense and puff up, ready to lead his "dogs" into battle.

None of this would happen consciously, of course, because pack structures actually existed below the level of thought, more of a reflex or an instinct. It happened in a very brief window of time, and before the conscious mind kicked in. It was subject to immediate changes and modifications, dependent on far too many variables to calculate: the demeanor of the approaching individual, the attitudes or moods of any members of the pack, the safety of home court advantage, whether they'd just eaten, whether their leader was riding high in their opinion or whether his reign was at its nadir. The group would pass beyond meaningful structural analysis when minds got in the way, becoming amorphous and unreadable.

By the time that happened, though, Joe had already gotten a pretty good read on the group.

The alpha was a chisel-faced, slender white guy, maybe eighteen or nineteen years on the clock of life, with ratty dreadlocks in his bleached, to orange, hair. A pierced nose and two facial tattoos—a stylized *666* to the side of his left eye and a jigsaw puzzle piece on his cheek—suggested a level of not-giving-a-damn that sent alarm bells ringing in Joe's mind. The guy neither tensed nor relaxed as Joe approached. If anything, he looked utterly indifferent.

Joe watched the other members of the group to see how they reacted, instead.

The remaining six kids, ranging from short and fat to tall and gangly, made the tiny movements that Joe had pretty much been expecting, with the "muscles" flexing and the "brains" assessing. There were four figures that really needed to be watched: three muscles and the alpha. The other three betrayed their fear—and with it, their lack of confidence in their own abilities if things got violent. One of them even flashed his eyes around, as if looking for an exit route. It still left four kids who might be inclined toward causing Joe immediate harm, but the "muscles" were back-up-the-alpha types, and that meant an extra second or two in Joe's favor as they organized themselves into a fighting formation.

Joe stopped in front of the group, gave them a warm smile, manufactured the pheromones that advised them to treat him with caution and said, "Hey, guys. Look, I'm sorry to drop in on you like this, but my name's Joe and I heard that you might be the ones to come to if I need a little . . . if I could, maybe . . . if you . . . Aw, heck. Look, I need to buy some kids. You got any you could sell me?"

<*))))><

He'd started with the social worker who'd flagged the disappearances, but it uncovered little more than Abernathy had already told him. That was one of the things about Abernathy: he was thorough.

The social worker had been a determined, compassionate woman fighting against impossible odds. Budget cuts had only made it easier for kids to fall through the system's cracks, and the only safety net that existed for them was life on the streets. Heck of a safety net. It made Joe wonder just when it was that the country lost its heart.

Joe got only background details on the missing kids: six horror stories that you'd think came from a lurid paperback novel, or from Mayhew's study of Victorian society, "London Labour and the London Poor," but surely not from twenty-first century reality. They were biographies that differed only in the types of abuses and tragedies suffered, the drugs and violence endured, the moment that all hope was lost and dreams dashed.

Joe had promised the woman that he would try his best to find them, and then he'd hit the streets.

The word *homelessness*—or its cowardly double word twin, *rough sleeping*—did little to describe the world that Joe encountered. Fall down all the rungs of the UK's socio-economic ladder and you landed, not on a soft mattress of second chances, or halfway house security, but rather on the cold concrete and asphalt of the city streets.

Joe had spent his first day talking to the homeless people of Luton, listening to their stories and trying not to let the details of each person's personal tragedy play on his conscience. Compartmentalization. Keep the political and emotional facets of the problem to one side, and concentrate on the question Abernathy had sent him here to answer: Where did the six homeless kids go?

<*))))><

His entrance, and conversational gambit, took the group by surprise, and when they didn't reply immediately, Joe pointed to the alpha kid's tattoo.

"Brave choice," he said. "A 666 tattoo. Brave, because it's six-six-six, and, I guess, because it's on your face."

"You know what it represents?" The kid asked, trying

for menacing, but missing by a yard, or so, because Joe had him rattled.

"Sure. It's what you get if you add up all the numbers on a roulette wheel." Joe grinned. "You in charge here?"

<*))))><

He'd quickly discovered that kids disappearing from the streets weren't as rare occurrences as you might think. And most of those disappearances had a pretty straightforward explanation behind them. There was a big difference between the types of homeless, for one thing. There were long-term and short-term street people and, luckily, most fell into the latter category. Being without a roof over their heads was a transient phase for these folks: kids found sofas to surf on or caring individuals who took a risk by putting them up or they discovered that squatting in empty houses was a better alternative to cardboard beds in shop doorways.

Others left, turning their backs on the city that had turned its back on them.

So there *was* a chance that the six names on his list could have found their own ways out of their personal predicaments.

Except, of course, it was *six* names.

All teens.

All had disappeared within weeks of one another, and no one had heard a word from them since.

Joe had talked to Abernathy, who'd been skeptical about his plan for a next move, but had ultimately agreed because the simple truth was that there really was no other way to proceed when all leads had gone cold. Abernathy had insisted on "a safety net" of his own, and had made some discreet calls to select numbers in Luton.

So, on his second day in in the city, Joe had become homeless himself.

He'd taken advice—and tips—from the social worker, raided a charity shop bargain bin for clothes, ditched his phone and cash in the cheap hotel room that was starting to look pretty darned homey in comparison to the life he was about to embrace, and then he'd hit the streets.

As plans went, it was a long shot at best. The one thing he had going for him was he was pretty much the same age as the missing kids. If there *was* a sinister cause behind the disappearances, and even that was uncertain, then maybe he could engineer an encounter with the same person that the other six had.

A long shot.

It took a little less than fourteen hours for it to pay off. Fourteen hours of boredom.

He'd just put his bed together for the night, arranging some flattened boxes he'd salvaged from the back of a supermarket, when it had started to rain.

"You listening, Abernathy?" he'd growled, knowing that *someone* at YETI HQ would be monitoring his inboard systems, tuned in to the open channel that was implanted in his head. "That's rain you're hearing."

"Joe," Abernathy came back a short while after, "how's my supertramp doing?"

"Hey, careful with the hatespeak. We don't like the word *tramp* around these parts. We prefer *residentially challenged.*"

"Raining, huh?" Abernathy said, ignoring him. "Bet you don't think this was such a good plan of yours, now, eh?"

"Abernathy, didn't you read the files the social worker sent us?"

"I'm sorry?"

"We got three dates that are supposed to be spot-on for three of our disappearances."

"And?"

"It was raining on two of them." Joe scanned the road, his brow furrowed. "Look, I gotta go. Stay where you are. I may have something."

Joe watched the taillights of a white van that was suddenly speeding up, getting farther and farther away. He was sure it had slowed to a crawl as it passed him. Just as he was sure that the same van had passed by a few minutes before. This time, he committed the license plate to memory—even though they called them "number plates" on this side of the pond. Joe had never managed to pick up the phrase. It wasn't even correct. The plates had a mix of letters and numbers. He settled down onto his cardboard bed and tried to look as miserable as possible.

"Okay, I have a minute," he told Abernathy. "A suspect van just did two drive-by look-sees. Could be nothing, but here's the tag." He gave Abernathy the plate number. It was already being run when the van came back around again.

This time it stopped right next to Joe. A thirty-something guy with dark hair and exaggerated eyebrows came toward him, hunching over, with his jacket pulled up to take the edge off the rain.

"Hey kid!" the guy said. "Are you okay?"

Joe felt a thrill of anticipation, but managed to hide it behind a veil of careworn indifference.

"Yeah," he said, "I guess."

The guy kept walking until he was just about standing in Joe's cardboard front room.

"You get kicked out of your house, or something?" The man had a concerned tone to his voice, but it was manufactured, no more than word-deep.

"Something like that."

"Bad scene, bro," the man said. "You don't have a friend with a sofa?"

Joe shrugged. "Already used them all up," he replied. "Friends and sofas, both. Thus . . ." He gestured around at the squalid surroundings.

The guy nodded, then shook his head. Not yes and no, but rather agreement followed by feigned empathy.

"Be lucky, man," the guy said, and started to turn away.

Joe thought he'd struck out, but then the guy turned back.

"Hey," he said. "I just thought of something. Some guys I know are hiring. Nothing glamorous, but at least it'll pay a few quid to get you back on your feet. I think they can even provide accommodation. Bed and breakfast. Again, nothing flashy, but better than . . ."

He gestured around to finish the sentence.

"What sort of work?" Joe asked.

"Light manufacturing or assembly or some such. They'll train you. It's a bed for the night . . . Maybe a chance at a new beginning."

"How do I get in touch with them?" Joe asked.

The man looked at his wrist, where a pretty high-end watch made its home. Rolex. Gold. This guy was into something. Unless all Luton van drivers made enough money to buy timepieces like that.

"Look, I've got a few minutes. I can take you there, if you want." The guy jabbed a thumb over his shoulder toward the van.

Joe found it incredible that anyone fell for such an obvious tactic. A stranger offering a new beginning, and all you had to do was get into the van with a man that wouldn't know sincerity or empathy if they bit him on the ass.

You'd have to be insane to get in that van, he thought. *Insane or very desperate.*

Joe tried his best to look grateful.

"Thank you," he said. "Thank you so much."

He had no belongings to gather, so he followed the man to the vehicle, got into the passenger seat, and the guy started the ignition and pulled away.

<*))))><

"Yes," 666 said, "I'm in charge. Now, who the hell are you and what are you doing in my gaff?"

To Joe, a gaff was a hook or spear, but he figured from the context that it probably meant "place."

"I thought I'd explained myself pretty well," he said. "Who am I? Joe. What am I doing here? Looking to buy some kids. You want me to text it to you, maybe with an emoji, to hammer it home, or have you got it now?"

He knew that he was pissing 666 and his buddies off, but it was a pretty good plan when you wandered into enemy territory, because it kept them wrong-footed and confused them about the power dynamic that was developing. Or maybe he'd already decided that this wasn't going to resolve itself peacefully and he was getting himself ready, mentally, for what was going to go down awfully soon.

"Sling your hook, wise guy," 666 said. One of his "muscles" did a teeth-baring thing that was more than a little weird, and nowhere near as threatening as he'd hoped. It was actually pretty funny.

"Sling my hook?" Joe asked. "See, to me that's interesting. A moment ago you said the word 'gaff.' A gaff is a kind of hook. Then you tell me to sling my hook. Coincidence? Freud would say that things like that are never completely accidental. Maybe you've got something about fish? Anyway . . . Kids. Cash money. Can we make a deal here?"

666 got to his feet, and it caused a ripple effect through his minions, but they were still seated, like they were in church for the first time and a hymn just started up and they didn't know the correct etiquette.

Joe logged each move, modeled the change of environment in his head, and took another step forward. He was already accessing the chip in his head for combat strategies, and felt the digital suggestions gelling with his own, natural ones.

"You're a nutter, mate," 666 said. "A bloody lunatic. I reckon it's time you turned around and got out before things get a little tasty."

Tasty was a bit of slang Joe knew, but its usage here was sloppy. It was used to describe a person that was good at fighting, as in "he's a bit tasty," but Joe had never heard it used as a threat. Still, it would be rude to let an opportunity to get things going slip away.

He unleashed the chip's potential and felt its effects on his muscles.

He smiled and then began.

<*))))><

If you're into something dicey—like kidnapping vulnerable kids off the streets, for example—then it's a bad idea to pick up a teen secret agent with a chip in his head that has, among other things, an open channel to HQ and a GPS-locating device.

That was the thatched-eyebrow-white-van-man's latest mistake, but judging by the cursory, even clumsy, way he'd picked Joe up, he was sure to have made more. Joe figured that if you went back through this guy's life, you'd find a whole lot of mistakes.

Still, as mistakes went, this was a biggie.

They'd barely made it two-hundred yards from their starting point when the van driver suddenly found himself boxed in between two SUVs, and by then, it was far too late. The trap was already sprung. A guy got out of the passenger side of each SUV, each carrying a pistol, and quickly moved to either side of the van. The guy on the driver's side tapped his gun against the window and used it to gesture for the driver to wind down the glass.

The guy with the eyebrows did as he was instructed.

The man leaned in.

"Save yourself a lengthy stay in an off-book detention center," he said, and pointed to Joe. "Answer the kid's questions."

The van-guy held out for a little over twenty seconds, then spilled his cowardly guts.

<*))))><

First, Joe moved right up close and personal to 666 and faked a punch, moving his right hand just enough to make it the expected move, before he reached out, grabbed two big fistfuls of 666's shirt, and pulled him sharply forward as he drove the crown of his forehead to meet him. It was called a head butt, or a Zidouken, or a Glasgow Kiss: a sharp, brutal way to put your opponent down. Fast. A simple use of two forces colliding—Joe's hard bone against 666's much softer face, with the surprise factor added into the mix. It was a perfect execution of the move, too: straight into the bridge of 666's nose. The kid was out with barely a second on the clock.

Two of the thug underlings hadn't even achieved standing, so they were next up. In Joe's fighting lexicon, "halfway out of your seat" was "critically unbalanced." His chip gave him both speed and power, and he pushed the first one back with a flat palm to the ribs, watching as the guy tumbled back and got himself all tangled up with the chair; then, pleased with success of the move, simply repeated it on thug number two.

A fist from the last of 666's rather predictable "muscle" whizzed past a cheek that moved too quickly out of its path for it to connect, and Joe took advantage of the heavy swing by grabbing the arm the fist was attached to, and helping its travel on its way by applying a fair amount of force. As a result, the guy stumbled forward—another thug unbalanced—and Joe stamped heavily on his left shin.

It was a leg that wasn't going to be functioning properly for a long time, and it put thug three out of the fight. Thugs one and two, of course, were only temporarily floored, but Joe made that a longer-term situation with minimum of effort and a precise exercising of force. In the case of thug one, that was a simple matter of waiting until he lifted his head from the floor and putting it back down with the stomp of his boot measured to keep him prostrate without risking serious injury. In the case of thug two, it was a body slam across the abdomen that took all the air—and fight—out of him.

Joe got back to his feet, looked at the other three kids who were sitting as if welded to their chairs. They'd seen how easy the fighters of the group had gone down. None of them were going to offer up their own bodies to a war that was already over.

"Where are the kids?" Joe demanded, pleased to find that he wasn't even breathing heavily.

One of the seated pack pointed out toward the bowling lanes. Joe narrowed his eyes in a silent "are you sure?" and got a full round of nods in response.

He headed into the bowling alley proper as the three still capable of movement scurried out the door, into the hands of the authorities waiting outside.

<*))))><

The human ability to be a complete asshole and somehow think it's all right to behave like one just because it benefits you, never ceased to amaze Joe. It was the reason for a whole bunch of the world's problems including crimes and other atrocities. As soon as you put your own needs and wants over the needs of wants of others, you were well on your way to becoming a sociopath.

Empathy was what the world needed, the ability to see other people as equally deserving of all the things that you, yourself, want and definitely don't want. If Joe had one wish for the world, it was a sudden outbreak of empathy.

He certainly saw little of it in evidence today, here, at a crappy bowling alley in the badlands of Luton.

Two whole lanes were taken over by a huge metal cage in which a bunch of kids toiled. This was where the missing kids had ended up.

In a cage.

Joe felt anger boiling inside him as he approached. Through the bars, he could see that the kids were thin and malnourished, dirty and defeated, with a glazed look in their eyes and a near-robotic quality to their movements. They wore a uniform—white T-shirt, white slacks, and white shoes. There were benches inside the cage, and the kids were attached to the benches by wires attached to bracelets on their wrists. Anti-static wristbands that grounded the wearer to protect delicate components from electrostatic discharges that would damage them. Most of the kids had soldering irons in their hands, and they were working on circuit boards under fierce fluorescent lights, hunched over to concentrate on their tasks. The others were assembling the completed boards into plastic towers.

It was a sweat shop. A factory that had found a new way to make its products even cheaper than farming them out to the China or Korea.

Slaves.

Picked up off the street with promises of a new beginning, then locked into a cage and forced to work.

None of the teens even noticed Joe as he approached. He saw that some had bruises on their faces. He took in the buckets in the corner of the cage that they used as toilets. He saw the folded camp beds and thin sheets that would act as their beds when the shift was over.

"Hey!" he said, and the kids looked up from their work. "I'm closing this place down. Anyone wanna clock out? Permanently?"

He watched confusion turn to hope, and wished he'd smashed 666's face even harder.

Then he called in the cavalry. The *go* phrase was: "Drawbridge down."

Five minutes later, the kids were free. Most of them were crying, not from the horror of their situation, but from the sheer joy of being released.

Sometimes being in YETI meant Joe got to save the world. Today, he'd saved about a dozen kids.

He wasn't sure which one felt better.

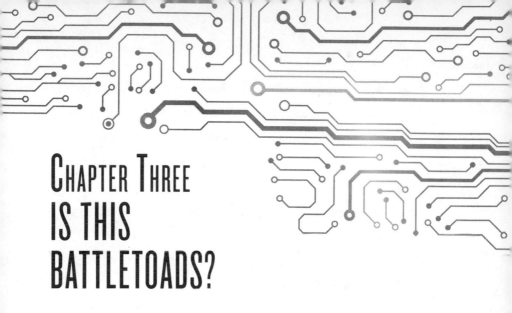

Chapter Three
IS THIS
BATTLETOADS?

Ani was frustrated.

She told Gretchen about it over dinner.

"I'm getting nowhere." She said. "And I mean *nowhere.*"

Gretchen chewed her hickory-smoked tofu and put down her fork.

"It's only been three weeks," she said. "Depending on the time frame of the next phase of *victorious*'s operation, that might be just what you'd expect."

"But they're getting ready for something," Ani said. "I mean, I know they are. I feel like I joined too late to be considered for inclusion in it."

She put her cutlery down, too. They'd eaten a huge medley of vegetarian fare and, honestly, she'd probably eaten enough about ten minutes before. It made her think, suddenly, of home in Cambridge. It was no longer the homesickness that had gnawed at her for her first week or so in London, but rather a gleeful feeling of how things had changed for her. Her dad had never been a good, or even frequent, cook, and she had often ended up eating whatever was left in the cupboards, however mismatched and unappetizing that might be.

She felt herself smiling as the other changes played through her mind.

"What?" Gretchen asked, noticing a shift in her, and becoming concerned.

"Nothing bad," Ani said. "Just thinking about my new life and how it kicks the hell out of my old one."

"Your old one just didn't quite fit," Gretchen said. "It was a couple of sizes too tight for you. You're just growing into the life you deserve."

"I don't want to lose it, that's all. Not now that I know I really *really* want it."

"You're not going to lose it."

"Well, I'm hardly making progress breaking into *victorious*, now, am I?"

Gretchen thought about that for a couple of seconds, then asked, "Look, if a piece of software you build isn't working for you, what do you do?"

"Go back and look at the code, see if I can find another way to get it to behave. But that's a logical system . . ."

"Hey, Ani, people are systems, too. And they can be pretty logical if you know what makes them tick. It's the same with their organizations. So what do you do?"

"I change the approach. I inject myself into their plans, and make them think it was all their own idea."

"When the best leader's work is done, the people say, 'We did it ourselves.'" Gretchen agreed.

"Fortune cookie?"

"Attributed to Lao Tzu, Chinese philosopher and poet. But yeah, I got it out a fortune cookie. Or a book. I can't remember."

Ani laughed.

"Because you're *so* renowned for having gaps in your memory I bet you can point me in the direction of six or seven books that contain that quote . . ."

"Eleven," Gretchen corrected, "not counting books of quotations. Dessert?"

"Sure, why not?"

<*))))><

After getting a thumbs-up from Eddie Wells, Ani had expected things to happen pretty quickly, but the reality turned out to be far from the actual triumph it was supposed to be. She'd been sent a scuzzy piece of code to clean up—it had taken her about ten minutes, surely a test but not a particularly demanding one—and they'd sent her links to a couple of addresses that were little more than holding pages for tor.onion sites that were yet to be constructed.

In terms of entrance to the secret world of *victorious*,

it was little more than a series of dead ends. The only person whose face she knew was Eddie's, and he was back in Yeovil, and surely not high on the *victorious* pyramid.

"How about this?" Gretchen said, when they were sitting in front of her computer. "There are all kinds of hackers in the world, from techies who just love the challenge, through the mischief makers, right up to career criminals. How does *victorious* select the ones they want to become . . . more involved in whatever it is they're planning? How do they select out the ones they don't?"

Ani thought about that. "Damn it," she said. She should have spotted have spotted it herself. "It's probably not from the recommendations of people like Eddie Wells."

"In business, companies often hire other recruitment agencies to find staff for them to fill their vacancies," Gretchen said. "It saves a lot of work for the human resources department of the company by suggesting people who could fit the job, and weeding out those that just won't. They find a group of people who match the company's needs. They'll check their references, interview them, set tests, all the background stuff, but at some point, the eventual employer will probably want to interview the candidates themselves. Give their own tests."

"So Eddie's just a scout," Ani said. "A low-level member of the group who suggests other members to the . . . to the *management*."

"Exactly."

"Where's the follow-up interview, then?" Ani asked. "I mean, are they just slow? Or did I do something wrong?"

"Maybe they've already arranged the interview," Gretchen suggested, her voice slightly higher in pitch, the words coming slightly faster. She was no longer rolling ideas around; she was homing in on something, Ani was sure.

It got her thinking harder, to keep up. And then she saw it.

"The code. The .onion sites. They're the interview. The test. Like Cicada 3301, that alternate reality game of puzzles and cryptograms that appears on the net every year. They're a set of puzzles to solve."

"Could be."

"Okay, okay," Ani said, pulling out her YETI-issue laptop and opening up the code she'd been sent. "What if the exercise wasn't to tidy up the code?"

"Talk me through it," Gretchen said, encouraging her to continue.

"They sent me some code and asked me to improve it," Ani started, staring at the code she'd been sent and the code she'd sent back, side by side. "But what if it was their way of setting a trick question? What if it wasn't the improved code they wanted but, instead, for me to do something with the original code?"

"That would work," Gretchen said. "Carry the thought through. What can you do with a few lines of code that are pretty much missing their context within their larger program?"

Ani chewed at her lip as she scrutinized her screen.

"I could try to finish the program based on the snippet they sent," she said, then shook her head. "No, there's not enough data here to make that kind of leap. It must be something else."

"Something else . . . ?"

"Yes. Look. If this bit of code is a clue to something, then it must be findable. Probably online. Maybe . . ."

Ani facepalmed and sighed.

She copied the code to the tablet's clipboard, then opened a new browser window, typed in an address and a search box appeared, under a minimalist banner heading:

CodeHub

She pasted the code into the box and pressed ENTER.

"CodeHub?" Gretchen asked.

"I can be awfully dumb, sometimes. CodeHub is a search engine, but not for the usual page titles, keywords and metadata. It's for code. If there's a website out there with this code on it, CodeHub will find it."

"Could it be that easy?" Gretchen asked.

The search results came back.

The answer was yes.

One hit, followed by half a dozen mirrors of that main site. Ani clicked on the main link and it opened onto a flash game, with retro 8-bit graphics and a soundtrack that sounded like something that a kid's toy keyboard might make.

There was no doubt that she'd reached the right site.

The name of the game?

`victorious.`

"Guess you'd better play it, then." Gretchen said.

<*))))><

Level one of the game was a pretty basic "endless running" side-scrolling platformer, that required the player's character—a basic stick man—to hop across gaps and up onto ledges, avoiding occasional boulders and fire balls from above. There was a JUMP key for crossing gaps, hopping onto ledges, and avoiding ground obstacles, and a DUCK key for avoiding things that were at head height. That was it.

It wouldn't get many stars on Google Play or in Apple's App Store.

The game was terrible to look at—its background was untextured black and the level design was rudimentary—and it was very, very difficult to play. The ramping up of the level speed was merciless, going from slow "getting a feel for the controls" to brutal "no time to think, just to act" within the first twenty seconds.

Ani was no slouch when it came to video games, but this really was hard. She crashed and burned so many times that she was starting to contemplate a possible alternative approach to many a flash game—programming a bot in Python that could play it for her—but, instead, she calmed herself down, worked on slowing down her breathing, visualized the screen behind closed eyes, thought about the stakes she was playing for—infiltrating deeper into *victorious*—and then opened her eyes, pushed a lock of hair from her eyes, and announced, "I got this."

Gretchen replied, "I know."

With only two moves available, it was all about timing and Ani had spent years, and quite a lot of her YETI self-defense classes, developing that very thing. Hand-eye coordination required a perfect synergy between, 1) the parts of the central nervous system that related to vision, 2) her sense of touch, and 3) the muscles controlling her hand; *synergy* being the idea that "the whole" of a system becomes greater than the sum of its parts.

By controlling her breathing, and in doing so reducing the stress of the game's intense speed, Ani was able to approach the game in a different way. Her moves were no longer frantic twitches of panic but, instead, became more controlled, more definite and, it turned out, a heck of a lot better.

It took Ani three more tries before she beat the level.

Level 2 was easier. A "Match 3" game mashed up with *Tetris*, where oddly-shaped blocks randomly changed every three seconds. It just meant that she had to make a quick survey of the board, find the best place for the descending block, and quickly slot it into place before the three seconds expired. It was almost too easy, but then her visual/spatial skills had been honed by years of similar games. She finished the level on the first try.

Level 3 was a tile flipping game. She needed to flip identical tiles, revealing one of eight different symbols on the other side. Flip two that didn't match and they flipped back. Match two symbols, and they stayed flipped. Take too long and the tiles reorganized themselves, and the tiles she'd matched flipped back, putting her back at square one. Her short-term memory was pretty darned good, so she pretty much sailed through Level 3.

Before Level 4 a line of text flashed across the screen: Final Level – victorious.

Then: No retries. Fail, and it's back to the start of Level 1.

The level started, and it took a good twenty seconds before Ani worked out what she was even supposed to do. A text block of code scrolled down the left-hand side of the screen, while another block of code scrolled up the right. They looked the same, but on closer examination, were slightly different. The trick was to highlight, exactly, the parts of code on the right that differed from the code on the left. The arrow keys of the keyboard moved the cursor around the text block. TAB selected each mismatched piece of code, and RETURN made the selection final. Easy enough, if the speed of the game wasn't absolutely punishing. Ani's fingers moved lightning fast, almost dancing across the keys, but she viewed them only peripherally, keeping her gaze fixed on the screen and relying mainly on muscle memory.

The first problem was that by the time she'd worked out the point of the game, and the keys she needed to navigate to play it, she was already playing catch-up, which meant she needed pure concentration and total accuracy. The second problem was that there was no gauge or bar that showed her the progress she was making or how many mistakes until the level would end in defeat. The third problem was that she'd already been mashing keys for a while now, and her fingers were starting to feel tired.

Still, she'd be damned if she was going to play through all of those other levels again.

She focused her mind, letting her fingers move and her eyes observe. After what seemed like forever—with the speed and complexity of the tasks increasing until it felt like she was running on automatic—the level finished.

The feeling of relief that accompanied the sudden Game Complete, Well Done. was profound, but soon gave way to a crushing sense of disappointment.

Because that was all there was.

Just those words at the top of the screen and a whole void of black below.

And nothing else.

There was no "Welcome to *victorious*. Prepare for your

first mission." No link to an encrypted server with all of *victorious*'s secrets. Nothing.

"Aaargh." Ani growled. "I thought that was it."

Gretchen stroked her chin and grimaced.

"You did well," she said. "And you went where the clues led you. It can't be a coincidence that you ended up here, playing this game. What else is there you can do? Here, now."

Ani looked at the screen.

Game Complete, Well Done.

Then she smiled.

"That's a heck of a lot of blank real estate," she said, pointing at the black screen below the message.

"What are you thinking?"

"Something could be hidden in all that black."

"Ah," Gretchen said. "Steganography."

"Dinosaur writing?"

"You're thinking of the Stegosaurus, which actually shares its origins with the same prefix. 'Stego' means 'covered' or 'roof,' like the plates that covered, or roofed, a stegosaurus's back. But in this case, I mean using 'covered' as in 'hidden.' Steganography is hidden writing."

Ani used the laptop's left mouse key and track pad to select the black void on screen. The selection highlighted an area in the screen's center where a black-on-black message was made visible by the highlighting: #180808 is #ICEI4D

"Like that?" Ani asked.

"Absolutely," Gretchen agreed. "But what are they? Twitter hashtags?"

"I think they're HTML color codes," Ani replied. "Tags that refer to a specific color on web pages." She searched online for a list. "There we go." Ani pointed at the screen. "It turns out that #180808 is a shade of black, while #ICE14D is a rather fetching shade of green."

"So the code basically says 'black is green'?" Gretchen asked.

Ani thought about it. "HTML is an acronym for HyperText Markup Language, it's the way you specify the contents of a web page to the web browser."

"It's an initialism," Gretchen corrected reflexively. "The word 'acronym' ordinarily refers to something pronounced as a word, like NATO or LASER."

"Noted," Ani said. "Anyway, maybe I need to go back to those web addresses?"

She got them both up in separate browser windows and put them side by side.

She pointed to the one on the right-hand side of the screen.

"This one has more black on it," she said.

"So how is that green?" Gretchen asked. "The message said 'black is green.'"

"Watch."

Ani took her cursor arrow up to the VIEW bar of the browser window, selected DEVELOPER from the dropdown menu, and

VIEW SOURCE from the submenu. The screen changed into a crowded window full of the code. Ani pressed the COMMAND and F keys and input the first color code into the FIND search box that came up. FIND found three matches, and Ani navigated to them, changed the first color code into the second one three times, then toggled back to the web page.

Now, instead of pure black on the web page there were three groups of letters visible, in green.

ddder

xglirl

fhnvnv.

Ani shook her head.

"Great," she said. "The answer just makes everything more confusing. It's gibberish. Or a code that might as well be gibberish, because there's no key to solve it."

"Hmmm," Gretchen said. "Maybe there *is* a key. Why don't you do the same color substitution to the *other* web page? There's a bit of black on it."

Ani repeated the VIEW SOURCE/FIND process and replaced black with green again.

Another message was revealed, although this time it was a lot shorter:

13 < and below it was a green text entry box with address written in it.

"Thirteen is less than . . ." Ani said. "Less than what? Fourteen? Forty? Four million?"

Gretchen grabbed a pad of paper and a pencil off the

desk and put it down in front of Ani. The pencil was one of Gretchen's stock of Palomino Blackwings—her favorite brand of pencil, which she ordered in bulk from the US. This one a #725 in Fender Stratocaster sunburst colors, a limited edition issued as a tribute to some folk festival.

"The number thirteen," Gretchen said. "An interesting number for a lot of reasons. First, it has a lot of superstitions attached to it, and it's often thought of as unlucky. Many buildings are constructed with twelfth floors and fourteenth floors, but skip the thirteenth. *Triskaidekaphobia* is the fear of the number thirteen. It's also the smallest *emirp*—a prime forward, and backward: thirty-one. It's a Fibonacci number, a happy number, and is one of only three Wilson primes that have been discovered."

"And this is helping us how, now?" Ani admired Gretchen's library brain, but it did need bringing back from the far edges of *so what?* occasionally.

Gretchen smiled apologetically.

"More relevant to this situation, though, is that it is half of twenty-six."

"And there are twenty-six letters in the alphabet," Ani said.

"In *our* alphabet," Gretchen corrected, and it looked like she was winding up for another lecture on the different alphabets of the world before she thought better of it. Instead, she pointed to the pad of paper. "Write down the first thirteen letters of the alphabet."

Ani did.

a b c d e f g h i j k l m

"Now look at the 'less-than' sign on the website," Gretchen said. "Couldn't that be a directional arrow?"

Ani squinted at the screen again.

"I guess," she said uncertainly.

"So put the next thirteen letters of the alphabet *underneath* the first thirteen, but going backwards."

Ani did as she was told.

a b c d e f g h i j k l m
z y x w v u t s r q p o n

"There's your key." Gretchen said. "A equals Z. B equals Y. G equals T. It's called the Atbash Cipher. Low level cryptography, even without the 13< clue it wouldn't have been difficult to crack."

It only took a minute for Ani to decode *ddder xglirl fhnvnv* using the new key and find that it spelled out *wwwvi ctorio usmeme* and two seconds longer to put them together into one string *wwwvictoriousmeme*. From there, it was just a matter of entering a couple of periods, before the address, www.victorious.meme, was retrieved from what once had been chaos.

"Shall I?" Ani asked.

"It really would be rude not to," Gretchen said.

So Ani entered www.victorious.meme into the search box she had revealed beneath the final clue to the puzzle, and pressed ENTER.

Chapter Four
CHALLENGE
ACCEPTED

Abernathy was happy, and that was so rare that Joe thought it might need Instagramming, if it weren't for the fact that he'd be fired from YETI for putting a picture of his boss anywhere near the Internet. Oh, and the other fact that he'd never Instagrammed anything in his life.

And that wasn't just because the intelligence services needed to keep a low profile.

Most forms of social media activity baffled Joe, but top of his list of "You Could Explain It to Me Until the End of Time and I Still Wouldn't Get It" was the need to capture a moment and share it with the world. Maybe it was just the spy in him, but geotagging your location on selfies and letting the whole web have a look seemed like stupidity of the highest order. All those people worrying about the surveillance state and about how Big Brother was watching them, and it turned out that they just reported their own locations and activities willingly. Twitter and Facebook and Instagram might as well have been dreamed up *by* the intelligence services as a way of getting people to voluntarily surrender to a program of surveillance and then to run it themselves.

Still, there should be some way to record Abernathy's delight over the Luton operation—a glee which Joe was sure had more than a little to do with the fact that the other intelligence services had thought it didn't deserve any attention. Instead, he just grinned back.

They were together in the briefing room at YETI, going over the details of the fallout from the Luton job.

Any triumph, of course, did not last long.

"There's a problem," Abernathy said, fixing Joe with one of those looks that meant it wasn't just *a* problem—soon it would be *Joe's* problem.

"What kind of problem?" Joe settled back in his seat. If this was about to become one of *those* sessions he wanted to get comfortable.

"The crew you busted were middlemen at best," Abernathy said. "They didn't have the wit, the bank, or the imagination to come up with all of that by themselves. None of them are talking, other than to say it was all their own idea, but they're certainly protecting someone. Still, they'd rather take the fall than talk. Offering them deals has failed. What does that tell you?"

"That they're smarter than you give them credit for?

Hang on. What am I saying? The guy in charge had a 666 tattoo on his *face*. So we're looking for the next tier up, huh?"

"Among other things," Abernathy said, tersely. "Now, I know I said they're not talking, but one of them sort of did. He tried to make a deal, but didn't have enough information to make it worthwhile. He mentioned the name of the Mr. Big he claimed they all answered to but, according to him, none of them had ever met the guy. And even if it's true, it seems unlikely that the name the kid provided is anything but an alias."

"And the name was . . . ?"

Abernathy shuffled some papers on his desk, but Joe knew that he had the name memorized.

"Emmett. The kid didn't even know if that was a first name or a surname. Whichever it is, it rings exactly zero bells with any law enforcement or security services databases. Around the world. And as I said, it's either an alias or a red herring. In lieu of Emmett, this is our leader."

Abernathy waved his arm and the briefing room screen lit up to display a picture of 666 smirking at the camera. His dreadlocks framed his bony face, looking like the legs of a crab.

"666," Abernathy said. "Or Gordon Clarke, as he was christened. A habitual crook with a string of arrests that all fall under the heading 'petty' and a life plan that seems to stretch no farther than an eventual extended incarceration in one of Her Majesty's prisons."

"Bad childhood?"

"No, as far as I can tell, he's just a bad person. He had a loving family, plenty of opportunities, and a whole load of second chances, but he turned his back on them all. I guess he decided a life of crime was better than a nine to five, and that his fellow lowlifes cared for him more. Or feared him. Some people will take power over love every time."

Abernathy gave Joe a knowing look. Joe supposed it was a sideways reference to Victor Palgrave and how he'd treated his son, Lenny. The whole *dotwav* affair still gave Joe nightmares, how close YETI had come to a major disaster in Hyde Park. Joe had expected YETI to be exposed in the aftermath of that disaster, and for humanity's outlook to change in the light of their exposure to what had visited earth on that weird, terrifying day. But to his shock, nothing really changed.

The organism that had descended over London had taken all traces of its existence with it when it took off back into the voids of space, including all digital data on cameras and phones, leaving just a load of conflicting testimonies without documentary evidence to back anything up. No video clips hit YouTube, because there were no videos to post. No photographs went viral because there were no photos to share.

And the testimonies that were recorded were so wildly different that they could have been referring to different events altogether.

No one, it seemed, could agree on just what they had seen that day. Indeed, it was as if the creature had appeared as different things to different people. So when the government issued its cover story—that Victor Palgrave had been a terrorist, and that he had unleashed an experimental toxin at an open air concert in the center of London, one that had been dispersed, causing mass hallucinations—it seemed to fit the facts better than any other explanations and had been accepted by all but the conspiracy theorists. And no one listened to them, except other conspiracy nuts.

As it turned out, for once, the conspiracy theorists were right: a vast cover-up clicked effortlessly into place. Strings were pulled on a global scale to mask all satellite and telescope data. Reports were redacted until they were just files of pages full of black marks. A campaign of disinformation buried a truth that sounded crazier than the lies.

The world spun, the people on its surface got on with their lives, and few knew that a strange part of the universe had come down to earth, leaving behind more questions than answers.

"But there's something odd about this Luton affair," Abernathy said, pulling Joe out of his reverie. "First, let's detail what we know about this enterprise. Gordon and his crew abducted kids off the streets and forced them to assemble computers. Hundreds of computers, maybe thousands for all we know. What shipping manifests we found—and it should be no surprise that this gang was anything but diligent about keeping exhaustive records—tell us that the computers were then sent all over the country, and to locations all over the world."

An almost dismissive wave of Abernathy's hand caused the image on the screen to change. A photo of one of the computers, disassembled, replaced the one of 666.

"Ordinary computers," Abernathy continued. "Not even particularly good ones. Pay your workforce peanuts and you get monkeys. Grab that workforce off the street and keep them locked up, you get grudging work. And none of the kids that assembled these machines were computer technicians. If they were, they probably wouldn't have been homeless in the first place. So the computers are no better than something a novice hobbyist would throw together quickly at home."

"Even so, it must have taken a chunk of change to get this operation started," Joe observed.

"You are very right, Joe. And that's the first worrying thing we have to confront. It's not the strangest, though."

"What is?"

Abernathy waved again and a picture of a heavily-filled circuit board appeared on screen.

"What we're looking at here is a motherboard," Abernathy said. "The main printed circuit board for these computers. It's pretty ordinary, at first glance at least. A lot of generic parts—mostly Chinese and Korean—but there're some American components, too. It has a reasonably fast processor, and a fair amount of RAM. The Shuttleworth brothers will have to tell you more about it. I think I've just exhausted my knowledge. Except about this . . ."

Abernathy moved his arm again and the image zoomed in on a part of the circuit board occupied by what looked to Joe like a large, black microchip. Although his computer expertise was probably as slight as Abernathy's, he could tell by scorch marks and cracks on the surface of the chip that it had burned out somehow.

"That doesn't look good," Joe said. "A faulty chip? Or was it badly placed on the circuit board?"

Abernathy inhaled a deep breath through his nose and then let it out so it was part exhale, part sigh.

"This is where it gets weird. We cataloged all the evidence at the scene, the bowling alley/slave cube, you know what I mean. We cataloged these computers. I've got a photograph of this very motherboard. Look, here it is."

Another image appeared next to the first. The evidence document number was the same. The motherboard was the same. Everything was the same.

Except the black chip was intact.

No scorch marks.

No cracks.

"Did we test this computer? Burn out the chip?"

Abernathy shook his head. Then his arm. Dozens of images filled the screen. Dozens of motherboards. Dozens of the same chip.

All scorched.

All cracked.

"It's the same with every computer we seized," Abernathy continued. His face had settled into a scowl. "The way we figure it—and by 'we' I mean the Shuttleworths—these chips were destroyed remotely. Someone realized we'd seized them and sent a kill signal that burned them out."

Joe whistled.

"So what are they?" Joe asked. "Why would someone burn out those chips?"

"Whoever burned them, *really* burned them," Abernathy said. "We have no idea what they were. The Shuttleworths are running all sorts of tests that I neither understand nor hold out much hope for. But Joe, this puts a whole new complexion on our case. A bunch of computers assembled by a slave workforce is one thing. Opportunistic and cold, but comprehensible. But add these chips into the mix—chips that the Shuttleworths don't recognize, that burned themselves to avoid closer inspection—and it pushes us into a whole new realm of criminal enterprise. Whatever those chips are, I think it's safe to say that someone doesn't want us to get a good look at them."

"So what are self-destructing chips doing in slave-assembled computers in a bowling alley in Luton?" Joe asked.

"Shall we go and ask our resident geniuses?" Abernathy asked, brightly.

<*))))><

In the R&D lab of YETI headquarters, the Shuttleworth brothers were absorbed in working their singular form of technological magic on the computers from the bowling alley. When Joe walked in, they both turned from what they were doing, stood to attention, and said, "Sir!" to Abernathy. Then they grinned from ear-to-ear, and said, "Joe. Good to see you."

In unison.

Sometimes, it was easy to imagine that the Shuttleworths were simply two halves of the same person. They often finished each other's sentences, laid out their workspaces as a mirror image of the other's, and they were both bona fide geniuses who excelled in kitting out YETI operatives with innovative equipment that made Benji Dunn's gear from the Mission: Impossible movies look like Tinkertoys.

There was, of course, a major difference between them: Geoff Shuttleworth was tall and lanky and gave no more shape to the lab coat he wore than it got from the hanger, while Greg Shuttleworth was short, squat, and tested the breaking strain of the buttons on his own coat.

"Hi, guys," Joe said. "Geoff, there's something different about you today."

Geoff gave an awkward shrug.

"I have been working out . . ." he said in a deep voice.

"He's keeping fit," Greg said in an altogether higher pitched voice.

Joe narrowed his eyes and looked at Geoff head-to-toe. There was no sign that working out had had any effect upon his body at all.

"I was thinking of the 'no glasses' thing." Joe laughed.

Geoff put a spidery hand up to his eyes, then nodded furiously. "Of course, of course," he said. "I'm breaking in a pair of contact lenses . . ."

". . . to varying degrees of success," his brother finished. "Although, what's wrong with glasses, I honestly don't know." He pushed his thick-lensed glasses up the slope of his nose to emphasize the point.

The brothers exchanged a glance that told Joe that the contact lens issue was far from settled, before snapping back to the matter at hand.

"The burnt-out chips are a secondary processor," Geoff told Abernathy and Joe. "At least, that's what we think. It's tech we haven't seen before . . ."

". . . and the computers we . . . *impounded* . . . work just fine without them," Greg added.

"We have tried to determine their purpose," Geoff said.

"But they were destroyed to prevent us from doing that very thing," Greg said. "The remote signal detonated the very heart of those components. Someone really didn't want us to examine them."

"So how can you tell it's tech you haven't seen before, then?" Joe asked.

"Because the remote signal detonated the very heart of those components," Geoff explained, and Joe wondered if he'd deliberately copied his brother's exact words, or if it was just part of their unique double act. "You have to ask yourself why someone would go to all the trouble of killing each one of those chips if they didn't contain something that someone didn't want anyone else to see."

"Are there any identifying marks on these chips?" Abernathy asked. "So we can ask the manufacturer directly?"

"We've got good news and bad news on that front," Greg said. "Which would you like first?"

"Say 'the bad news.'" Geoff advised. "It's a better story that way."

"The bad news, please," Abernathy said, but his face told the true story of the way he wanted the information relayed.

"Well, the chips burned out, did we mention that?" Greg asked. "And that was obviously part of the function of the remote destruction. So any maker's mark was destroyed, too . . ."

"Although, why there would be a maker's mark on such secret chips is a question I can't answer," Geoff said.

"But," Greg said.

"But," Geoff echoed.

"We *did* find a partial mark. So small, we needed a

microscope to make it out on one of the chips that didn't *quite* burn the same way as all of the others."

"Have a look." Geoff waved to a microscope on his desk.

Abernathy bent down, spinning the focus wheel to the disapproval of the Shuttleworths.

Then it was Joe's turn. He put his eye to the eyepiece and saw the surface of a chip magnified into a textured landscape of anthracite black, with a design printed on it in white ink, split down the middle by a crack, but still readable for all that.

It was a stylized letter *D* in the middle of a triangle with its points rounded off.

"Can we trace the mark?" Abernathy asked.

The Shuttleworths looked at him oddly.

"You don't recognize it, sir?" Geoff asked.

"Should I?"

"It's the logo of Dorian Systems." Greg said.

"Dorian . . . ?

"C'mon," Joe said. "Even I've heard of Dorian Systems, and they were before my time. You must have heard of *Space Dementia? Centipeter? Missile Storm? Echelon Warriors? Grathna's Revenge?*"

"I'm assuming that those are the names of video games," Abernathy said. "I can't think of anything else that would parade under such juvenile labels. Or get two nerds and a kid so excited."

"That's like saying 'I'm assuming this Mona Lisa you're

talking about is some kind of doodle,'" Geoff Shuttleworth said. "Dorian games are high art, the kind of games you'd get if Bach and Da Vinci and Shakespeare coded."

"I thought you said one of them was called *Centipeter*," Abernathy said, sounding like the word, itself, was distasteful to his delicate sensibilities. "That hardly sounds like high art to me."

"That's because you're not a gamer," Joe said exasperatedly. "We're talking some way retro gaming here. I've played all the Dorian classics. And not just for some kind of ironic laugh-at-how-bad-this-game-is reason. They are unlike anything else out there. Dorian is the Orson Welles of gaming, and *Centipeter* is his *Citizen Kane* . . ."

"*Grathna's Revenge* was his *Kane*," Greg objected. "It has a strong environmental message that came at a time when the Green Party had only just started gaining any kind of traction, and it played like an RPG . . ."

"Rocket propelled grenade?" Abernathy asked.

"Role-Playing Game." Greg said. "Anyway, *Centipeter* is great, but less socially relevant, so it's more like his *Touch of Evil*."

Abernathy made an exasperated sound. "If we could stop playing pop-culture-reference-tennis for a minute, could someone please tell me why Dorian chips are being used in these computers? And why someone felt the need to blow them up to prevent us identifying them?" He turned on his heel and headed for the door. "Briefing room, ten minutes," he barked. "I need background info, and I reckon I know three fanboys who are just the people to give it to me."

<*))))><

As it turned out, it was mainly the Shuttleworth brothers that filled both Joe and Abernathy in on Dorian's company background. Joe's knowledge was limited to the games, themselves, and that kind of knowledge was composed of words like *cool, amazing,* and *awesome,* none of which provided the kind of detailed analysis that Abernathy expected at a briefing.

Luckily, it didn't matter.

Dorian games seemed to be one of Greg and Geoff's specialized subjects.

"Richard Dorian was eighteen when he designed his first computer game," Geoff told them. "It was 1983, and Dorian was starting his first term at Trinity College, Cambridge when he bought an Acorn computer with the last of his savings from two years of summer jobs, and a decent chunk of his first grant check."

"He said in an interview, years later, that he ran the numbers and decided that a computer was more important to him than food and drink," Greg offered.

"It was a BBC Micro Model B," Geoff said, and Joe smiled at the ease with which each brother picked up the thread with scarcely a gap between the other's sentences.

"His lively, enquiring mind latched onto the possibilities that home computing offered, and before the end of his first year at college, he had already coded *Missile Storm* entirely in Assembly."

"Assembly?" Abernathy barked. "What are you talking about, man? Universities don't have assemblies."

"Er, I think they mean the programming language," Joe said. "They're not suggesting that he was designing a best-selling video game while sitting on the floor in the school auditorium while a policeman or fireman visited."

"Oh," Abernathy said. "Carry on."

"A lot of people started programming in BASIC," Greg explained.

"BASIC is a language that makes programming easier, but it's like coding through an extra layer between you and the computer," Geoff further clarified.

"And you have to remember that computer memory was incredibly limited back then," Greg said. "BASIC took up working memory, and The Model B had just 32 kilobytes of user RAM. That's 0.032 of a megabyte, a minuscule amount. To gain complete control over every last byte for game design, Dorian decided to forgo BASIC and learned Assembly, a symbolic representation of the binary commands that make up machine code. He effectively ditched the layer between the programmer and his computer, talking directly to the CPU."

"I weary of the nerdy delight in things I don't need to

know." Abernathy cautioned. "Put it in words that a human being can understand."

"It gave him turbocharged games compared to those written in BASIC," Geoff said. "As a result, *Missile Storm* was blisteringly fast."

"It also had great gameplay, and a clever story," Greg said. "But there was one thing that set it apart from most games of the time. It didn't just speed up to make the gameplay harder. It developed, it adapted, it *grew* as the gamer improved. The shift was fair. It was rewarding. And the reward was that you got to watch as the plot unfolded around you, complete with twists. Remember, this was long before the "Would You Kindly" twist of *Bioshock*, or the "one of the characters I was playing as was the killer all along" twist of *Heavy Rain*, but it's probably safe to say that the developers of those games whet their storytelling appetites on *Missile Storm*."

"Which is why it sold by the truckload," Geoff said. "Dorian raised his own capital by tapping the resources of his fellow undergraduates—or, more specifically, their dads—and set up his own software company, Dorian Systems. As a result, midway through his second year at Cambridge, Dorian was running a hugely successful company that made finishing his studies irrelevant. He left without graduating, and poured his energies into developing more and more elaborate, entertaining games."

"Or more and more elaborate wastes of time," Abernathy

said. "I guess I like to deny to myself that people actually make money out of these electronic gewgaws."

The Shuttleworths both rolled their eyes.

"Modern games can cost hundreds of millions of dollars to make," Greg told him.

"And can still turn huge profits," Geoff added. "I think it's time they were acknowledged as something more than mere *gewgaws*."

"Come back for that acknowledgment when they stop fetishizing violence and demeaning women," Abernathy said.

Geoff Shuttleworth looked on the verge of explosive anger, or as close to it as he could get, but his brother patted him on the shoulder, gave him a glance and an almost imperceptible shake of the head, and Geoff calmed down immediately.

Abernathy carried on, oblivious. "So, the long, tall, and short of it is that Dorian made lots of money by making and selling video games to people old enough to know better."

"Yes," Geoff said, through slightly gritted teeth. Joe didn't think he'd ever seen one of the Shuttleworths angry with Abernathy, or with anyone for that matter. It was kind of interesting to see how one of them remained calm enough to stop the other from saying something he might end up regretting. Once more, it seemed almost like they were two halves of the same individual, yin and yang.

Joe, however, had no qualms about calling Abernathy out on some of his pompous B.S. "While I'm certain that times were a lot more intellectually rewarding in the rosy-tinted past you seem to compare the modern age to," he said, "when kids ran down the bridleways with a hoop and a stick, or entertained themselves trying to get balls into cups or hitting balls with bats that were attached by rubber bands, I don't think you can seriously dispute that computer games are just another example of humanity's ingenuity and are a legitimate art form all of their own."

"I certainly can," Abernathy said, but Joe was relieved to see he was smiling. "If *Pac-Man* is art, then the term has become next to meaningless."

"But you're judging an entire genre of entertainment on its earliest examples," Joe said. "You would never have gotten the *Mona Lisa* if it weren't for the cave paintings at Lascaux, but you wouldn't judge the entire history of painted art on the strength of the horses daubed on the walls there. And if you look at the difference between those cave paintings and the *Mona Lisa* you'll see it took seventeen thousand years to refine the artistic techniques that led from one to the other. In the case of *Pac-Man* to, say, *Grand Theft Auto V*, I think you'll find it happened in less than forty."

"So stealing digital cars is the computer game's version of the *Mona Lisa*?" Abernathy said. "Although, I have to admit I was impressed when I found the hatch from *Lost* in the ocean near the San Chianski Mountains."

Joe did a double take. "Wait a minute, you can do that in *GTA V*?" He asked.

"If you use the submersible," Abernathy said, grinning. Then he rolled his eyes. "Newbs." He turned to the Shuttleworths. "So, enough of that. The important question is, I think, what is Dorian doing now?"

There were a few moments of bemused silence as the brothers digested the revelation that Abernathy had not only heard of *GTA V*, he'd also played it to such an extent that he'd found something that only die-hard gamer nerds would, and then Greg pulled himself together.

"Dorian made a lot of money from his games, poured it into a massive expansion program swallowing up a lot of smaller software and hardware manufacturers in the process, and ended up doing what a lot of high-tech companies end up doing: he took his business overseas. Dorian has two offices in California—one in Palo Alto, the other in LA which is hardly surprising . . ."

"Why is that 'hardly surprising'?" Abernathy asked.

"Dorian games are the kind of cutting-edge tech that means they belong in Silicon Valley, but their games are becoming more and more like interactive movies," Geoff replied. "They're huge productions now, with movie-sized budgets and A-list celebrities providing voices, and use motion-capture acting. It stands to reason that the company needs to be where all that talent—and money—lives. Having a foot in both Silicon Valley and Hollywood just seems appropriate."

"Dorian is reinventing what it means to be a global

entertainment brand," Greg said. "He has the best of the high-tech *and* entertainment industries at his command. He's been talking about a merging of games and film for a long time since his games have always been story-based. If you look at the video game landscape today, you can see that convergence is already happening."

"With games like *Heavy Rain* and *Beyond: Two Souls*, the French video game developers, Quantic Dream, have already blurred the distinction between 'game' and 'interactive movie,' and with *Until Dawn*, Supermassive Games raised the bar even farther with a 'butterfly effect' system for branching the narrative based on the decisions of the player." Geoff was flapping his arms around, which suggested to Joe that he was *very* excited about this direction for video games.

"Dorian is set to blow them all out of the water with the release of *NeWToPia,* a game that promises to blur that line even further. A-list voice actors, multiple storylines that can completely alter the overall plot based on decisions the player makes. In *Until Dawn,* the story, itself, was set in stone. Your decisions only affected small parts of the story—mainly how many characters would survive to the end of the game—but the early buzz with *NeWToPia* is that the stakes are different. By following a set of decisions, the player can discover one facet of a larger plot, and by following another set, he or she can discover other completely different content. The plot, or rather the game engine, adapts to your choices. Passing up one set of choices closes off a branch of the story, but opens up another."

"The word is," Greg continued, "that there is no right or wrong way to play it—no single set of decisions that will lead to an ending—because the game has so many paths and so many endings, that even a set of wrong choices will still lead to a pretty satisfying, if sometimes bleak or disturbing, conclusion."

"It sounds like an overpriced version of one of those Choose Your Own Adventure books," Abernathy said. "If you want to hit the dragon with your sword, turn to page 189. If you want to run away from the dragon, turn to page 96. Hardly the dawning of a new multimedia age now, is it?"

Geoff shook his head. Vigorously.

"That's like saying an iPhone is like an old brick Nokia because it can make telephone calls. The difference is the tech. The story in *NeWToPia* is *adaptive*. You can make so many choices, that it's like the game is able to adapt to those choices and spin off in new and interesting ways."

"Clever software," Joe said. "I've read a lot about the game, but I hear that it's going to be very expensive."

"That's because it's not just software," Greg said. "At the heart of the *NeWToPia* experience is a new piece of tech—a peripheral that hooks up to your PC or console. Something that Dorian has been working on for *years*."

"And what is it?" Joe asked. "This new tech that's going to have me forking out all this extra money?"

Geoff and Greg shrugged in unison.

"You won't believe the secrecy surrounding the specs," Greg said. "I mean the next iPhone is practically open source compared to this bad boy."

"And the secrecy means that, instead of actual information, the Internet is rife with rumor and speculation," Geoff said. "The web is saying that it could be anything from a little add-on memory to a neural net via total immersion virtual reality and quantum computing."

"What now?" Abernathy said.

"A bunch of science fiction ideas that certainly won't be in the add-on," Greg said. "The point is, no one knows."

"But it could have . . . I don't know . . . a new kind of Dorian chip in it." Abernathy said, cutting through all the clutter and homing straight in on the heart of the matter.

Joe saw where he was leading and whistled. "You think that maybe there's a connection between the computers we seized and the new Dorian game? But how would a bunch of lowlifes get a hold of something that no one else on the planet can?" Joe asked.

"And why would they?" Geoff asked.

"I guess we need to know whether the chip that didn't completely self-destruct is indeed Dorian's latest tech, and if it is, we need to know exactly what it does." Abernathy said.

"And how are we going to do that?" Joe wanted to know.

"Field trip," Abernathy said. "You, me, and the Brothers Shuttleworth are going to America to ask."

"But Dorian is notoriously reclusive," Greg said.

"He's never seen in public," Geoff continued. "He prefers to let his games do the talking for him."

"He had some kind of health scare in the '90s that led to him slipping out of the public eye, and he liked it so much . . ."

". . . he's kept it up ever since. He doesn't do interviews, so he's not going to . . . Wait, what did you say? You want us to . . . ?"

Greg Shuttleworth looked like his legs were going to collapse out from under him.

"That's right." Abernathy said. "You're coming, too."

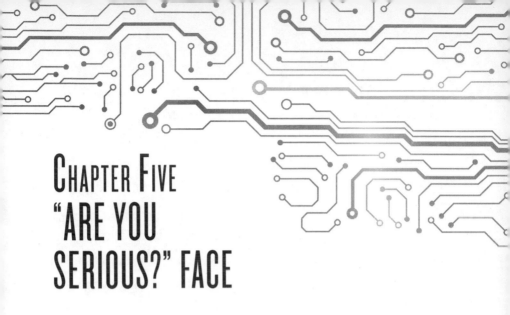

Chapter Five
"ARE YOU SERIOUS?" FACE

Ani realized that she watched too much TV.

The source of this revelation was the disappointment she felt when the physical address given to her by the *victorious* website turned out to be in central London. She'd been hoping for something cool, like an abandoned arcade in a dilapidated fairground, but knew that was only because it was the location of the headquarters of *fsociety* in *Mr. Robot*.

But where she found herself now couldn't be farther away from that lovely fiction. She was standing in front of an anonymous pile of glass blocks that an architect had probably convinced his client looked visionary, but turned out to be so bland, that it managed to recede back into an already quite dull section of Tottenham Court Road.

It was the type of managed office suite that one rented on a month-by-month basis to give your business more prestige than a unit on an industrial park or a home office ever could. Your monthly payment bought you as much square footage as your budget would stretch to, a broadband and phone package, and a part-share in a receptionist who would answer the phone with your company name, but certainly wouldn't make you tea or coffee or run errands for you.

VTR Industries was a vague enough name for a high-tech company that no one would give it a second look, but it had enough of the letters of *victorious* in it to make her sure she was in the right place.

The digital interview had led to the website, and that had led her here. The only other information had been a time and date (now) and the instruction:

come alone. dress nice.

If the message had been meant for her, alone, based on her recruiter's recommendation, then it seemed like a pretty damned sexist instruction, so Ani clad herself in black—smart, expensive clothes (a YETI salary was a pretty amazing thing) that managed to cover over every curve and most of her flesh, but still managed to look "nice" in a hacker-chic kind of way. She'd even finished the outfit off with some black, knee-high, lace-up boots that were very much in the Raven Adler vein. She'd broken the fem-hacker stereotype of "little-to-no make-up" by going for full-on war paint.

Reflected in the mirrored glass of the offices, she thought she looked pretty good.

Way better than just "nice."

She took a deep breath and entered the building.

The reception area was spacious, modern, and functional. It was hard to say anything else about it, really. Sure, there were a sprinkling of chairs, sofas, and low tables to give the illusion of the space being designed for humans to inhabit, but in truth, it was all too corporate and staged to feel comfortable.

Behind a desk on the far side of the room, a bored blonde tried to embody a whole bunch of stereotypes by ignoring Ani's entrance and fussing with her nails with a polka dot emery board. She lost marks off her professional rating when she carried on filing her nails as Ani approached. The only way she could have made a worse impression was if she'd been chewing gum.

"Hi," Ani said, and the woman looked up, but continued her manicure. "I have a meeting at VTR."

"Name?" the woman said in a voice that proved that "bored" wasn't just a look this woman cultivated, but a holistic diagnosis of the woman's entire personality.

"And a good afternoon to you, too," Ani said. "No name. Just an invitation code: 57A18."

The woman made the simple act of reaching for a phone look like a physical inconvenience.

"There's a girl here," she said, after lifting up the handset and making a pantomime of pressing a button. "That's right. Yes. Yes, she has a number. A7 . . ."

She frowned, then looked at Ani and raised an eyebrow of rude inquiry.

"57A18," Ani repeated.

"578 . . ." Eyebrow raise.

"57A," Ani said slowly.

"57A . . ." Eyebrow raise.

"18," Ani finished.

"57A18," the woman said into the phone, and listened for further instructions. "Sure. I'll send her up."

If the woman was embarrassed by her inability to remember and repeat a five-character sequence, then she didn't show it. Instead, she pointed to a glass-fronted elevator and said, "Fifth floor. Ask for Mr. Ian Black."

The finger she pointed with had a nail that looked like it needed more manicuring.

As Ani walked to the elevator, she thought about the name she'd just been given. Mr. Ian Black? Seriously? Mystery in black? She wondered if everyone in *victorious* was handed out cheap puns as Secret Squirrel names.

Ani turned back to thank the woman, but she was already deeply involved in buffing her nails, so the youngest YETI operative shrugged, entered the elevator when the doors opened, and hit 5.

<*))))><

Ani knew, deep down, that she was being overly harsh in

her judgment of the woman on the desk. She was, after all, probably earning something close to minimum wage and was just trying to get through her days. Ani knew that she was just generally a bit irritated today.

She knew why, too.

When she'd dropped by YETI to report her progress, Abernathy had been distracted and, for the for the first time since joining up, she'd felt that her days as the new girl—with all the novelty value that afforded her—were already coming to an end. It had been a whirlwind few months of adjustment and learning, but the thing that had gotten her through was the feeling that her skills made her somewhat indispensable. She'd kind of gotten used to being the golden girl, so Abernathy's brusque treatment had made her feel more than a little deflated.

She'd caught up with him in his office, and when she told him about her meeting with members of *victorious*, she could tell his mind was on other things.

"That's great, Ani," he'd said. "We really need to make some headway on this, and this sounds promising. Really great."

From anyone else, that might have sounded like positive encouragement, but Abernathy's eyes had never left his computer screen and his voice didn't *quite* match his words. It had sounded too much like the voice of a parent humoring his kid while trying to watch TV.

Sure, she understood that Abernathy—and YETI—had

a whole bunch of cases going right now, but when she'd returned from the Yeovil operation, she'd felt like hers was, at least, reasonably important, if not critical.

She'd already reached the door when Abernathy spoke again:

"If you've got a few minutes, I have a couple of urgent tasks requiring your expert skills," he'd said. "You know Leeza Marsh? Of course you do. She'll fill you in on the details."

More urgent than preparing for a meeting with the inner circle of victorious? Ani had thought bitterly.

She was ashamed to find that she felt disappointed as she left Abernathy's office.

It probably wasn't personal. She knew that.

Still, she'd done the jobs that Abernathy had asked of her—insinuating information onto a couple of networks—but she also punched the crap out of a bag in the gym before leaving.

<*))))><

She was met at the door of the left on the fifth floor by a reasonably handsome twenty-something who'd decided that slicking back his hair needed to be done with so much gel that it looked like it was sculpted out of a single solid block. He had a warm smile, a firm handshake, and the inability to look Ani in the eye for longer than about a second.

"So, you're the newest member of our little cell, huh?" he said warmly. "I'm Ian. Ian Black."

"Ani," she told him. "Er, did you say cell?"

She was confused by a couple of things. First, could the man's name actually *be* Mr. Ian Black? And, second, by his odd use of word *cell*.

Ian nodded, met her eye for another brief moment, then turned away and started off down a white corridor.

"Follow me," he said. "I'll give you the grand tour."

Ani followed him past a couple of closed doors on the right, before he swerved through an open door on the left.

Ani had read a lot about boiler rooms, those less than respectable call centers where unscrupulous scammers sold dodgy stocks and shares over the phone, often to retirees probably just happy to be talking to anyone. She had always pictured them as crowded, chaotic environments, with rows of workstations piled into small spaces.

The office she walked into was almost perfectly matched that image, except instead of plying their trade on telephones, the thirty or so people in the room were tapping away at keyboards with only small sheets of plywood between them to give the impression of individual workstations.

Ian gestured around the room.

None of the keyboard jockeys even looked her way.

"Welcome to the bear pit," he said. "Everyone here is a bona fide legend of the keyboard, and it's rare, indeed, that someone impresses us enough to get a seat here." He looked Ani in the eye for the longest time he'd managed so far: a full three seconds. "Good to have you aboard," he said.

Ani nodded. "It's good to be here." She ignored the mixed metaphors of animal cruelty and boats. "Wherever and whatever 'here' is."

Ian Black gave her a lopsided grin. "This is the head-quarters of London's first Dead Cell."

"*Dead Cell* as in what makes up dust?" Ani asked. "Or as in characters in a video game by Hideo Kojima?"

Black looked surprised, and maybe a little impressed. It was hard to tell because he never looked her way long enough for her to get a proper read on him. If it was the latter, then he was a little too easily impressed. Kojima was a legend, and she'd played every game in the Metal Gear series. Most of them, more than once. Dead Cell were an anti-terrorist strike team in *Metal Gear Solid 2* but, Ani thought, it seemed a telling detail that Dead Cell were the bad guys, or at least the tools of the bad guys, in the game.

Was that deliberate? Or just not thought through?

"The latter," Black said. "You see, *victorious* is organized into cells that we call Dead Cells, with each Dead Cell acting with little or no knowledge of the activities or personnel of any of the others. That way, if one cell is compromised, it's *only* one cell that's compromised. Like a Hydra, we have many heads. Cut one off, another will grow in its place. Welcome to the dawn of a new era in hacktivism: the good guys win."

Ani nodded, but wondered if Black had noticed he'd just invoked the name of another fictional bunch of bad guys— Hydra, from Marvel Comics—or that his bragging about the way that *victorious*'s cells were organized was exactly the same way a lot of terrorist groups acted.

Abernathy had warned her that they were encountering a new kind of hacktivism, but Ani had doubted that they were anything more than a bunch of disenfranchised kids with a little too much time on their hands and a sparkly new banner to parade their skillz under.

Seeing this number of hackers working together in an office—hackers were by pretty much self-definition, loners—made her wonder if Abernathy hadn't been on to something.

"We're going to be having a strategy meeting soon," Black told her, "and you'll get your first task assigned to you then, so how about I get you set up at a workstation and you can familiarize yourself with our system here? Maybe meet some of your partners in crime?"

He smiled to show that his last remark had been a joke, but Ani couldn't help but think it might also be entirely accurate.

Black led her to an unused desk pretty much in the center of the room, and gestured toward the scuzzy office chair in front of it.

"Your place in history awaits," he told her, obviously overdoing it with the macho crap. "It's all set up and ready to go. Your new screen name is *RedQueen*, capital *R*, capital *Q*, and your password is *cedar*, all lowercase. I suggest you change it now. Strat-meet in about twenty. See you in the conference room."

He turned and walked away, back to a desk on the far side of the room where he started punching the keyboard.

Induction over, then, Ani thought. *Strat-meet? What about 'egy' and 'ing' is so difficult to say that you have to drop them from the ends of words?*

She sat down, pulled the keyboard closer, and looked at the screen.

The computer was a ho-hum, generic PC running a version of Kali Linux, designed for security testing of networks through an arsenal of penetration tools, among them, some pretty sophisticated password crackers, packet analyzers, and port scanners. YETI's hacking kit was largely made of the same stuff, and she clicked through the system trying to note the differences, just to kill time.

It was a workhorse computer, nothing special, but it seemed capable of doing all of the things she'd be asking of it. She was, truthfully, a little disappointed by it, but maybe she was just spoiled for tech now.

She changed her password, yawned, and looked around her. An eager pair of eyes magnified by thick lenses in black frames, met hers from the desk to her right.

"New, huh?" the guy said, a short and squat teenager

with a complexion that said too much junk food, not enough daylight: a pallid monitor tan shaded in with blackheads.

"Yeah," Ani said. "First day."

"It's like being at work." The guy winked, and then extended a pudgy hand. "I'm the Count of Ten."

"RedQueen," Ani said, taking the hand and shaking it, making a point of not wrinkling her nose when she felt how clammy it was.

"Excited?" the Count asked.

"Not yet. I'll save that for the briefing."

"El Capitan Black *loves* his briefings," the Count told her. "Still, this one should be good."

"Oh?"

"Phase Two." the Count explained. "When we start taking this whole enterprise a little further, a little more publicly."

"How was Phase One?"

"DDoS attacks on a bunch of heavy hitters' servers. Worms, viruses, and Trojans injected into the body politic. The groundwork."

"For?"

"I, for one, am looking forward to finding out. Phase One was a limbering up exercise, apparently. Checking our tools against the enemy. Phase Two is where it all starts to make sense. At least, that's what I've heard. Guess that's why they brought you on board. You must have some pretty mad skillz."

"I try."

"Just make sure you bring your A game"—the Count turned back to his screen—"or they'll be looking for someone else to fill that desk. Just like the guy before you."

Ani gave him a quizzical glance, but the Count didn't turn back. Ani thought about what he'd said—*It's like being at work*—and decided that was a pretty accurate assessment of the operation here. Which was, it had to be said, pretty damn weird. Sure, you could treat people like staff if they were getting paid for it because . . . well, because that was the very definition of *staff*, but hiring and, apparently, firing people, cramming them into an office, that didn't sound like a hacker paradise. It sounded . . . *wrong*.

She didn't deal in stereotypes, but some of them came about for a reason. One of the most prevalent stereotypes of hackers was that they were loners, spending all their time in their rooms because of social inadequacies. Ani knew this to be false. Lots of the hackers she knew were outgoing, with lively social lives, lots of friends, and were actually pretty socially adept. In truth, good hackers *had* to be socially adept. A significant weapon in a hacker's arsenal wasn't her computer, or her software, but rather her ability to make people trust her. Social engineering got around many computer security systems. A firm could have all the security in the world plastered onto their network, but a phone call to an employee that got him to divulge his username and password could circumvent all of it.

Hacking, itself, *was* a solitary act. Pretty much by necessity, it was perpetrated by individuals sitting alone at their computers. The concentration needed could be intense, but so was the purpose behind it. Curiosity. The search for information that no one else had seen, for digital forbidden fruit. It wasn't really a team sport.

But hacking wasn't this. It wasn't a room packed with people, organized to appear like a workplace. This went against her every instinct.

She didn't like it.

She didn't like it at all.

<*))))><

The briefing was about an hour later. Everyone got up from their workstations and filed through a door on the left beyond which was a meeting room with a table and chairs at the front and a bunch more chairs arranged audience-style to face them. Three people sat behind the table and Ani was surprised to see that none of them were Ian Black; he was squashed into a plastic seat like everyone else from the office.

The guy on the left was wearing a Metallica T-shirt and looked . . . well, pretty much as you'd expect from the T-shirt: long hair, tattoos, plug earring in an overstretched hole, ripped jeans, and bullet belt. Probably about eighteen years old. In the middle was someone who looked more like an accountant than a hacker: male, mid-to-late twenties, sharp suit, expensive accessories, preppy flick in the hair, and cold, calculating eyes. Rounding out the trio was a girl, probably about the same age as Ani, wearing army surplus camo, a leather jacket over an ALL CAPS, ALL RAGE, ALL THE TIME T-shirt, sporting a blonde Mohawk.

They waited until everyone was seated and had quieted down, and then the guy in the middle stood up. All eyes were on him. The room was deathly silent. *Unnaturally silent*, Ani thought. No coughing, chattering, or whispering.

"Today is a good day," the man said, in a mellifluous voice, not loud but somehow still commanding, with the hint of an Eastern European or Scandinavian accent. "It is the day that we begin our journey out of the shadows and into the light. Up until now, *victorious* has just been chatter on the web, vague hints and allusions, but nothing concrete, with no visible members. To most, it is nothing more than a digital urban legend.

"All movements start small. One or two people banding together over a shared vision, dream, or ideology. In time, the movement grows. A tiny branch falls from a tree on a mountain slope, it makes a snowball, a snowfall, then an avalanche. The avalanche is only the first visible sign of the chain of causality that came before. And our movement has followed that exponential growth. From one to few to many. We are almost ready to earn the label 'movement.'"

He turned to the girl, who reached down beneath the

table and retrieved the flight case she'd obviously stowed there. She opened it, took out a piece of tech and, with some effort, placed it on the table: a large rectangle of plastic that Ani *sort of* recognized as a 3-D printer, but it was sleeker, and more compact than the ones she'd seen before. The woman plugged the unit in, inserted a memory stick into a port on the side of the printer, pressed a few buttons and the machine started doing its thing.

Whatever its *thing* might be.

Ani hoped it wasn't a My Little Pony, or a bust of Yoda, which seemed to be the most popular things on her quick scans through 3-D printing videos on YouTube. Whatever it was, it was going to take a long time, that much Ani knew.

When the printer was underway, remarkably quietly, the woman sat back down.

Mr. Metallica stood up.

"So, I say '*Anonymous*' and you know exactly who I mean," he said, in an oddly high-pitched voice that didn't fit with the rest of his image. "Of course, *we* all know them through their work, but the general public is aware of them, too. Tell me why?"

There was a self-conscious silence in the room, with no one wanting to answer a question obviously directed at them. It was like being in school. After ten seconds of uncomfortable silence, Ani thought it was time to put them all out of their misery.

"The *V for Vendetta* masks," she offered. "They backed

up their attacks on The Church of Scientology—Project Chanology—by appearing in public, in their thousands, hiding their faces behind Guy Fawkes masks. It gave the movement a single face: and it gave Anonymous something they hadn't had before: a brand."

A few of the people in the audience nodded as if it was *exactly* what they were about to say themselves.

Mr. Metallica nodded, too.

"Couldn't have put it better myself," he said. "Thank you. *Anonymous* branded themselves, and hid their identities at the same time. It's tremendously economic. They burned themselves onto the cultural landscape and gained true anonymity at the same time."

He looked at Ms. Hacker at the other end of the table. She shook her head, checked the printer, and held up two fingers.

Ani was puzzled. It looked like Mr. Metallica was waiting for whatever the 3-D printer was generating, but Ani knew that couldn't be the case as those things took ages to print anything.

"It may not be original," Mr. Metallica said, "but we are entering Phase Two of our endeavors, and that means it's time that we, too, did something to brand ourselves. To project ourselves onto the cultural landscape. With an image that will confuse, anger, provoke, but that we can all hide our faces behind.

"If you think about the Guy Fawkes mask that has become ubiquitous, you can see that it both serves and undermines its own purposes. For a group with an anti-capitalist agenda to use masks that make money for a large corporation, Time Warner, seems a little self-defeating. But we can see the reason: Guy Fawkes is a potent image of anti-government action, and the fact that he didn't succeed in blowing up the Houses of Parliament is neither here nor there. The message is clear. The status cannot remain quo. It must be brought down, and society made fairer. Just because we use computer keyboards instead of explosives merely demonstrates the dramatic way the battlefield has changed."

He looked over at Ms. Hacker and she nodded.

"So," he said, somewhat overdramatically, "a symbol, A brand. Something to hide our faces and convey a message that cannot be ignored.

"But we will not be rallying behind Guy Fawkes. Rather, his modern counterpart. Ladies and gentlemen, I present to you our new symbol. Our brand. Our disguise."

Ms. Hacker opened the printer and put her hand inside. Again, Ani couldn't believe that the printer had completed its task so quickly. Especially for something the size of a human face mask. It gave her a strange feeling in her stomach, a knot of concern.

The knot cinched tighter, however, when the hacker girl pulled the completed mask from the printer.

Ani felt appalled, angry, sick and more than a little afraid.

The mask was a 3-D-printed replica of a face she knew all too well.

It kind of explained the name *victorious*, too.

It was the face of Victor Palgrave.

Chapter Six
I DON'T KNOW
WHAT I EXPECTED

Joe had never been to LA before, but there was no time for any sightseeing that couldn't be accomplished from the window of the limo as they drove from LAX. A place that Joe had always wanted to visit flashed by so fast, it might as well have been anywhere.

Even Luton.

Or Des Moines.

Abernathy was unusually quiet, just as he had been for the twelve-hour flight. Joe didn't know if it was just that he didn't have anything to say, or if travel always had this effect on him. He knew so little about Abernathy outside of his role as the head of YETI, and had hoped that maybe traveling together would allow him a deeper insight into just what made the man tick. So much for that. Abernathy read books on a YETI tablet like Ani's, slept sitting bolt upright, and occasionally looked out the window, but apart from that was an island unto himself.

Joe read, too. He played games on his PS Vita, then read some more. He tried to sleep and failed miserably: it was hard to relax in a tin can hurtling over the Atlantic. Flights were like being stuck in limbo.

So, too, was a limo drive from the airport.

They were both so passive: put your trust in the guy in control and the rest was simply a matter of waiting to reach a destination.

World Way had led onto Sepulveda Boulevard, then the One-Ten.

Joe sat back and let it all blur by his windows. It was a procession of flat, near-featureless hardtop cars, electricity pylons, and palm trees. The intermittent buildings on both sides of the Harbor Freeway were squat and similar. It was like those backgrounds in cartoons that are looped to save on drawings.

The limo stopped in West Hollywood, across the street from the LA office of BuzzFeed and next to a high-end yoga studio. The bright black on red Dorian logo was hardly subtle, stretching across the whole front wall.

Abernathy pushed open the doors and they walked into a reception area that was a lot smaller than the size, and ostentatious logo, of the exterior had suggested it would be. A waiting room that looked designed to discourage waiting. Bare. Minimalist. The only furniture was two wooden benches that looked more like pieces of corporate sculpture than anything you were actually supposed to sit on. A woman sat behind a glass screen, a corporate smile plastered across her face. Joe wondered if it was hard to show real emotions when you faked it all day, then realized that that was pretty much the description of an undercover agent and made a note to stop being so judgmental all the time.

"How can I help you today?" the woman asked with the sort of enthusiasm that comes from training seminars and regular reviews.

"We are here to see Mr. Curtiz," Abernathy told her in his most aristocratically-inflected voice, even fleshing out the contraction "we're" to add gravitas. "I believe we are early."

The woman checked one of three screens, then nodded.

"I have you booked in for three," she confirmed. "So yes, you're early. I'll see if he's free."

She picked up a phone and spoke quietly into the mouthpiece. She listened for a moment and her corporate mask slipped a little, revealing the human being that lived behind the façade. She'd recovered her mask before she hung up, but Joe guessed she'd just received a dressing down from someone with direct influence over her future with the company.

"He will be free in a moment," she told them. "We seem to have misplaced the . . . er, someone forgot to enter the reason for your visit into the system."

Abernathy did an excellent impression of someone insulted by this admission. It was all in the arch of an eyebrow and the downward turn of the mouth. Anyone would have thought that he'd really *had* an appointment before Ani surreptitiously entered one onto the company's server just before they'd left YETI HQ for the airport.

"Still, it's not a problem . . ." the woman added hurriedly. "And I really must apologize."

"No need," Abernathy said in a voice that suggested precisely the opposite. "Do we wait here?" He pointed at the medieval torture seating. The woman nodded.

Abernathy and Joe sat down. The benches were slightly less comfortable than they'd looked. There were no magazines, papers, or corporate screens.

"Play with your smartphone," Abernathy whispered to Joe. "Just make sure it's on camera mode, and that you get a shot of our receptionist, and anything—or anyone—else that looks interesting."

Joe wanted to tell Abernathy that this wasn't his first rodeo, but in the end did as he was told, getting his phone out of his jacket pocket and acting like any other bored teen.

"I'm surprised you haven't gotten a camera embedded in my brain yet," he joked out of the side of his mouth. "It would be easier."

"Oh, we're working on it." Abernathy replied.

<*))))><

Ten minutes later, a door opened to the left of Reception.

The guy who came out was shaggy-haired with a wide, snouty face. He looked to be in his mid-forties, but was dressing a good twenty years younger, as if that was ever going to help him stay young. Joe thought it was the guy they were here to meet, but instead of coming over to them, he threw a quick quip at the receptionist—her professional demeanor didn't slip for a second in any place but the eyes—and then made for the exit. Joe snapped a couple of photos of him, more out of hope than in expectation that he was anyone important, and then slumped back into waiting.

It was a full five minutes before the door opened again, this time enough of a crack for someone to stick his head and shoulders through. A thirty-something executive with a slick suit, a Beverley Hills hipster hairdo, a deep-water tan, and a humorless face. He eyed Abernathy and Joe, then raised an inquiring eyebrow at the receptionist. She nodded and the guy gestured for them to follow him using only his head and neck in a textbook display of managerial economy.

Follow him they did. Joe held his smartphone loosely in his hand, video camera running. Like the astronauts who'd first walked on the moon and taken such amazing pictures with cameras fixed to their suits, Joe had practiced this move a lot, making it look as if it was impossible that he *was* filming. He knew the angles of the wrist that he needed to get good footage of anyone or anything.

On the other side of the door was the secret that the

reception area was keeping mighty quiet: a vast, open plan office area spread over four floors, all high modernism, polished chrome, clinical lines, and glass. The man led them through the bustling environment and Joe started picking out discreet working zones that were only suggested because of the lack of concrete, physical demarcation zones. The nerds were the easiest to locate: their zone was filled with the kind of stuff you'd expect—computers with huge screens, action figures, a foosball table—along with a few things that made Joe feel pretty envious—a pinball table, three arcade machines, assorted beanbag chairs and soft furnishings, and what looked like a Starbucks counter.

The man led them through the space without commenting on any of it, taking them up a couple of staircases that seemed to defy gravity, and into a glass cube with informal seating and no desk. The man gestured to a couple of chairs before taking one himself.

"Sebastian Curtiz. Welcome to Dorian Interactive."

They were the first words the man had spoken since they'd met him.

Abernathy introduced himself and Joe, using their actual names, and then launched into some tedious, but well-intentioned small talk about traffic, the building and—inevitably—the weather.

When he was done, the man brushed at his trousers and asked, "And how can I help you today?"

This was the moment that Joe'd been waiting for—

Abernathy's cover story. Joe was betting on an article for a too-good-to-refuse magazine, which provided an easy in, an eager-to-please interviewee, and a perfect excuse to ask questions.

So he was surprised when Abernathy cleared his throat, reached into his pocket, took out the offending burnt-out Dorian chip, tossed it to Curtiz, and said in his driest, most penetrating voice: "I don't suppose you'd care to tell us what this is, would you?"

Chapter Seven
COINCIDENCE? I THINK NOT

The guard looked at her ID, squinted, held it up to the light, clicked his tongue, rotated it in his fingers, sucked his teeth, held it closer to his eyes and still couldn't find fault with it. It wasn't for lack of trying. It was a pretty important looking document that had been messengered over to her, accompanied by another document that the guard had given the same amount of scrutiny, and had also failed to find fault with.

So the man gave her a long look, comparing her actual, physical self to the tiny photographic reproduction of her laminated on her ID, then handed it back to her with a click of his tongue and a bewildered shake of his head.

"S'pose that's you," he said in a grudging tone that suggested he'd far rather it hadn't been. "You're a bit young for this, aren't you? Does your mum know you're out?"

Ani bristled. In her experience, patronizing was never a good conversational maneuver.

"Two things," she said. "First up, too young? Is that what you take away from a person presenting you with ID that puts her on the same level of intelligence clearing as James-bloody-Bond? Her age? And, secondly, my mum? Really? Do spies really tell their mums when they're on missions? Doesn't that kind of negate the whole 'security' bit of 'security services'? I suggest you work on your interpersonal skills, especially with regards to being patronizing to young women, and I'll keep your attitude out of my report. Deal?"

The guard looked nonplussed, which Ani suspected was pretty much his default setting. She sat down without another word and waited for her name to be called.

When it was, she felt a moment of self-doubt, which was quickly followed by a wave of fear. She rose above the first feeling, squashed the second down, and was shown into the interview room. A small, perfunctory space with no concessions to comfort, just a graffiti-scarred table and two institutional-looking chairs. On the other side of the table, she faced a man dressed in a prison jumpsuit

The man looked up as she entered.

He did an ugly thing with his mouth that was based upon the concept of the smile, but seemed to have a few more levels of meaning.

"Ani Lee," Victor Palgrave said. "How delightful. You must really be in trouble to come to see me."

<*))))><

Abernathy had been out of the country, so Ani was put through to someone named Minaxi Desai. She'd seen the woman around YETI HQ: tall, elegant, aloof. They'd never actually spoken, but you'd never have known that from the warmth of Ms. Desai's greeting.

"Ani, how lovely to hear from you," she said. "Minaxi Desai, but you simply must call me Mina."

"Okay, Mina," Ani said, grimly. "Are you up to date on the *victorious* case?"

"I believe so," Mina replied. "As up to date I can be with Abernathy, anyway. He can forget to keep people in the loop when he gets focused . . ."

"Or when he just forgets," Ani joked. "Look, the case just took a disturbing twist, and I need to talk to someone about it."

"Try me."

"Okay."

Ani took in a breath to calm the panic she was experiencing. That she'd been experiencing ever since Ms. Hacker pulled the mask from the 3-D printer.

"*victorious*," Ani said. "They just revealed the face they're going to hide behind. Literally. It's a 3-D-printed mask. The face of Victor Palgrave."

"Palgrave?"

"Yeah, they're calling him the new Guy Fawkes. Using his face as the symbol of the next phase of their operations."

"And do you what know what that next phase is?"

"Not yet. It was my first day at a *victorious* cell, more like corporate orientation with a side order of menial hacking. We were told that the targets are big and that the world is going to change when we are done. It's either an exaggeration or a mission statement. I figure the latter, but then I'm paranoid."

"Is it a coincidence that 'victor' features so predominantly in '*victorious*'?"

"I don't think so. Everything about this seems . . . purposeful. Strategized. And the tech is extraordinary. The 3-D printer I saw was tiny and lightning fast, like nothing on the market. I suspect that the organization is bigger, and better bankrolled, than anyone previously thought. And I'm worried that there's something more behind it than simple mischief. Something much scarier."

"What?"

"An ideology," Ani said. "A bunch of hacking geniuses is one thing, but they're disparate. Contrary. They don't play well with others. They fall out over the most trivial things, and they all have different ideas about what to hack and why they're doing it. Having them band together under a single flag, not a loose consensus like Anonymous, makes me uneasy."

"So how can we help?" Mina asked.

"I need to find a handle on the whole Palgrave connection," Ani said. "It seems too coincidental that they have adopted him as their figurehead. And I hate coincidences.

I think . . . I think someone needs to interview Victor Palgrave. See if he knows anything."

"Okay," Mina said. "Good idea. I'll get you a visiting order. Whether he chooses to see you or not is, I guess, up to him."

"Me?" Ani was dumbfounded. She was just trying to get YETI to follow another lead. She hadn't been expecting to be the person to actually interview Victor Palgrave. "There has to be someone with more experience with these things."

"Maybe," Mina said, "but I've been reading your training reports and you are already an exceptional operative. Most of our agents require vast amounts of training and resources, and they still won't achieve the level of tradecraft that you possess pretty much intuitively. I read Joe's reports about the way you handled yourself on the original Palgrave case, and I find it incredible that you haven't been in the field for years. Add to that, Abernathy thinks you have the potential to become the greatest asset we've ever had. Of course, he'd never tell *you* that.

"I think you're the best person for the job. And I'm in operational control while the boss is out of the country, so I'd like you to visit Palgrave and see what you can find out."

"When?"

"No time like the present. It shouldn't take more than an hour to organize everything. I'll messenger you over everything you'll need."

<*))))><

"So what have I done to deserve this visit?" Palgrave asked as Ani sat down opposite him.

"'Deserve' is overdoing it," Ani said. "Why do I suddenly feel like Jodie Foster in *Silence of the Lambs*?"

"Weird that you see me as Hannibal Lector, don't you think?"

"Guy with a huge ego who's committed multiple murders, and is now incarcerated? I don't know, seems pretty spot-on."

"You *have* missed me," Palgrave said, folding his arms on the table in front of him. "So, tell me, what provoked Abernathy into sending you to see me? Joe too busy? Or your masters thought that your ethnicity would unsettle me?"

"I had a day off," Ani said. "What do you know about *victorious*?"

"I would have thought you'd had enough of music festivals," Palgrave taunted.

"Not the festival. The hacking collective."

"Ah. Then the answer would be, nothing."

"Fair enough." Ani got up from her seat. "I guess that's all I wanted to know."

She started toward the door, but Palgrave obviously changed his mind about being unhelpful. "I've heard of them. Enough to know they're dangerous."

Ani stopped, turned around, and waited. It wasn't enough information to get her back in her seat, but it was a start. Just as she'd hoped. Palgrave's ego wouldn't let him allow her to just walk out. Maybe Mina Desai was right. Maybe she *was* good at this.

"Dangerous, how?" she coaxed.

"Dangerous, because they think I'm a hero," he said, motioning to the empty seat.

She sat down.

"And how would you know that?"

Palgrave laughed.

"This is a British prison," he said. "Not Guantanamo. People *can* contact me here, you know. They do, all the time. Some just want to know the truth about what happened in Hyde Park. Others want me to know that they support my views. *victorious* wanted to know if they could use my face. The request was kind of hard to resist."

"So does *victorious* have a racist agenda like you did, then?"

"Tut tut tut, Ms. Lee. My agenda wasn't racist, it was nationalist, and I still find it amazing that having pride in your country can be transformed into racism through the bizarre alchemy of political correctness. Control of language sounds the frontline weapon of a totalitarian state to me."

"Political correctness is just an attempt to render language less discriminatory," Ani said. "It's basically saying 'try not to be a dick.' A sentiment I agree with."

"Of course you do. Never mind that it's become suspect to fly a St. George's Cross flag, but you can fly an ISIS one with out impunity . . ."

"In the dreams of *Daily Mail* readers, maybe. I still can't believe that you tried to take over the country using a sound from outer space, but your motive came from the lowest common denominator ravings of the far-right press, the stuff they print that even *they* don't believe, just because it sells copies of their papers." She shook her head in exasperation. "What else do you know about *victorious*? And if you say, *'quid pro quo'* I'm out of here."

Victor Palgrave seemed to weigh the negligible difference between her staying and leaving.

"Ah, what the hell?" he said. "When I was a member of the Aeolus group, I heard intel about a well-funded computer collective with a series of very specific targets and a deep strategy for hitting them. But here's the thing: they were leaving me alone, so I returned the courtesy."

Ani studied Palgrave's face. He seemed to have aged a couple of years in the few months of his incarceration. His face was stubbled in a way that it wouldn't have been on the outside. There were lines around his eyes and bags beneath them. And it was in those eyes that she saw that although he was telling her the truth, he wasn't telling her the *whole* truth.

"So let me get this straight," Ani said. "It will just make the whole report-writing thing a lot easier. You became aware of a parallel threat to national security, and you didn't use your powers as head of the Aeolus Group . . ."

"Consultant to, not head of," Palgrave interrupted. "My leadership has not been sufficiently established."

Ani rolled her eyes.

"Okay, as de facto head of a private security firm," she said. "You didn't deploy *any* resources on the investigation of that threat?"

Palgrave laughed. "I was very cruel about you the last time we met," he said. "I can see that I underestimated you, and let my prejudices get in the way of seeing you for what you really are. You'd have made a fine addition to Aeolus, and I can guarantee it would have paid a lot better than Abernathy's ragtag band of misfits . . ."

"A band of misfits who did, I don't know, bring you to your knees."

"Okay," Palgrave said, holding up his hands in mock-surrender. "So let's say I *did* reach out to a few . . . acquaintances for some background information on the hacker group who have obviously raised YETI's hackles to the extent that they'd send you here to talk to me. Why would I share that information with you? I guess what I *am* saying is, '*quid pro quo*.'"

"I have no authority to offer you anything," Ani said.

"Oh, I don't think that's true." Palgrave leaned back in his chair, hands laced behind his head, and gave her a predatory look. "When the case is done, the dust has settled, your report filed, and the bad guys put behind bars, I want you to come back and tell me all about it. Not a detail left out. Do we have a deal?"

Ani thought about it. Her loathing for the man, his lunatic plan, and the things he'd put his own son through for his own political agenda made her angry beyond reason. It had then, and it still did now. She thought about him standing there in Hyde Park, pressing the button that turned a crowd of kids into a living weapon, and wanted to slam out of the room and get as far away from him as possible.

Six months ago, she probably would have.

But she was a different person now. She was learning a whole new set of core skills, and one of them was that there was nothing more important than the mission. Even personal safety had to take a passenger seat, which wasn't to say that she was going to take any *unnecessary* risks, but if the mission demanded something of you, then you needed to try your best to satisfy it.

So although visiting Victor Palgrave in prison again was far from the top of her list of things that she wanted to do, if he gave her some useful intelligence, then it was worth the discomfort.

"Sure," she said. "It's a deal."

Palgrave smiled. In his mind, he had won a personal victory.

Fine. Let him think that.

"Do you have a pen, Ms. Lee?" he asked. "I have an FTP server address for you, a username, and a password."

"I have a pretty good memory."

"You get one shot at logging on. Make a single, tiny mistake and it will lock you out. Anything you want to know will be gone. Forever. I suggest you give me that pen."

"As I said, I have a pretty good memory, and no pen."

It might have sounded vain, but it really wasn't. Gretchen had been helping her turn her memory into a useful tool and, although she was still leagues below Gretchen's near-superhuman memory skills, she was certainly more than capable of remembering an FTP address, login, and password.

She listened to Palgrave as he gave her the details she needed, then she thanked him, promised she'd be back, and left.

Just to be on the safe side, she borrowed a pen and paper from the guard and jotted the information down.

She had a good memory, sure, but she wasn't stupid.

Chapter Eight
FOLLOW *ALL* THE CLUES

Joe was on another flight, heading somewhere else, feeling like international spying was a pretty tedious affair.

Okay, he was sporting a bruise on his cheek, a couple of painful ribs, he'd torn some of the skin on his right knuckles. And he was going to have a pounding headache in the very near future because of a scuffle while waiting at the airport, but he hadn't worn a tux, driven an Aston Martin, or even stopped long enough to check into a hotel.

After leaving Dorian Interactive, Abernathy had gotten a call and told Joe he was heading back to London, leaving Joe to wait three hours in the departures lounge, only to get on another plane headed to Eastern Europe to follow the trail of a lead that didn't sound particularly promising.

"Ani's made some disturbing headway on the *victorious* case," Abernathy had explained. "I need to get back to HQ to see if I can help make any sense of it."

"Disturbing . . . how?"

"You know the *Anonymous* masks? The Guy Fawkes disguise popularized by *V for Vendetta*?"

"Of course," Joe said, surprised that Abernathy even knew about *V for Vendetta*.

"Well, *victorious* has just revealed the masks they're going to be hiding behind this season."

"Let me guess: Darth Vader. Too dated. No, wait, Deadpool."

"Victor Palgrave."

Joe thought he'd misheard. Palgrave's name just seemed like a non sequitur, as if he'd missed part of what Abernathy had said.

"I'm sorry, Palgrave masks? Crap, why not just go for Hitler masks and be done with it?"

"Add 'ious' to the former MP's first name. I think you can see why this just became a lot more serious."

A cold feeling played slide guitar up and down Joe's spine. The hackers had named themselves after a man who had, as far as the public was aware, unleashed nerve gas on thousands of kids at a rock concert, all in the name of a racist ideology that was about closing the UK's borders to refugees and migrants.

It was in pretty bad taste.

Making a symbol of a man like that.

So Abernathy had needed to fly back to the UK to coordinate things there, and Joe couldn't disagree with the decision. Did it make him feel a little abandoned? He'd be lying if he said it didn't. But he still understood.

They parted at the airport. Abernathy was absorbed in dark, complex thoughts, but shook Joe's hand, and said, "Take care of yourself out there. It might be nothing, but it might be something. My intuition tells me it's the latter."

"I'll be careful," Joe told him. "What about the Shuttleworths?"

"I was always pretty sure that LA was where we'd make our progress," Abernathy confessed. "They were a contingency plan for the remote chance that we might need them. I sent them along with some photos of the chip, but I wasn't expecting anything much."

"So why send them at all?"

"Do you know how many days the Shuttleworths have taken off since the start of the year?"

Joe shook his head.

"None. They don't think personal time is important. So I saw an opportunity to get them some downtime, in Silicon Valley, where they will have to wait twenty-four hours to see anyone at Dorian."

"You *made* them take a vacation?" Joe said, incredulously. "That is some pretty sneaky work."

Abernathy shrugged. "They were getting too narrowly focused," he said. "Not seeing the rainforest for the trees. Hopefully they'll be back in a couple of days with a new, wider perspective."

"When did you last take time off?" Joe asked.

Abernathy smiled and headed toward his gate.

<*))))><

When Sebastian Curtiz looked at the chip Abernathy handed him, his brow furrowed.

"Where did you get this?" he asked, his voice almost a whisper.

"You recognize it?" Abernathy asked.

"Of course I do." Curtiz looked visibly shaken. "This is the new Dorian processing chip, the B23/Heuris. It's going to be the centerpiece of the new tech for *NeWToPia,* our next interactive adventure."

"You seem surprised to see it." Joe observed.

"That's because I am," Curtiz said. "Where did you get it?"

"We pulled it out of some black market computers we confiscated in a raid," Abernathy said. "Part of an urban slavery ring. Homeless kids kidnapped and forced to assemble computers including this chip."

"That's not possible," Curtiz said. "This tech is top secret. We have eight of the units they're central to on premises, and they're signed out and signed back in every day. They never leave the building."

"But there aren't only eight in the world?" Joe asked. "Where are the rest?"

"The programmers at our Palo Alto office have more, but they're treated with the same security measures we use here, and we would know if a single chip went astray. The rest are at a secure location, with even less of a chance of being removed."

"And where is this secure location?" Joe asked.

"That's a company secret," Curtiz said.

Abernathy shifted in his seat, obviously unimpressed with the man's evasive answers. "Can you at least tell us just what this B23 chip *does*?"

Curtiz shook his head.

"Let me guess," Abernathy said. "That's a company secret, too."

"There'll be announcements as we get closer to *NeWToPia*'s release date," Curtiz said, brightly.

Abernathy let out a deep breath. "Perhaps we need to talk to Mr. Dorian, himself. We are, alas, getting nowhere, rather quickly."

"I'm afraid that's out of the question." Curtiz sounded like he was pleased with his level of obfuscation. "Mr. Dorian isn't even in the country right now."

"Well, where is he then?"

Curtiz said nothing. He didn't need to. His job, it seemed, was not to provide information past what you could read in a company brochure, only to deflect questions about the things that you couldn't read about. Joe understood that corporate espionage was a huge problem, and that information that wasn't guarded tended to be leaked. He knew that many companies relied on their innovations to keep themselves going, and finding out a competitor has stolen your idea, and has gotten a leg up on you after all of that investment of time and capital, had to be a terrible experience. But Curtiz's caution was getting them nowhere, and Joe couldn't tell if it was just the stubbornness of being a company man, or if it was deliberate obfuscation.

Joe assessed the man in front of him. Curtiz was a top-level executive, with the ego that accompanied such a position. He liked his position, and he would have a high sense of loyalty to Dorian. The ego expansion would be a front, though, and Joe suspected that there was a fair amount of neurosis and self-doubt lurking beneath the manicured exterior.

Joe accessed the chip in his head and cranked up his pheromone factory, mixing *encourage* and *respect* with a high concentration of *urgency*, a trifecta calculated to make Curtiz open up more than he might otherwise would have, while still feeling important, in control, and—more than anything—*needed*.

Pheromone deployment was based on some amazing tech, but its practical use was often more of an art than a science. Joe found that he needed to use intuition, followed by trial and error, to manufacture the right chemicals to get the result he was after. It wasn't always effective—some people were impervious to its subtle chemical cues—but it was always worth a shot.

"Is there any way we can catch up with him? It's pretty urgent." Joe asked, each word calculated to work with the pheromone flood. "These are some bad people we're talking about, and we really need to get ahead of them. You're our only chance."

There were a few seconds where it looked like Joe had failed and they were just going to get more evasions, but then Curtiz leaned forward.

"We have a factory in Eastern Europe," he told them, almost conspiratorially. "Near Braşov, in Romania. That's where we manufacture the chips, and it's also where Mr. Dorian is now."

<*))))>

Joe bought a ticket for a plane bound for Bucharest, and sat down to wait a couple of hours before he could even check in.

He'd sat there until he got bored, then went to the men's room, partly to take some pressure off his bladder, partly for something to do.

He'd stood in the bathroom, did what he'd gone there for, then turned to find the sinks, and had seen three guys in Lakers shirts that he hadn't heard come in. Big guys, with more muscle than brains, two white, one black, watching him with the kind of cold scrutiny that rarely foreshadowed a friendly outcome.

Joe had nodded at them. It seemed to be an act so provocative that it required all three guys to punish it. The biggest of the group, a scar-faced white guy with a fist like a brick and a body like sacks of concrete—moved straight at him, while his pals boxed him in on either side.

"Er . . . is everything okay, guys?" Joe asked, going for a full New York accent without a hint of colonial Brit. He figured it might just stop the thugs long enough to let him talk his way out of this.

He figured wrong.

The three ignored him and kept moving.

Joe had no idea what breach of etiquette had put him in this position, or why they were so silent without even a little bit of macho posturing or riling one another up. It looked like they were just itching for a fight, and Joe was the unlucky one who fit their criteria: pick a kid, any kid, and bash his head in.

To be honest, Joe thought he could use the workout.

Nothing too strenuous and nothing that was going to slow him down or make him miss his flight. It needed to be quick. Minimal damage to his assailants, and without serious enough injuries to get airport security involved.

As he accessed the fighting programs in his chip, he checked the bathroom for CCTV cameras. He was pretty sure that Congress hadn't gone totally insane and let them put cameras in restrooms, but the way House members voted these days baffled him. Finding no surveillance, he got himself into position.

Fighting three people at once was always a hard task, especially when you're a seventeen-year-old kid and your opponents are in their twenties and built like outhouses. It was a simple equation: two hands versus six hands equals a short fight. But, Joe knew, that he could win as long as he fought them one at a time. Three fights one after another was a more manageable proposition. The three guys were close now, close enough that Joe could smell body odor and beer. And if he let them get any closer, he was going to come out the loser, so he needed to change the dynamic.

Joe figured the guy on his left was the weakest link. Sure, he was built like a rain barrel and had a brass knuckles on his right fist, but he wasn't close enough to his comrades, and that meant that there was enough of a gap to buy Joe a ticket out. Joe feigned right and immediately threw himself left, aiming for the space between Knuckle Duster and Concrete Hands. Knuckle Duster lifted a fist, and created a perfect opportunity for Joe to drop to his knees and slide through the gap.

Joe spun on the ball of one foot the second he was through, and took a second to breathe as he stared at three backs. This was what his fighting instructors had called *breaking out*—physically getting out of the tight spot you'd been maneuvered into. Now he needed to separate one of the guys from the pack. Joe stepped to his right on a slight diagonal until he was standing next to Knuckle Duster, who'd made the mistake of turning his body so it followed Joe's escape route. Which meant his back was to Joe, who took advantage of the slip by hammering his fist into where he was pretty sure Knuckle Duster's kidneys hid beneath his bulk. There was a raw meat thump and a satisfying *uuuffff* sound and Knuckle Duster stumbled forward into the middle guy as he tried to turn to face Joe.

But Joe had the three attackers in a straight line now, and that was exactly what he'd wanted. Still, three big guys to fight, yes, but now one at a time.

As long as he made it quick.

So quick they didn't have time to make their numerical advantage pay.

He bent his knees and popped his whole body forward, slamming his shoulder into Knuckle Duster's side and pushing hard into his ribs. He felt something come loose in there and rolled off ducking as the thug wheeled his arms around in a panicked attempt to land a blow. Knuckle Duster's problem was that it's a lot easier to connect with a target if it's in front of you.

If you can see it.

Joe was making a point of keeping out of the guy's line-of-sight and moving so fast he couldn't see what was coming.

Joe saw an opening to bring some pain to the guy's calf,

and he thought it would be rude not to take it. He dropped low and put his weight behind a swift kick, making perfect contact with the back of the guy's leg and eliciting a meaty sound. Knuckle Duster fell forward again, slamming into the middle guy. Joe rose to his full height, used Knuckle Duster as a route to his friend, his head becoming a springboard for Joe's leap, and hit Cinder Block Hands in the face with an open palm.

Cinder Block Hands let out a string of expletives and swung wildly. Joe was glad to discover that the guys *were* capable of speaking, even if it was in playground swears that were more embarrassing than threatening. He dodged the hands and prepared to finish him off.

He was just making sure that the third guy was still on the wrong side of the second when a hand closed around his ankle.

Joe had thought Knuckle Duster was down for the count—he'd bounced off the guy's head, after all—but some thugs just had other ideas about lying down and quitting. He held Joe tight and that gave Cinder Block the opportunity to land a couple blows, one to Joe's ribcage and one to his cheek.

It was the blow to his face that could have turned the tide of the fight. Joe's vision swam, but he slammed the chip into rage-mode to compensate, kicked the hand free from his ankle, took Cinder Block down with a two-handed swing to the jaw (scraping his knuckles against the guy's teeth), slammed Knuckle Duster back to the tiles, and then stared at the final guy with all the intensity that he could manage.

"Are we done?" Joe barked. "I can see that you're not really committed to this, so how about you stand down? That way, I'll leave you standing up."

The black guy tried to hold Joe's stare, but what he saw in Joe's eyes was too much trouble, all bundled up with a lot of crazy, and he looked away and did as he was instructed.

Joe stepped over the other two guys, washed his hands in the sink, and left without another word.

<*))))><

He endured another long haul, with a couple of hours to kill in Munich before his connecting flight, and landed in Romania. He tried to sleep on both flights, but managed fitful snatches at best. As a result, his body clock was trashed, and a combination of exhaustion and pain from the fight back at LAX was making a mess of his body, but he still had another two-hours ahead of him before he reached his destination, Braşov.

Joe found a cash machine that gave him a handful of Romanian leu notes, grabbed a shuttle bus to the train station, bought himself a ticket, found the right platform, and found the right train.

The car was neat, clean, and reasonably modern. He

had no idea why this surprised him. Was he so ignorant of other countries that the mention of Eastern Europe suggested Communist-era infrastructure?

Maybe.

He was too tired to care that much, and the pain in his ribs was a constant nagging drain on his energy reserves.

Life was blurring around the edges, becoming processes rather than experiences. The visit to LA where he'd seen nothing but airport, Dorian Interactive, then airport again. Now, this dreamlike passage from the USA to Germany to Romania—it was all just noise, without meaning or message.

He had to get some sleep. He just needed to stay awake on the train, a taxi ride to a hotel, then he'd be able to relax.

Right now, he felt adrift. The faces he saw on the train were just like the people he'd see on a train in any big city in the world. The language difference, notwithstanding, people were people were people. They did what they did, wherever they were.

Jesus, man, you really need to sleep. People are people are people? Very profound.

He rubbed his eyes.

Looked out the window.

Bucharest rushed past him, and Google helped him understand what he was seeing: the city's history told in architecture. From the splendor of neo-classical buildings, through the whimsy and beauty of Arts Deco and Nouveau, through the communist era of high density pre-fabricated tower blocks, into a present of characterless post-communist capitalism. Joe had heard how bad things had been under the iron rule of Nicolai Ceausescu, the communist dictator overthrown in 1989, but had never thought he'd see the city where so much turmoil and totalitarian control had existed for so long.

Now the city had thrown aside its terrible history, where the *Securitate*—the dictator's secret police—had cast a long shadow of fear and violence over the country; now there was a sense of a country awakening from a nightmare. Unfortunately, Google also informed him that nearly sixty percent of Romania's citizens found the reality of capitalism to be stressful and confusing, and they actually missed the certainty of totalitarian rule.

Joe found himself dozing as the city gave way to countryside, and it was only when the train arrived in Braşov that he realized he had slept for most of the journey. The sleep hadn't done him much good, though. His head felt muddy and his body was a patchwork of aches and pains.

He found a taxi outside the station, gave the address of the hotel that Abernathy had booked him into, and left the driver to do his thing. Joe's knack for small talk was gone. When the driver tried to engage him, Joe was monosyllabic until the guy gave up and drove in silence.

Eventually, they arrived in front of a modern glass-and-stone building with a high concentration of neon lighting. Joe paid the man from his wad of notes, over-tipping out of guilt over his own rudeness. The man looked pleased, and Joe guessed that cash was probably more useful to him than the conversation would have been. The man waved as he drove off.

The journey from the road to Joe's room was a blur, and although he meant to find something to eat before turning in, that plan was sabotaged when a quick lie down—to take a load off—turned into a long and dreamless sleep.

<*))))><

He slept for fifteen hours straight, fully-clothed, on top of the bed. For the first thirty seconds or so after he awoke, he genuinely had no idea where he was.

Then his memory kicked in, a flipbook-style procession of images and impressions of his journey. His body no longer just ached where he'd been punched, it now ached where it hadn't, too. He groaned, stripped, took a hot shower, and started to feel human again.

Just.

He checked his phone, which needed charging, but the room had some two prong adapters, and it wasn't a problem. He had a few texts from Ellie, a couple from Abernathy telling him to be careful on his visit to Dorian's European plant in case the chip thieves were there and didn't take kindly to his nosing around, and a bunch of emails that were hardly worth the energy of opening them.

He replied to Ellie and acknowledged Abernathy's communications, then went downstairs to find some food and the envelope that would be waiting for him at the reception desk.

<*))))><

Dorian Europe was some ten miles outside of Braşov, and the cab driver seemed delighted that Joe had never visited the area before. As they followed a narrow road leading up a mountain through dense forest, the man asked, "You like Dracula?"

"I don't know about *like*," Joe replied, "but I'm certainly aware of him."

"These are the Carpathian Mountains," the man said, pointing out the window at the spine of rocks looming across the horizon. "And you are traveling through Transylvania. Of course, the real Dracula was nothing like the one you see in the films."

"The *real* Dracula?" Joe asked. "You mean Vlad the Impaler? The guy Bram Stoker allegedly used as a template for Dracula?"

The cab driver shook his head.

"Vlad Tepes—you call him 'The Impaler'—is still celebrated as a hero by most here. He fought the Ottomans to keep the homeland free of Turkish rule. The real Dracula, to us, was Ceausescu. It was only with his fall that we even discovered the existence of the book, *Dracula*. For us, Ceausescu was the real vampire, sucking the lifeblood from our country. And vampires aren't even a big part of our folklore. We have *strigoi* and *moroi*, but they are more related to ghosts and witches than they are to vampires. We're more a werewolf kind of people."

"But I saw a poster for Dracula's Castle back at the hotel."

"Ach, that's for tourists," the cabbie said. "Bran Castle: it looks creepy, but probably has no actual connection to Vlad Tepes, unless you count him being a prisoner there for a very short while. Certainly, no connection to vampires."

"Oh."

"We have bears and wolves though," the man said brightly.

"Where?"

The man indicated the woods on either side of the road.

"Oh," Joe said again.

<*))))><

The building that housed Dorian Europe was the kind of structure that arose when function dictated form. The only vision for the place was the enclosure of the space needed to do . . . well, whatever Dorian did inside.

The factory was located at the end of a long private road that cut through the forest into a clearing—a vast, featureless collection of white boxes, with the only concession to aesthetics being a slightly fluted roof. A twelve-foot fence, crowned with barbed wire surrounded the property, with a security office at the end of the road.

The cabbie became less and less talkative as they approached their destination, commenting once that there were no locals employed at the factory. It all sounded a bit Willy Wonka's chocolate factory to Joe, but he sympathized about the local economy, and the man seemed to welcome the comment.

He dropped Joe off, took the cash, and drove away.

Quickly.

Joe approached the gates with a lot less urgency.

Chapter Nine
I CAN HAS
CHEEZBURGER?

Day 2 at *victorious* HQ dawned, and Ani made her way to Tottenham Court Road on the Tube, feeling too much like a city commuter for comfort, while her mind was a blizzard of creeping apprehensions and terrifying doubts.

The ftp server had coughed up its digital payload, providing her with just enough information for her to be worried. On the phone, Minaxi Desai had, likewise, been somewhat unsettled by its contents.

Victor Palgrave's investigation into the hacking collective had been far more successful than YETI's, and it had uncovered some potentially alarming facts: that *victorious* was remarkably well funded, with a war chest running into the millions of pounds; that it was global, well organized, and decentralized; and that it had masqueraded under a few other names before finally settling on *victorious*—first *Gaia* and then *golem*.

She'd heard both of those words, but it had been Gretchen who had provided the useful capsule definitions of them.

"Gaia is the original earth mother," she'd said. "By which, I mean she was the goddess from which the earth, itself, sprang. The universe, too. In Greek mythology, she was the personification of the planet earth, itself. Although, for all that, she is now consigned to the discard pile of 'gods that failed,' the ones no longer worshipped, along with Odin, Zeus, Osiris, Baal, and Jupiter.

"But the idea of Gaia was given new meaning in the 1970s, when James Lovelock, a chemist and inventor, whose instruments can detect CFCs and look for life on other planets, formulated what he called the Gaia Hypothesis. The simple version is that the earth, itself, is a self-regulating system that responds to feedback from the creatures inhabiting it in order to maintain an environment in which they can survive."

"It does what now?" Ani asked.

"Basically, the idea is that there is a constant series of complex interactions taking place between all living creatures and their non-living surroundings and, indeed, the planet itself. Earth becomes a kind of living organism, or as close to one that there's no real difference; it nurtures life, maintaining the perfect ecologic balance for creatures to exist."

"Are you saying the planet is a lifeform?" Ani asked. "But that's just silly."

"And that was pretty much the view taken by a lot of emi-nent scientists when the hypothesis first saw the light of day. The problem is, the theory captured a kind of post-hippy strand of the zeitgeist. It was new age-y, but with a sugges-tion of a scientific basis. And it is a pretty comforting thought that the earth is a living life-support system. So Lovelock's idea took off. His book sits on an awful lot of shelves. It became part of the New-Age, pagan, pseudoscientific para-digm, where ideas don't have to be true to be believed."

"Down on the hippies much?" Ani laughed. "Next, you'll be telling me you don't like homeopathy . . ."

"Do *not* get me started on that." Gretchen said. "It'll get very loud for a very long time."

Ani grinned. Gretchen was pretty easy to bait if you knew the right targets to aim for.

"So Gaia is a way of viewing our planet as a living organ-ism?" Ani asked. "Why would *victorious* ever have thought that was a good idea for a name? Sure, it's a bit hippy, but it sounds pretty harmless. What about Golem? Wasn't he in Lord of the Rings?"

"You're thinking of Gollum," Gretchen said. "Although, I'm sure Tolkien was, at least subliminally, thinking about the mythological golem when he named the character. The golem was a creature made of mud and powered by magic and—at least in the version of the story I'm most familiar with—it was a defender of the Jewish people in the city of Prague in the sixteenth century. Legend has it that there were a series of pogroms and anti-Semitic attacks in Prague, and a rabbi called Judah Loew ben Bezalel built a golem out of river mud to help put a stop to them. Of course, like in all good monster stories, the golem ended up going on a rampage and had to be stopped."

"So the group was going to name themselves after a living planet, then a monster made out of mud, but decided to honor a racist lunatic instead? I guess the mask must be better."

"Palgrave is a symbol," Gretchen mused. "It's probably not his right-wing views, but rather the idea that he *is* kind of a modern analogue for Guy Fawkes. I guess that Gaia and the golem were symbols, too. But where Palgrave is more about destruction, perhaps the other two were more to do with the idea of protection. A nurturing planet, a defense against violence . . ."

"Although the golem did go postal . . ."

"There is that. But maybe we can track a group's ideology through the images it chooses to represent itself, even the ones it discards along the way. Perhaps the destruction implied by the Palgrave mask is donned in defense of something important to the group. The planet. A persecuted minority. These are certainly causes that people might fight for. Maybe we need to be looking at an environmental agenda or—"

"Wait. The golem was made of mud, right? And what is mud but wet earth? What if the golem symbolizes the earth, itself, getting its own back? It could be *wholly* environmental. Greenpeace gone cyber."

Gretchen had just nodded.

Sure, it was possible.

But Ani knew that she needed evidence to back it all up.

<*))))><

Back at her desk, she found a Victor Palgrave mask waiting for her on her chair. Around the office, people were actually wearing the bloody things. Ani put hers on the floor beneath her desk and settled in front of her computer. There was a list of tasks on a Post-it note attached to the monitor—a few networks to probe for vulnerabilities to exploit—and it got Ani thinking about how to use *victorious*'s computers as a weapon against them. She needed to scope out how closely the network was monitored without raising suspicion. Would 'I'm a hacker, what did you expect?' cut any ice if they were scrutinizing network activity, or key-logging, or screen capping the terminals? If it was just a bunch of similarly-minded individuals, it probably would, but she wasn't so sure that that was what they'd collected here.

Palgrave's ftp site had shown her that there was a significant financial investment in this project, and that it was being run along the lines of a corporation or business. Cells in different locations, rather like branches in business terms, Ani had no idea why the people behind *victorious* felt they even *needed* offices.

It was one of the weirder things about this outfit. She still thought hackers were better at home, in their bedrooms.

They didn't tend to flock.

Most of them had jobs and perfectly ordinary home lives. Hacking was just something they did in their spare time.

Bringing them into an office, where the benefits of working together were, as far as she'd seen, utterly negligible, seemed bizarre and unnatural. It was like forcing square pegs into round holes not because you needed them there, but simply because you could.

Or because, for some as yet undiscovered reason, you felt that was where they should be.

As she worked through the first task on her list, she realized that her computer was more powerful than she'd first thought. And more powerful than it had looked from its system profile. She opened up a console window and was even more surprised. If the computer was struggling with CPU load then it simply took more processing power from the other computers in the room that weren't using it. Distributed processing. A nice touch, and really well-implemented. She made a mental note to get more info and, maybe, the specs for the boards the *victorious* computers were using.

As the novelty started to wear off, she started thinking about how this whole office set-up was the way most companies worked. They provided a workplace and the work that was to be done there. It was as if *victorious* was not only modeled on the way corporations behaved, but a slave to it. The people behind *victorious* clearly thought it was the way to get things done, but that surely showed that they were more familiar with the characteristics of the business world than they were with those of the hacking community.

So why were all these hackers here? That was the question she still couldn't answer. Sure, they probably jumped through similar—or the same—hoops she had to earn her place, but was that really enough to keep them engaged? Were their egos being fed by the fact that the people in this room were the London cell? That out of all of the people in the city, only *they* were the chosen ones? The reasoning seemed thin, but then wasn't hacking as much about ego as ideology or adrenaline?

Ani knew that she hacked networks for the same reasons other people climbed mountains, sailed solo across oceans, or walked in space. They relished the challenge despite the difficulty, the fear, and the fact that maybe small, evolved hominids weren't even *meant* to do such things. It was about overcoming big obstacles, about coming out on top. About knowing that you were the first to achieve something, and the bragging rights that inevitably sprung from that.

Which was all possible, but the people here seemed so . . . joyless. There was no bragging, no displays of ego of any sort. This was like work. Work that they weren't even getting paid for . . .

She stopped.

Assumptions.

Why did she keep making them?

If her experiences with YETI so far had told her anything, it was to question the kind of assumptions that people made every day as a matter of course.

The assumption here was simple: that no one here was getting paid.

What if that wasn't true?

Hackers had jobs to hold their lives together, to keep their families fed and clothed and housed, to buy the tech they needed. *victorious* was bankrolled by some pretty hefty financial backers. Put those two facts together. If you want a random bunch of outsiders to suddenly play nice with one another in an office that looked more like a job than a cause, then maybe you just needed to pay them.

And pay them well.

Never mind that she hadn't been offered money: that was the thing that had made the assumption possible. She was here because she'd passed the *victorious* test and because she'd showed up when they told her to . . .

Wait a minute, she thought. *Hold the phone.*

Was what she was thinking *possible*?

There were a lot of people in this room, but were they even all top hackers? It seemed statistically unlikely. Even more so when you considered that they sat here compliantly, largely in silence. Could *victorious* really be paying people to make up the numbers? That didn't sound likely either. The details were running around in her head, and she couldn't make sense of it all. But there really was something *off* about this whole thing.

She turned to the guy she'd met yesterday, the one who had been rechristened the Count of Ten.

"Hey!" she said. "How's it going?"

The Count looked up from his screen and then looked around the room, warily. What, was the guy scared to be talking to someone else? Or just scared to be talking to a girl? Ani gave him her most disarming smile and leaned in toward him.

"Weird briefing yesterday, huh?" she said. Start with small-talk.

"W-weird?" the Count stammered. "What do you mean?"

"There was a lot about the masks, but Phase 2? Not so much."

"I guess it's still filed under 'need to know,' or something." The Count looked like he really wanted to return to his computer screen, but didn't know how. Ani couldn't tell if it was how he always behaved or how he behaved when talking to a girl or how he behaved when talking to this particular girl.

"I guess," she said. "It's probably that I'm new here . . ." She raised the pitch upward at the end of her sentence, just like Joe had taught her in training, to leave the impression of a question dotted through her conversation. So what if it made her sound like an Aussie surfer? It also provided a subtle conditioning for the listener to answer. ". . . but I'm struggling to understand why we need to do this . . . well, here, I guess. I mean, surely we could do the same stuff better at home?"

The Count looked puzzled, as if he'd never questioned such a thing before.

"They need to keep eyes on our work," he finally said. "You know, make sure that everything's coordinated for when we go after the big fish . . ."

"That's what I'm itching to get to," Ani said. "These systems they have us probing, they're not exactly exciting targets now, are they?"

"You're lucky," the Count said. "At least you get to probe networks. A lot of the other guys here, they just work all day on memes."

"Memes?" Ani thought she'd misheard him.

"Well, if we're being precise, we should probably call them image macros. You know the difference?"

Ani nodded. Of course she did. A meme was an image, phrase, or idea that spread across the web, from person to person. An image macro was a kind of meme—a subset—that had a picture or photograph overlaid with text. Often deliberately misspelled in LOLspeak.

Memes could be funny, but Ani could see no reason why *victorious* would bother taking up office space to make them.

Then she remembered the web address that had led her here: www.victorious.meme. That, in itself, was interesting, but now that her mind was focused on the word *meme*, she recalled something more—the message board that had given rise to *victorious* in the first place. The knock-off of 4chan called dot2me.

dot 2 me.

dot 2 x me.

dot and then two *mes*.

dotmeme.

What was it with *victorious* and the word *meme*?

She hid her excitement by asking the Count in an almost disinterested tone, "So people here produce memes . . . sorry, macros?"

"Yeah, a bunch of us, actually." The Count managed half a smile. "So count yourself lucky that you're doing any hacking at all."

"I love a good meme," Ani said. Sometimes a person had to say the exact opposite of how they felt to get where they wanted to go. "Do we produce those 'WHEN YOU SEE IT' ones here?"

The Count's half smile turned into a full-fledged grin.

"Did you see the one where there's a messy flat, with rubbish strewn all over the place, and when you look closely, you can see a face between all the tissues and pizza boxes?" he asked.

"Was that one designed here?"

"No, but it was a good one."

"So how do I see the in-house memes?"

"Dot2me," the Count said, snatching another quick look around. He saw that Ian Black was staring at them, and then snapped back to his monitor like a kid caught with his hand in the cookie jar.

dot2me, again.

Ani didn't give the site much credit. Since they'd started the investigation, she'd spent a lot more time there than she would usually have, but she'd been looking for mission critical chatter rather than pictures with funny captions. It seemed like she'd missed something. But what?

Image macros were one of those odd things the net threw up, but she had never really become a fan. They drew their actual name from the fact that they used images from stock sites with captions applied using something close to a macro—computer speak for a series of input commands that gave a different, pre-programmed output.

The first popular image macros were probably the LOLcats from 4chan. The image of a fat, happy cat with the slogan I CAN HAS CHEEZBURGER? was probably the first megastar of the image macros: the cute cat picture that launched a thousand memes. It was good for a smile, maybe, but hardly a logical choice of weapon for *victorious* to use, so why were they wasting people's time creating them?

Ah, *victorious*, where every discovery brought another series of questions.

<*))))><

There was a "disaster" around midday when the whole computer network went down. Every terminal in the room just decided to stop talking to the Internet. A red-faced tech ran around babbling about "hardware integration problems" and "server load," but the long and short of it was that lots of people went home, and Ani was pretty close to the front of that line.

She ended up walking with another member of *victorious* to the Tube station. The guy was screen-called Touchshriek, although he confessed that his real name was Brian. He had an easy manner and was a lot more approachable than the Count, so Ani chatted away with him and ended up pretending she was heading the same way as he was on the Central line, in reality heading away from where she wanted to be.

"It's crazy," Brian said, when they'd found seats and the train had left the station. "I really don't know if I'm cut out for this office-style approach to bringing down capitalism." He laughed. "There's me, raging against the machine, and I end up in an office of the guys who make me rage in the first place."

"It's a bit weird," Ani said. "The guy next to me seemed terrified to talk with me earlier, as if he was sure a supervisor was going to come along to tell him off."

"You've just joined the good fight, haven't you?" Brian asked, wiping a curl of mousy hair off his brow. "I mean, I haven't seen you around before."

"I just started yesterday," Ani said. "But I've been fighting the good fight on my own for as long as I can remember."

"Did you stumble into it, or were you recruited?"

"Recruited, I guess. You?"

"A puzzle on a website that led down a rabbit hole into an alternate reality game of emails and more websites. I thought I'd stumbled onto the next Cicada 3301, but it was just a recruitment drive, I guess. Still, it's kinda cool to be on the cutting edge of . . . well, whatever this turns out to be."

"It seems like a pretty well-organized hacking team."

"It's a bit more than hacking," Brian said, then quickly glanced around the car as if checking no one was listening. "I mean, sure, the hacking's part of it, but there's something else going on. There's also a meme factory and a homebrew gaming division . . ."

"I heard about the memes. Seems a bit weird."

"I reckon there must be some kind of steganography or something going on in the images, and the memes are just a disguise. Or maybe it's all some colossal wind-up and we'll be on the next series of Derren Brown."

Ani laughed. "It does feel a bit like some hidden camera stunt, doesn't it? And you say there's a gaming division?"

"Yeah, but it looks pretty crude. 8-Bit *Sims*-looking stuff that they've got a few people working on. Again, I'm thinking it's a way of hiding some kind of messages, like a spy's dead letter drops but, like, digital. There're some camera apps in development, too."

"Someone must have some serious bank to be hiring out an office and filling it full of computers," Ani said. "You kind of wonder about the endgame."

"I'm hoping that we bring down the whole capitalist mechanism. If not that, I hope it's an interview for a big security company."

"Well, those are diametrically opposed ambitions."

"So what are you in it for, then?" Brian raised an eyebrow with Spock-like efficiency.

"I just can't keep out of other people's networks. It might be that I'm part-anarchist, or just that I'm just nosy as hell and don't know how to take no for an answer. Most people buy a computer and think 'What games can I play on this? or 'Oh, incognito mode on my Internet browser—result!' Me, I think 'Where can this get me into?'"

"I know what you mean." Brian looked around again. *Paranoid, much?*

He sighed. "I swear that it's taking all my willpower to not hack into *victorious* to see what they're really about."

"Snap."

"You, too?" Brian looked relieved. "Thank the Flying Spaghetti Monster that I'm not alone."

"Is that still a thing?"

"What?"

"The Flying Spaghetti Monster."

"Haven't got a clue. Although, you know what they say?"

"What do they say?"

"The Internet's forever."

"Yeah, but who is this 'they' that keeps saying all these things?"

Brian "Touchshriek" laughed. "The wizards. The ones that run the Internet through unicorn magic."

"Wanna grab a coffee?" Ani asked.

"I think that's about the best idea I've heard all day."

<*))))><

When you're an operative for a top-secret government task force, the simple act of asking someone out for coffee means something completely different from its use in everyday, civilian life.

It's a weapon.

Ani had even taken a course about it.

That was her life now as a YETI operative. Two-and-a-half days a week taking intensive school lessons, cramming a whole curriculum into half the usual time, the rest spent learning how to charm your way into a building, break a man's arm, or interrogate a suspect.

The fact that Brian was pleasant, funny, and seemed to know his way around networks that he really didn't belong in were secondary considerations. That was one of the odd things about being a spy. Something as commonplace as social interactions with strangers became a double game where the surface goal was having fun, but the real goal was gathering intelligence.

Ani had always been good at playing two roles at the same time.

It was something you learned being biracial in the UK, by being the daughter of a petty criminal in everyday society, and by being a hacker in a world that misunderstood the whole hacking scene. She had learned to hide parts of herself from just about everyone, presenting a normalized version of Ani Lee that was more surface veneer than actual, living breathing person.

That being said, it still took a lot of getting used to: the idea that most of the people you met were simply conduits through which—that word again—intelligence could flow.

It sure took some of the shine off of a coffee date.

They got off the Tube at St. Paul's and took in the majestic sight of the old cathedral as it failed, spectacularly, to blend in with its modern surroundings. They stood and looked at the massive dome and its Baroque trappings, brought to silence by the sublime building and its glass and concrete restraints. It took a while before Ani could bear to break the reverent silence. As a new inhabitant of London, she still found the historical architecture pretty humbling and, at times, overwhelming.

"Sometimes disaster has another side," she finally said.

Brian gave her a confused look.

"The Great Fire of London," Ani explained. "It cleared the city's canvas and allowed this building, and others, to rise from the ashes. Sir Christopher Wren and Nicholas Hawksmoor took advantage of the chaos to make a thing of beauty."

"I never looked at it that way before," Brian admitted. "But how many people had to die before the phoenix could rise from their ashes?"

"Apparently, the answer to that question is six," Ani said, showing off her nascent memory skills and some trivia she'd read in a guide book months before. "Six confirmed deaths during the whole of the Fire of London. Of course, that doesn't take into account those that died of indirect causes . . ."

"So you think the sacrifices of the few are justifiable if the end result is positive?" Brian was surveying her with an intensity that made her feel uncomfortable.

"It was an accident," Ani said. "People made the best of it. If the question is would I sacrifice those six people to make the rebuilding of London possible, of course I wouldn't."

"Thank goodness for that," he said. "I thought you were one of *them*." He looked around again.

Looked like the money for coffee wouldn't be wasted.

Ani located a nice non-chain coffee place, got some drinks and pastries, and then asked him who *them* were.

"Ah, you haven't been in the *victorious* HQ long enough to have met any." He took a sip of his cappuccino, leaving behind a white mustache that he wiped away with the back of his hand. He ended up still leaving behind a toothbrush mustache that Ani rubbed off with a napkin.

"There is a sort of . . . attitude . . . among some of the *victorious* faithful," Brian continued. "A kind of 'ends justifies the means' outlook that leaves me kind of cold. I guess that's probably why I overreacted to the whole Fire of London thing. I'm sorry about that. I just don't think it's true. I think the means are pretty damned important. My uncle—my mum's brother—was at the back of the Tavistock Square bus on 7/7. I don't really remember him that well. I was . . . what, six when he died, but I see the 'ends' of that atrocity in my mum's face all the time. It leeched some of the joy from her, and sometimes I think that she'll never get it back.

"Now, I'm pretty sure that the Islamic Fundamentalists who detonated the bombs that day were clear where they stood on the issue of ends and means, and do you know what? They were wrong. A hundred percent wrong. If innocent people get hurt in accomplishing your goals, then you've lost sight of reality, whether you're a terrorist, a government, or a hacking collective. You have to have values, and there is no sane value set where innocent people suffer. End of. Simple as."

"I'm so sorry." Ani said, reaching out and touching his shoulder, giving it a gentle squeeze. "That's horrible. I can't even imagine how it affected your family."

Brian gave her a weak smile that was a combination of pain and gratitude. "When I hear people at *victorious* talking about 'collateral damage' and 'acceptable losses,' it makes me angry. And I know it's probably all bluster. We're hackers, not terrorists, and we hurt systems, not people. But I just don't want to be part of a club where losses like that are ever acceptable."

"I can see that," Ani said, realizing her hand was still on Brian's shoulder and retracting it quickly before it got embarrassing. "But, as you say, it's systems we're attacking, not people."

Brian waved her closer, and she leaned in until her ear was next to his mouth.

"I have doubts," he whispered. "Suspicions. And I hope they're wrong, I really do . . ."

"Suspicions about what?"

"*victorious,* I guess. Did you see the people who came in yesterday: the heavy rocker, the suit, and the caricature of an anime hacker?"

"Yep."

"Never seen them before. Happens all the time, people

turn up with tech or software that I've never seen before, and they're like 'this is for Phase 2', but no one ever tells us what Phase 2 is. It's like this important event we're working toward, but we're not even allowed a glimpse of the finish line: the thing we're supposed to be fighting for.

"And that 3-D printer, what the hell was that? There's no company coming close to making something that prints that quickly and is that portable, so who's behind this? And if you have the resources to manufacture something like that, how come you're giving the tech to a bunch of hackers?"

"The Palgrave masks were in pretty bad taste, too," Ani added. "At best, that looks like poor judgment, at worst . . ."

". . . they're glorifying a racist lunatic? Yeah, I thought that, too. It hasn't made me feel any happier about the situation."

"So then, why stay?"

Brian shook his head and fixed Ani with a solemn stare. His eyes were incredibly blue. "I don't know. Maybe I just think that I'm better in than out. Does that make any sense to you? If *victorious* look like they need reining in, then maybe being on the inside is the best place to do that. Sometimes, you've got to stand up and be counted, even if it means you end up standing alone."

"Screw that," Ani said. "You're not alone. Looks like this is the first meeting of the Dead Cell *inside* the Dead Cell. We'll keep our eyes and ears open, and the first sign of anything sinister, we take it to the authorities and let them sort it out."

Brian looked at her with something close to admiration. Those blue eyes offering up that kind of reaction made Ani feel a flash of guilt for all the things she wasn't telling him. Only a flash though.

"You going to eat that muffin?" Brian asked.

Chapter Ten
HAS SCIENCE
GONE TOO FAR?

The guard at the gate looked at Joe's paperwork with impatient incomprehension. Goodness only knew what pressing tasks he was being kept from accomplishing, but it was pretty safe to say that they weren't earth-shattering, because the guy had been reading a racy paperback when Joe arrived. The guard had stuffed the book under his desk, so Joe couldn't say for certain, but he looked like the type who moved his lips when he read.

"You're from Dorian Interactive," the guard said, repeating it in the hopes, it seemed, that it might make sense this time around. "But you don't have an appointment?"

Joe looked stern, oozing authority—literally, it was an absolute pheromone blast of it—and tried again. In his closest approximation of a California accent, because that was the accent that went with his cover story.

"An appointment would hardly be useful for a security spot check, now would it?" he said.

The guard looked him up and down. "You don't look old enough to be in plant security."

"And that's why I'm so successful." Joe cranked up the authority another notch. It tended to blur into arrogance if he went any higher. He'd need to offset it with a little flattery to throw the guy off, then launch into a threat. "Look, I shouldn't be telling you this, but you look like you're elite security material, so here's the skinny: some top secret Dorian chips from this very establishment have turned up on the black market, and I'm here to find out how. Now, do you want me to inform Mr. Dorian that I was stopped from carrying out that duty by a— Sorry, what's your name?" He reached into his pocket and showed the guard enough of his phone to make sure his message was heard loud and clear.

The guard had a craggy face with a sloping brow, a hard kind of face that was probably the reason he got hired for security to begin with. But Joe saw it soften and become compliant with those last three magic words and that partial reveal of his phone.

"So, who do I tell that you're here?" the man asked.

"No one," Joe said. "Again, that's the point. We have no idea who, or how many people, are involved in this breach of security, so from here on out, it's a case of trust no one."

"So I just let you in and . . ."

"And I do my stuff," Joe said. "I'll call you when I need you. It'll look good for you if you're the one to take the thieves down, and it might save your job . . ."

The guy flicked a switch, and the barrier that stood between Joe and the factory suddenly was no longer an issue.

"You'll do that?" the guard asked.

"Of course. Now, if anyone asks . . ."

The guy zipped his lips.

And Joe walked into Dorian Europe while the man who was tasked with keeping him out had not only let him in and would keep quiet about it, but also felt grateful to Joe for the privilege.

<*))))><

Of course, that was the easy bit.

The bit that Joe had been able to plan in advance.

Inside the fence, everything was about to get a little more . . . improvised. Or fluid.

Or make it up as you go along.

There was a big main door in front of him, but it was behind a high fence with turnstile gates and ID card readers, so that wasn't going to work. Instead, he turned to the right and went up the side of the building, looking for a window, fire door, or loading bay. He found none of the above—just a long, blank, plastic-clad wall that was at least the length of a couple of soccer pitches.

Joe followed the wall, aware that the forest on the other side of the fence was getting thicker and darker, and that something large was moving around in the undergrowth. He didn't know enough about Romania to know whether the cab driver had been pulling his leg about the wolves and bears, but Joe didn't feel like meeting up with it either.

He was almost to the back of the building when a clearing appeared through the fence and Joe saw what had been moving parallel to him: a large, brown shape, like a hairy pig, with curved horns jutting up from its bottom jaw. A wild boar, foraging in the forest. Joe had never seen one before, and he took a moment to watch as it continued on through the trees, soon disappearing from view. Sometimes nature just snuck up and surprised you like that. Joe was still pretty glad about the fence, though. Despite being a big furry pig, the wild boar had looked pretty mean, and those tusks . . .

The back of the building opened out onto a large concrete area—obviously a loading dock. There were a couple of freight entrances, raised to allow the trucks' containers to pull right up to them. One door was open. Joe peered through, but could see no one on the other side, so he hopped up and through and he was inside the building, easy as that.

Now he was standing in a loading bay, but there was no loading taking place. There weren't any people to do any loading, either. The place was empty. Which saved him a lie. Off to the side was a forklift and dotted around were some hand-operated pump trucks, stacks of wooden pallets, and piles of boxes with the Dorian logo emblazoned on them.

Joe had been expecting to have to talk his way past a couple of surly dispatchers, who would probably have been surprised by his unorthodox entrance into the building, but it felt weirder that the space looked deserted. Still, there weren't any trucks pulled up, either, so perhaps this area was only staffed when there was actual loading to be done.

He made his way quickly but quietly across the loading bay, toward a door on the far wall. Turning the handle, he opened the door a crack, leaning in to peek through to the room on the other side.

There was a vast open-plan factory and warehouse with boxes and shelving and workstations, but no one was working at any of them. He opened the door and slipped through into the factory proper.

His senses were on full alert as he moved through the area, but the place looked totally deserted.

Which was very weird.

The workstations were divided off from the factory with suspended walls that gave the suggestion of rooms. He looked up and saw the system of cables that held the walls in place, and at the anchors in the floor that completed the job. It was a practical solution, a balance sheet fix, but Joe guessed that was true of a lot of modern design: cheap and functional, giving the illusion of worker comfort, but nothing more.

He stopped at one of the workstations, which was prepped with tools and electrical components, circuit boards, and a soldering iron. A full coffee cup sat to the right of a computer that seemed set up for some kind of electrical testing. Joe picked up the cup and tested the liquid with his little finger. It was lukewarm. Definitely not room temperature.

Which meant someone had been there pretty recently.

He put the cup back on the ring it had formed on the desk, and moved on.

More workstations, more signs that people had here recently been there. A sweater slung over the back of a chair, a jacket over the back of another, a soldering iron left switched on, a computer running its testing procedures.

Just no actual people.

It made Joe feel uneasy and unsure as to how to proceed.

Still, an abandoned jacket was a good start. He rifled through the pockets, but there was nothing useful. At least, not what he'd been hoping for: an ID badge or maybe a key card. The kind of thing that YETI had been unable to provide him on such short notice. Biometric data. Site-specific ID. Stuff that would grant him passage beyond the plant's security doors and into the executive areas behind them. Instead, there was a wishbone-shaped piece of metal that looked like some kind of tool, a pen, and . . . that was it. No candy wrappers, chip bags, cough drops, tissues . . .

And the vast area was still devoid of people. There was something unsettling about being alone in a building like this. It felt wrong. First there was the obvious primal dread of being somewhere you really shouldn't be. And then there was the fact that the place was like a ghost ship—the *Mary Celeste*—that Abernathy had told him about after YETI HQ was compromised. Together, they made Joe painfully aware of how exposed he was here: not just in the factory, but the country, too. He was rolling with no plan, and had no tech support, no back up, and no Plan B.

He set out to find the storage area where they kept the Dorian chips that had set this particular mission in motion, leaving the workstations behind him and heading toward the towering shelves of what had to be the fulfillment department.

Every sound he made seemed amplified by the stillness, echoing around the empty building as if inviting discovery.

Why was the place empty?

Was there some kind of national holiday that meant everyone had stayed home? The security guard hadn't mentioned anything like that and, anyway, that hardly explained the lukewarm coffee and the abandoned clothing. So was the workforce simply on a break, or meeting up in an executive office for a training session? All possible, and all would mean that people would be returning soon.

Joe thought about what the cabbie had said, about no locals being employed at Dorian Europe. That was a little weird, but perhaps the man was exaggerating, or repeating a half-baked rumor. He thought about the remoteness of the location and how he hadn't seen any other buildings for miles, but that wasn't helping his general sense of ill-ease, so tried concentrating on the here and now.

It was ironic, he thought, that the bug in his head that allowed Abernathy to listen in, and even comment upon, his actions had always been *slightly* irritating, always feeling like his privacy was being invaded. But now, when he'd gladly welcome input from Abernathy, he tried to establish contact and had failed. Joe had never tried connecting from abroad before—he hadn't needed to in the USA since Abernathy had been right there. Maybe the chip didn't work outside of the UK, but it ran on Wi-Fi, so surely it *should* be working. Maybe Abernathy wasn't back in the office yet, and he was the only person who used the communication method, or maybe it was that there was simply no Wi-Fi signal here. Joe took out his phone: there was a symbol for no connections possible, not even a voice call.

Well, if his phone couldn't get a signal, the chip in his head probably couldn't, either.

The warehouse was bounded on three sides by high shelves stacked with cardboard boxes, and plastic bins containing components. Everything was marked with location codes, to tell workers where to find the parts stored on the shelves. There were some four-wheeled carts with plastic bins incorporated into them that Joe figured were for picking components from the warehouse for delivery to the assemblers' workstations.

He was about to investigate one of the bins when there was a sudden high pitched noise—an abrupt pattern of bleeps that sounded like the world's loudest alarm clock. It only lasted a few seconds, but by the end of it, Joe heard people moving, en masse, toward him. For a moment, he worried that the bleeps had been a security alarm and the people he heard moving toward him were coming to intercept him, but then he saw workers heading back to their designated stations, so he relaxed.

A little.

Of course, now he'd have to explain his presence if anyone asked.

But the people just passed him, even the ones working in the area he was standing in. It wasn't just that they passed by though; they totally ignored him, returning to the tasks they'd recently left. Within minutes, the factory was back to what was probably its normal pace, and the contrast with the empty space just moments before was surreal.

It was made more surreal by the fact that people still didn't so much as acknowledge his presence. Even among themselves, there was no communication at all: no laughing or joking, no conversations, nothing.

The way these people were acting just wasn't natural. Maybe it made him uneasy because the behavior of the workforce reminded him a little too much of the cult-like spaced-out emptiness of the .wav people from the Palgrave Affair. Of course, the connection there was spurious: the creature . . . whatever the hell that had been in the sky over Hyde Park . . . had departed, taking with it every vestige of its influence. None of Palgrave's altered sound file remained on earth. Everyone affected by the sound had gotten better. Whatever this was had nothing to do Victor Palgrave and his crazed delusions of grandeur for a new British Empire.

But.

Palgrave's name had come up again very recently. What was it Abernathy had said about hackers using masks of his face to hide behind? Could there be some connection?

Joe shook the thought away. It was nothing but a dumb coincidence. Palgrave was in prison, his organization was in tatters, and his great weapon was out in space somewhere, living happily, if that's what sound creatures from space did.

This had absolutely, categorically, nothing to do with *that*.

Maybe this was just how people in Eastern Europe worked. They'd had their downtime—that's why they'd been absent, it had been a break—and they'd done all their chatting and messing around, and now it was back to work.

Except.

Except the cabbie had said the workforce wasn't local, and the guard at security had had an American accent. And now that he thought about it . . .

Joe looked around the factory at all the signage that was meant to inform, educate, or just show people where things were or where things went. It was all in English, with no Romanian translation for those not one hundred percent up to speed on every nuance of the English language.

Did "no locals employed here" actually mean "no Romanians employed here"?

That seemed a little unlikely. The entire management team might not be local, but surely it wouldn't be cost-effective to fly in a whole workforce for your factory. You'd use the local skilled workforce. You'd have dual-language signs. Wouldn't you?

Unless the level of technical ability was so high that Dorian couldn't source local talent to do the work, but then why set up shop in Romania in the first place? It seemed to Joe that you'd build your factory somewhere you could have access to workers with the right skill sets. And the ware-house guys? The guys in dispatch? Job agencies would be full of people with the right training and knowledge to ful-fill those not so technical positions.

His mind suddenly flipped back to the thought he'd had in the cab about Willy Wonka from *Charlie and the Chocolate Factory*, and a line from the Gene Wilder film version of the book popped into his head, the one about how nobody ever went into the factory, and how nobody ever came out.

That led straight to another thought about something he hadn't seen since arriving at Dorian Europe.

Cars.

He hadn't seen a single car on the premises.

Now, maybe there was a staff parking lot on the left-hand side of the building, but he was pretty sure he'd have noticed it. There certainly hadn't been any cars parked by the freight entrances.

So? So what? Maybe the staff came in on company-financed buses.

If that was the case, buses from where? They didn't employ locals, so how far away did you have to live to be "not a local"? Braşov was ten miles away, minimum. So this entire workforce came in on buses from, what? Twenty miles away? Twenty-five? Thirty?

Joe did a quick headcount and came up with a couple of hundred. Minimum. What was that? Five buses? Six? It seemed like a whole lot of trouble to staff your factory.

Joe realized his heart was pounding in his chest. He stared at the workers. Rows of assemblers. Warehousemen moving boxes, shuffling paperwork. Pickers at work collecting components from the shelves, working from iPad-like devices as if they were checking high-tech shopping lists and filling their carts.

Everyone was dressed in the same outfit: blue coveralls or jumpsuits. Everyone was working without speaking. Everyone was focused only on the job at hand. No goofing off. No one even taking a quick rest. Or a yawn. Or a cough.

And they . . .

And they all . . .

And they all looked . . .

And they all looked *the same.*

They had the same general build, the same haircuts, the same facial features. There were slight variations, sure, a longer face here, a fatter face there; a stockier build here; longer hair there; but they all looked far too similar for it to be a coincidence.

And they were all men.

There was not a single woman in the place.

Joe couldn't process the information. Unless they company was drawing their workforce from a single family, the composition of this workforce was impossible.

It *was* impossible.

Joe took a step backward and knocked into a cart that had been wheeled to rest behind him. A bin containing components spilled from its frame, clanging to the floor.

That was when Joe realized the other odd thing about the factory.

It was utterly silent.

It took a loud noise to let that thought break through.

A loud noise, echoing around the factory.

Suddenly, every face was turned toward him.

Every face was looking right at him.

Joe felt fear like none he'd ever experienced before.

And then the horrible thing happened.

Looking at him obviously wasn't enough, because every person in the factory started moving toward him.

Theresa Madoff-Wood

+ no2sjws

So, let me get this straight. You don't believe in evolution because you 1) don't understand it, and 2) think it sounds like unicorn magic?

no2sjws

+Theresa Madoff-Wood

Have you heard of the Turing test?

Theresa Madoff-Wood

+ no2sjws

Of course. It's a test for Artificial Intelligence. If a computer passes, the computer apocalypse can begin.

no2sjws

+Theresa Madoff-Wood

2 things. 1. Computer apocalipse already begun. 2. Would U pass?

YouTube Comments

Chapter Eleven
WHERE CAN I DOWNLOAD MORE RAM?

Abernathy looked at Ani over his desk and seemed to consider her words as if balancing them on an invisible scale. When he'd contemplated them for a full minute, he finally spoke. "You think this . . . Brian chap might be an asset?" he asked her.

Ani nodded. "He's been there longer than I have," she said. "He seems to know a lot more about the things going on there, and he's worried, too."

"Worried, how?"

"He sees the skull beneath the skin. The face behind the mask of *victorious*."

Abernathy allowed a ghost of smile to haunt his face.

"Was that an Eliotic allusion?" he asked. "Of course, Eliot was talking about Webster's Jacobean dramas . . ."

"I have no idea what you just said." Ani confessed. "I just thought it was a pretty cool line."

"It certainly is, Ms. Lee. And a good image to encapsulate our mission plan: to see the skull that *victorious* is hiding behind its skin. Or, indeed, its masks."

He looked down at his desk, moved a sheet of paper a couple of inches to one side, and then looked up again. "So why him?"

Ani thought carefully about her next words. She could only try channeling Brian's impressions and anxieties, but with little evidence to back up anything he'd had to say. It was sketchy at best, because Abernathy didn't know the kid, hadn't talked to him, and didn't know how genuine his fears had sounded to her.

"I think that he could be an important ally," she said. "He's smart, suspicious of *victorious*'s motives, and he has some sweet hacking skills. I'm thinking that we work together, pool our resources, and try to get a look at the dark heart of their command structure. I won't tell him anything about YETI. To him, I'm just another concerned hacker. We have nothing to lose, and everything to gain."

"But can you trust him?" Abernathy asked, gravely.

Ani thought carefully about that, too.

"I don't know," she finally said. "It could be a test, for all I know, and showing my hand could severely jeopardize the mission. That's why I won't show it to him. And if it looks like I'm getting in too deep, I'll just apologize, say I've gotten cold feet, and look for another way to see what *victorious* is hiding."

"And you're entirely sure there's something to find? That *victorious* has a darker purpose?"

"I'm certain of it. And was that a Shakespearean allusion? Of course Lear was talking about dividing up his kingdom . . ."

"Touché, Ms. Lee. I knew there was a reason I hired you. Okay. Brian . . . Touchshriek, was it, is your new best friend. Limit your exposure as best you can, but work with him. Do we have a last name for him? I'll need to run some checks, just to be on the safe side."

"Hoke," Ani said. "Brian Hoke."

"Well you and Mr. Hoke have work to do. Keep me in the loop. In the meantime, I'll see what I can dig up about him."

"Thanks, boss." Ani said.

<*))))><

The house in Islington was empty when she got home, which was both weird—Gretchen was almost always home—and expected: Gretchen was away for a couple of days in Denmark as a special guest of the Danish royal family. It was just another detail in a long line about her landlady that blew Ani's mind.

"It's just a thank you for some consulting work I did a while back," Gretchen had explained. "It's no big deal. I'm really only going because I want to see if it looks anything like it does in those Nordic-noir shows you've got me hooked on."

She'd also said some nonsense about canceling the trip if Ani thought she needed her here.

Ani had shaken her head firmly. "I'll be fine," she'd said. "And I *do* need to know why so many murders are being committed in Scandinavia, so go. It's not as if this *victorious* thing is moving so fast that I need an extra brain on it."

Ani made herself a cup of tea, sat down in the lounge, and tried to get her own brain to shut off for a moment. She called her dad, then her Uncle Alex, and let the simple pleasure of family conversation eat away at her worries and yes, frustrations. She didn't say anything about her YETI life and how she felt like she was getting nowhere fast, instead just basking in the glow of normal conversation about people and places that weren't covered by the Official Secrets Act.

When she was done, she ran herself a bath, and let some lavender and other botanicals ease the tension out of her body. Then she put on a dressing gown, wrapped her hair in a towel, and went down to the little office that Gretchen had named hers when she'd moved in.

There, on her desk, was her moving-in gift: a top-of-the-line computer that had made her feel like swooning the first time she'd seen it.

She switched it on and booted into Tails from a flash drive, clicked YES to use its Persistence volume and opened up the TOR browser. It was a basic anonymity approach to computing. Tails was an open source Linux flavor that ran from the flash drive and left no trace on the computer's hard drive. Any data was saved back to the flash drive, hence the name: Persistence volume. The TOR browser was modified, but only slightly, and allowed one of the safest secure browsing experiences.

With the machine fired up, she settled in to hack *victorious*.

Their network was intricately protected, with layers of encryption that seemed unsurmountable, but she opened up a couple of bits of software and started studying the answers the server was throwing back to the questions she was posing. It took an hour or so of trial and error and blunt force attacking before she noticed anything even resembling a pattern. She looked back over the entire log of her actions to see if she was correct.

It seemed she was.

Each layer of *victorious*'s encryption protection contained the key to the next layer, except in anagram or palindrome form. All Ani needed to do was reply to each security layer with the same key, just with the alphanumeric code either mixed up, or reading back to front. Of course, that still made a heck of a lot of possible keys, but knowing the characters it contained meant her computer generated and tested them a lot faster than random guesses. She didn't know whether to be embarrassed for the person who thought that was a good security feature, or to be scared she was walking into a trap.

Still, she was hidden well enough to risk it, so she pressed on into the network. Unfortunately, after hours of work, she ended up looking at a protected file called GAIA, which was impossible to open through any method she threw at it.

All she had to show for her efforts was that she'd revealed the file extension of the GAIA file.

GAIA.meme.

She couldn't view it or download it. She could only see it there sitting on the server.

She gave up.

But it did remind her of something.

She opened her browser and pulled up the dot2me site, scrolling down the front page until she found the archive for *victorious* memes. She opened the link and put the images in date order, newest to oldest.

Presumably, at least some of those displayed were products of the *victorious* "meme factory," but if she'd been expecting anything that was going to crack the investigation wide open, she was sorely disappointed. Just a bunch of stupid captions in Impact font overlaying equally stupid images.

A picture of an armed uprising, caption: WHEN I WUZ A KID AN ARAB SPRING WUZ DONE IN AN GYMNASIAM.

A picture of a bee on a flower: NECTAR? AGAIN? THIS SUXX.

A waterfall, complete with lens flare spectra: NOW DAT'S WHAT I CALL STREEMING.

Just utter nonsense. Not even sort of funny. Or, at all.

If this was what *victorious* was creating, then it really was wasting people's time.

Deliberately.

She was about to close the window and turn in for the night when she remembered something her new friend, Brian, had said about how there might be hidden messages within the images, so she dragged a half dozen onto her desktop and opened them up in Photoshop. She tried adjusting balances and color codes, but it just made them look worse and threw up nothing, so she closed the programs and then, almost as an afterthought, opened up a bot program and set it to attack GAIA.meme.

Then she went to bed.

<*))))><

She'd been asleep for a couple of hours when her phone started ringing. She tried to ignore it, failed, and picked it up from the bedside table.

The caller ID said: Touchshriek.

She pressed ACCEPT.

"Ani?" Brian's voice sounded unsure, maybe about the lateness of the call, maybe about the reason he was calling.

"Brian? What's up?"

"Did I wake you up?"

"Yeah. No. A little."

"Sorry. I couldn't sleep."

"What's on your mind?"

There were a few moments of silence before Brian spoke again. "Meeting up with you, finding an ally, it kind of made me braver," he said. "So I thought I'd try to break into the *victorious* network."

Ani laughed.

"Me, too," she confessed.

"Great minds think alike. Anyway, I got to a single file . . ."

"GAIA.meme?"

"Color me impressed. So, you opened the file?"

Ani sat up in bed.

"You got it open?"

"Yeah, I just clicked on it."

"I tried that. Nothing."

"That's weird. Anyway, I got a bunch of random data, but none of it makes any sense."

"That *is* weird. You want to send a link, and share it with me?"

"I would, but . . ."

"But?"

"It *deleted* itself."

"You get any screen grabs?"

"Nah, it all happened too fast. By the time I worked out what it was doing . . ."

". . . it was already done." Ani finished. "It hasn't called home, has it?"

"What do you think I am, RedQueen Ani, a newb? It's not that . . . I don't even know how to explain this."

"Try."

"It's doing something. To my computer. I think it's changing my browser history. Bookmarking sites I've never visited. Can . . . can you come over?"

"Sure."

"And bring a laptop. I need to check a few things."

"Tell me where, and I'll be there as soon as I can."

Brian gave her his address and she told him to sit tight.

"I will. Oh, and Ani?"

"Yes?"

"Be careful."

<*))))><

She took a cab from Islington to Globe Town, Bethnal Green, and it dropped her right outside Brian's flat. She got a receipt from the cabbie who made far more of a performance of it than was necessary, but she needed the receipt to put in for a reimbursement from YETI.

She rang the buzzer for Flat 4, and Brian buzzed her in.

At one point, the rooms in this house must have been quite generous, but a landlord had seen the potential for easy money and had divided them up to maximize his rent revenue. Brian's flat was tiny, little more than a studio, really, and it was obvious it wasn't built for company. What with the bed and the desk, it must feel crowded with just one person in it; two of them in the space just made it awkwardly intimate.

Brian seemed relieved to see her, though, and she sacrificed personal space for practicality, opening up her laptop next to Brian's computer. There was only one chair in the place, and Brian offered it to her, but she shook her head.

"Show me what's got you worried," she said.

Brian sat down and started by opening his Chrome browser, Instagram, his Twitter feed, and his Facebook timeline.

"First," he said, drawing her attention to Chrome, "these bookmarks." He pointed to a row of tagged sites at the top of the browser. "They're not mine. They just appeared."

He clicked the bookmarks, and they all opened onto empty pages.

Ani squinted at the addresses, and plugged them into her own browser. Same result. Blank. They looked like holding pages. She ran the domain names through WhoIs and saw that they had all been purchased, but there was no information about who had done the purchasing.

"If I had to guess, I'd say that *victorious* bought the domains, but haven't gotten around to putting anything on them yet," she said.

"That's what I thought," Brian said, turning to his Twitter feed.

He showed her his post history.

There were three blank tweets, and they'd all been made in the last hour.

"I didn't send them," Brian said. "My computer did. And it's the same on Facebook."

"You have Facebook?" Ani said, arching an eyebrow. "How about MySpace?"

"It's just for family and friends," Brian said, going red. "I only opened it because the meme file seemed to crashing through all my social media . . ."

"Your secret's safe with me." Ani said, studying the blank posts on his timeline.

"Strange," she said. "And this happened after opening the meme file?"

"I think so. It all happened so fast."

"What was in the meme file?"

"Random junk. It was gone so quickly there was hardly time to take any of it in."

"Try to remember," Ani coaxed.

Brian rubbed his temples and closed his eyes. Ani had no idea if that particular combination actually aided memory-retrieval or if it just showed people watching that you were trying.

"There was a kind of compressed archive of website pages," he said after a moment. "Thousands of them: national, international, web news feeds. But once I opened it, they flashed by so quickly there was no way I could read any them. And there was a ton of social networking data, and huge number of photographs and video files."

"I don't understand any of this. Why would *victorious* be hiding a bunch of news pages behind so much security? You don't think this was a trap, do you?"

"It won't lead back to me," Brian said, but his voice wasn't quite as confident as his words.

"You don't sound one hundred percent certain."

"I'm not. I've never seen a file do what that one did. I've no idea if my security is good enough."

"Let me have a look."

She took a flash drive out of her pocket, inserted into one of Brian's USB ports, and opened up LogJump.

"What's that?" Brian asked.

"Just a little shortcut I made a few years back," Ani explained. "I had to scroll through a log file earlier and it took forever. Then I remembered this. After I needed it, of course." She typed a few commands into LogJump's window, then winked at him. "Still, my loss is your gain."

It took seconds to do its work, showing only the log parameters she wanted to see, screening out everything else. As a result, it didn't take long to study the information.

"You're okay," she said. "It didn't even try to squeal on you."

"That's a relief. I wouldn't want my cover blown."

"Oh, so now you're undercover, are you?"

"*We* are," Brian said.

"Oh, yeah. I just haven't received my decoder ring yet. So you really can't remember anything you saw in the .meme file?"

"Like I said, it just scrolled by so quickly."

"But you saw it all. I've been working on improving my memory recently, and it's surprising how much information goes in without us realizing it."

Brian looked at her, slightly disbelievingly.

"You're saying I might be able to remember what I saw?" The disbelief had leached its way into his voice, too. "It all went by *really* fast."

"Maybe." Ani said. "I think we'll need a bit of help."

Before Brian could object, she took out her phone and dialed Abernathy.

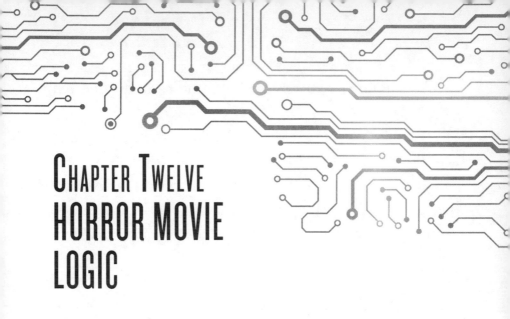

Chapter Twelve
HORROR MOVIE
LOGIC

Joe's first thought was: *I've lost my mind.*

His second was: *I'm dreaming.*

Closely followed by: *RUN!*

He was hemmed in on all sides, but the factory staff were moving slowly, so there were still a few gaps to slip through.

But only if he moved now.

He chose the closest gap and headed through it, bouncing off a workbench and bumping his hip. A spark of pain hit him and he used his chip to increase the level of endocannabinoids in his amygdala or, in non-Shuttleworthspeak, by suppressing the pain by chemical trickery in a part of his brain. Whichever way he phrased it, the relief was immediate and, while he was using his chip, he thought he may as well increase his escape abilities, too. He accessed the parkour routines programmed into the hardware and felt his body respond.

He hurdled onto a desk and slid down its length, hitting the floor on the other side and turning about ninety degrees so he was facing back toward the loading bay. Three workers lurched toward him, arms open but clutching at the air where he would have been if he hadn't slid under them and away.

Joe had always thought zombies in movies were a lot less trouble than people seemed to make them. They were slow, stupid, shambling creatures, and all you had to do to get away from them was walk a little faster. Sure, they could be dangerous in large numbers, but that meant you just needed to avoid crowds of them.

But zombies were exactly what he was thinking of now, because that was how the factory workers were behaving. Not the biting-at-flesh, groaning type of zombie, but the slave-type zombies of Haitian folklore—workers drugged into unquestioning service.

Slow, yes, but it seemed that what they lacked in speed they made up for in persistence. Ducking away from them didn't appear to enrage or frustrate them; it just made them pursue him.

Calmly.

He ducked and vaulted and slid past the closest workers, still heading for the rear of the building, but it was almost as if the workers weren't just randomly chasing him. If he hadn't known better, he'd have said that they were playing with him, blocking him from reaching his goal, delaying him.

Delaying him?

There was a table in his way, so he vaulted onto it, but instead of sliding across its surface, he flipped onto his feet and stood up. From a higher vantage point it was easy to see what he had missed on the ground. The workers engaging him—his immediate threat—were decoys. Time wasters. It was out beyond them that another far more insidious and dangerous threat was appearing.

Organization.

The rest of the workforce were arranging themselves into two concentric circles, with Joe and the few spare workers at their center. They had done it wordlessly, indeed soundlessly, and they had done it precisely. There were, in effect, two walls of people to be crossed if he was to reach his goal. But looking around, he could see that there was little chance of making it through that way without shifting from parkour to physical violence.

There was, however, another non-violent option. It wouldn't take him back the way he knew led outside, but it would get him away from the factory floor, and maybe get him a look around some more revealing areas of the factory.

Beyond and above the warehouse shelves was a walkway that seemed to lead along the wall, past a couple of doors. Joe couldn't see the stairs that led up there, but he knew it for what it was.

Another floor.

Just why there was a walkway up there he didn't know. Maybe management liked to stand there and look down on their minions. It didn't matter. Its existence was enough.

Which meant parkour it was.

He mapped the route in his head, knowing that it would look different when he hit the ground, and he was desperate not to waste time by taking even the slightest detour. This way, his chip could process the route, and all he needed to do was make sure that his body achieved the moves that the chip dictated.

A pair of hands reached for him and he launched himself forward.

He took three big strides when he hit the floor, dodged left, and then started his run up. His route took him awfully close to the inner ring of the human walls, but just as they moved to intercept him, he leapt up and planted one foot on a low shelf on the warehouse stack. Using his weight and momentum to push off with his right foot, and brought his left down on the shelf above it. He fought for balance and purchase with his hands, then repeated the process, leaving the clutching arms of his pursuers behind him as he scaled the shelving unit.

There was a moment when he stepped onto the top of the shelving that he thought he might have made a miscalculation. The walkway, surrounded with yellow safety bars and mesh, looked just a little bit farther away than it had from the ground. But there was no other option, really. Joe took a breath, steeled himself, then ran across the top of the shelves. The path was only a foot-and-a-half wide. On the ground, it would have been a simple action, but fifteen feet *off* the ground, he started to become aware of how precarious this plan was. Still, overthinking it was the surest way to have him plunging to the floor, so he just did it, reached the end of the shelving and leapt the gap to the walkway, arms outstretched to grab ahold of the railing.

He made it, but only just, and his hands weren't best-placed to get a decent grip. One missed entirely, but the other just managed to find a hold, and he tightened his grip while working his other hand into the mesh. His fingers hurt, but he held on, feet scrabbling for purchase. They found the lip of the walkway and he planted them hard, stiffening his entire body to keep him in place. He was hanging well over the heads of the workers whose faces were upturned, staring, unblinkingly at him.

Joe reached up, grabbed the top rail, and pulled himself up and over the walkway safety guard, onto the walkway itself. He looked back down at the factory floor, but the people there seemed uncertain how to respond to this latest development. And that was putting it mildly. They seemed frozen, staring straight at him, two hundred or so faces upturned and utterly blank.

The phrase that occurred to Joe was, *awaiting instructions*. And that stopped him in his tracks.

No one here had spoken, called out, or made a noise of any kind. They looked similar. They worked as a group, silently strategizing. They had organized themselves into rings to keep him enclosed, but as soon as he was out of their reach they froze. As if they had no idea of how to continue their pursuit.

It gave him a bad feeling.

A really bad one.

They were behaving like robots whose programming had just failed. Or like ants, controlled by the directives of a queen who was busy figuring out their next move. Whatever this was—whatever was going on here in this Romanian factory—it was far more serious, and far, far stranger than he or Abernathy had considered.

He had come here to find out how Dorian's top secret chips had disappeared from the factory's shelves, but to Joe, it looked like it wasn't just the chips that had been stolen.

The factory workforce's wills had been, too.

That was all for later, though. Right now, he needed to get some more information about what was happening here, and then he needed to get the hell out of the factory, back to Braşov, and then back to England.

And from where he was standing, none of that looked easy.

He tried the first door along the walkway, but it didn't open. There was a handle, but no visible locking mechanism. No card reader or keypad, either. He examined the handle, but could see no mechanism built into it. Maybe it only opened from within, but there was no buzzer, and surely it wouldn't rely on someone knocking on the door to get it open—that seemed archaic and unworkable. He checked the way the door sat in the frame. At least it opened inward. If it was outward-opening, there would have been little chance of him breaking through it.

He put his shoulder to the door and rammed it. The door didn't give even an inch, but Joe's shoulder certainly felt the impact. He retreated until his back was against the walkway's safety guard, then took a flying kick at the door just by the handle. There was a splintering sound, but the door held. Another kick yielded the same result: a sound, but no give.

Still, the splintering sounds gave him hope, so he smashed at it again and again, and on the sixth try, the door opened a couple of inches.

On the eighth, he was through.

He looked down over the walkway to the people below. Their faces were still upturned, but it looked for all the world like someone had thrown a switch and turned them all off for the rest of the day. The sight was eerie, unnatural, and it helped hurry Joe through the door.

The room on the other side was cold and semi-dark and smelled of burnt ozone. It was also long and wide and full of computers, with maybe a hundred racks of pretty hard-core processors all lined up in tight rows taking up most of the square footage. You could walk between the rows—just—but it looked like that would have only been for maintenance. An open toolbox on the floor seemed to confirm that, and Joe thought he caught sight of another of those wishbone things inside, which seemed to confirm it was some kind of tool.

He'd seen enough photos of supercomputers to recognize that that was exactly what he was looking at. The racks were all linked together with glowing cables, and the processors were all glowing, too, giving the room an unearthly, science fiction ambience. There was an air-conditioning unit in the walls, keeping the temperature the computers generated down.

There were no people here, just some unimaginably powerful processing power: surely far too much for the day-to-day running of a factory, no matter how high-tech its commercial output was. The hum of the processors was a deep vibrato that Joe felt as much as heard. He wandered among the racks, filming them with his phone's camera, with no real idea what he was looking at. He found himself wishing that Ani were there, or the Shuttleworth brothers, just so they could explain what this number of computers were capable of doing.

At the end of one of the rows of racks was a door.

NO ENTRY, some stern black writing on a yellow warning sign ordered.

An open invitation.

He tried the door and it, too, refused to open. Again, he could see no evidence of a handle or a lock, but this time there was a symbol engraved into the surface of the door, a kind of Y-shape, but with the diagonal arms becoming parallel and extending upward.

The shape was familiar, somehow, and he was about to use his chip to try to decode it when he realized that it was familiar for a more basic reason than it being some kind of symbol from a secret language. It was a picture of something he'd seen very recently. The wishbone tool in the pocket of the jacket he'd rifled through downstairs. And hadn't he seen one even more recently?

He backtracked through the room until he found the toolbox, and there, sure enough, was one of the strange-shaped tools. He picked it up, examined it for clues or operating instructions, and then took it over to the locked door. He placed the tool within the shape engraved upon the door, but it didn't trigger any magnetic locks, and the door remained resolutely shut. Joe groaned, wondering what he'd really been expecting. A symbol on a door that reminded him of a tool he'd seen downstairs. Had he really thought that was how this door was going to open? That sounded more like a door-puzzle in a *Resident Evil* game than an actual solution to a real-world problem.

Except, of course, the symbol on the door was an exact match—size and shape—for the wishbone tool. So maybe it was the way through.

Maybe he just wasn't using it correctly.

He studied the tool, turned it over in his hands, feeling its weight. He scratched it with his thumbnail, to see whether it was a soft metal or hard, and then his mind made a connection and he almost kicked himself. The answer was so obvious. Just because it was a slightly different shape and size to an object he knew and it was supposed to open the door, he'd completely overlooked what the object actually was.

He shook his head, and then held the tool by the upright of the Y and tapped the two tines on the door frame. There was a musical note, probably an A, concert pitch, because what he had in his hand was a tuning fork. He held the upright to the outline on the door, allowing the note to vibrate through its surface, and there was a definite *click* from within. He tried the handle and it opened without any security cards or violence.

A tuning fork door key.

Total *Resident Evil* logic, but utter madness for a real door in a real factory.

He made his way into the next room and weirdness piled itself upon more weirdness. He moved from the atmospheric semi-dark of the supercomputer room into the brightness of a science-fiction movie set, and the ozone smell changed to something harder to identify. Something cloying. Something coppery.

His first visual impression was of the stark, eye-assaulting, fluorescent lights in numbers surely too numerous for the space they lit. It was an impression probably heightened by moving from a dark room to one filled with light, but it stopped Joe in his tracks, and made his next discovery seem even stranger.

The booths.

There were ten of them arranged in two lines of five spread out along the walls of the room. They stood there, highlighted by the fluorescent strip lights above, just slightly larger than telephone kiosks, albeit telephone kiosks designed by someone from the future. Made predominately of molded plastic, curved glass, and polished steel, each kiosk had its own separate control unit and computer terminal attached to it by multicolored cables. The booths were big enough to fit a person inside, although not particularly comfortably, because much of their interior was taken up with even more banks of technology that Joe found incomprehensible.

He shot more photos on his phone and wished that he knew tech as well as some people at YETI did.

Whatever these booths were, it seemed likely that they were connected to the supercomputer in the previous room, but what could their function be? He was sure that people were supposed to stand inside them—thus the size, shape, and human ergonomics—but just what a person did inside a device like that Joe neither knew nor could attempt to guess . . .

He stopped, mid-thought. Maybe that wasn't the right way to be approaching this. Thinking about everything he'd seen since he'd gotten there, and especially the weirdly robotic behavior of the workers, maybe he should be thinking about what a device like that could *do* to people who got into it.

Could the booths *make* the staff act the way they had?

Some kind of mind control?

He'd started out looking for a security hole through which Dorian chips were being taken from the factory and finding their way onto the technological black market. He'd expected to find a couple of corrupt workers.

What he'd found, instead, at Dorian Europe (and to be honest, he still wasn't sure *what* he had found), was something far more puzzling, with a deeper reach and a hint of dark secrets that seemed to directly implicate the company.

He took more photos and video footage of the room with the booths, zooming in on panels and screens to capture any information that the Shuttleworths would be able to use to identify the devices. He walked the length of the room, filming everything.

And that's how he saw it.

The final booth.

It wasn't empty. There was something hunched over inside.

He stared through the glass at the thing on the floor.

The thing looked up at him.

Joe felt equally sick and scared.

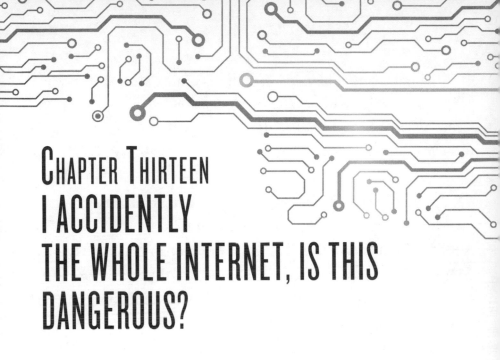

Chapter Thirteen
I ACCIDENTLY THE WHOLE INTERNET, IS THIS DANGEROUS?

Dr. Ghoti pulled the car into a parking space in front of a three-story townhouse in Greenwich. She said, "We're here," and shut off the engine. It had been a pretty uneventful drive, unless one counted going south of the Thames as a noteworthy event, which Ani was still new enough to the whole London thing that she kind of did.

Ani had heard that one of Abernathy's first actions in the wake of the dotwav affair and the seizing of YETI HQ by armed mercenaries, had been to set up a network of safe houses and alternative command centers, but this was her first time visiting one of those new facilities. Her first impression was . . . well, impressed, but that was just for the parking space being next to the building. Otherwise, the place was as nondescript as you'd expect of a secret facility;

a building that blended in with the others around it so well that you'd hardly give it a second glance.

Dr. Ghoti got out of the car and went to the front door, leaving Ani to wrangle Brian out of the back seat.

Ani had tried to soothe Brian on the trip over, but things were spinning so far out of the orbit that her cover story had even started sounding hollow to her ears.

He'd been suspicious as hell when Ani made the call to YETI. It kind of expanded the range of their newly formed cooperation to something that to Brian must seem like an amorphous conspiracy. Ani phoned someone and suddenly a "memory expert" was on the way over, she tried to imagine how she would be feeling in Brian's position.

The problem was he was now an *asset*. Even more so than he had been when she'd talked about him to Abernathy. Now Brian wasn't just a person with access, he was someone who had *intelligence*, albeit intelligence he couldn't remember. And that meant that, as much as she liked Brian or thought he could be a help, now his role was different.

And so was hers.

She had to know what Brian had seen, and it no longer mattered if he thought of her as a friend or an ally. All that mattered was him recovering as much of his memory of the *victorious* data as possible.

After the phone call, Ani realized that she had become something close to Brian's handler. So she reassured him, lied to him, was evasive where necessary, but she tried to maintain an atmosphere of trust, even as he must have felt such an atmosphere was rapidly dissipating.

Dr. Ghoti had said she'd be there in twenty minutes, but arrived in ten, which—with a few awkward silences and some heavy reinforcement of trust—was just about as long as Ani could have carried off the charade. Because she still couldn't admit to being a member of YETI, or of anything, and that meant that the "someone coming over to help" only added to Brian's anxiety.

The biggest aid to getting Brian back on board was the disarming nature of Dr. Ghoti herself. From the moment Ani had buzzed the doctor in, she'd played it perfectly, pitching her performance with precision and authenticity. Within a minute, Dr. Ghoti had Brian convinced that she was "Anya," a friend of Ani's mum, that it was a complete coincidence that she was doing a PhD thesis on memory recovery, and that an opportunity to put her theories into practice was something so rare and exciting that she would be forever in Brian's debt for his help.

Of course, getting three people into Brian's tiny room was something even a Tetris master would struggle with, so when the doctor suggested they swap venues, it seemed like the natural solution to the problem. They'd copied data over from Brian's computer to Ani's tablet, and got moving.

Brian had become less confident about the course of action in direct proportion to the number of minutes they drove. By the time they were parking, he was quiet, internalizing his feelings so efficiently that he was actually hard to coax out of the car. In the end, Ani had grabbed him by the arm and pretty much lifted him out of his seat. By then he was moving on his own, following her to the house's door.

On the other side of the front door was a pretty convincing hall, which led to a pretty convincing living room. If Ani hadn't known better, she'd have thought it was really Dr. Ghoti's house, and that it was really a home instead of a safe house.

The living room was about three times the size of Brian's whole flat, and it was decorated and furnished so well that Ani suspected that it was an exact copy of a picture of an interior designer's showroom from a brochure. Dr. Ghoti got Ani and Brian settled on a couch before bustling off to make them all a cup of tea.

"She seems nice," Brian conceded. "And this place? Wow."

Ani agreed, trying to keep things light and calm. She knew something that Brian didn't, and that really helped her be reassuring. She wouldn't need to keep up the façade for long.

The thing she knew was this: if a doctor from YETI was making a cup of tea, then there was going to be more than just tea, milk, and sugar in Brian's cup.

<*))))><

When the drug kicked in, it was like someone had just switched Brian off. Dr. Ghoti helped settle him back in his seat before turning to Ani. "So what are we dealing with?" she asked.

"He saw lightning glimpses of data, too fast for him to remember any of it," Ani told her. "I was hoping we had some kind of strategy for helping him recall just what it was he saw."

Dr. Ghoti shrugged. "It's a difficult one," she said. "Human beings seem to think that the memory operates like a camera—that the brain takes pictures of the things it sees and can recall them clearly and without error. And that's the problem. Our memories are nothing like photos, not really. They are subjective, easily fooled, and often wrong. We change memories, too. A recalled memory is as likely to mutate and distort as it is to provide us with more detail. So the bad news is that people searching for memories of the type you're looking for will probably end up with nothing."

"Oh," Ani said, "I was hoping for . . . well, something."

"I did say 'probably,'" Dr. Ghoti said. "And 'people.' I'm not 'people.' One of the extra ingredients that young Brian here ingested along with his cup of Darjeeling was an experimental compound codenamed 4t32h, which was developed to help amnesiacs improve their short-term memories. It affects the hippocampus, the area of the brain most associated with the translation of memory from short-term to long-term, and strengthens the coding pathways for new memories held in flashbulb memory."

Ani raised an eyebrow. "I thought flashbulb memories were memories connected to strong emotion," she said. "Like the JFK assassination or the Twin Towers atrocity. People remember what they were doing when they hear about a tragedy because of the emotions they feel then."

"Very good," Dr. Ghoti said. "But it's only part of the story. Flashbulb memory usually requires strong emotions to encode it into long-term memory, but not always. If we can get to a memory fast enough, before there's enough new data to imprint over it, then there's a chance that we can recover . . . something. 4t32h, named from its position on a strangely labeled laboratory shelf, can be seen as a biological filing manager, and it will give us our best shot at consolidating some of what Brian, here, saw into a more accessible memory form."

"How much of a shot?"

"Let's find out."

Dr. Ghoti knelt down in front of Brian and gently maneuvered him onto his back. Brian offered no resistance and he even made a sleepy sound that suggested he was only too happy to lie down.

"The worst effects of the sedative should be wearing off very soon," she said. "It should leave him relaxed, semiconscious, and highly suggestible. We have to gauge this just right, so I'm going to ask you to take over for now. I suspect he'll find your voice more reassuring than that of a stranger."

"I hope you're right," Ani said. "Now what do I do?"

"For now, the important bit: I need you to connect with him. We need him on our side a hundred percent. We need his trust. We need his belief. Say his name, tell him that everything is fine, and reinforce the idea that he's safe, comfortable, and doing well."

Dr. Ghoti took a device out of her pocket, switched it on, and placed it close to where Brian lay—a digital voice recorder with the recording light flashing.

Ani sat on the sofa next to Brian's head. She stroked his brow and did exactly as she'd been instructed, repeating his name gently, reassuring him often, reinforcing her words all the time by stroking his face and hair.

Brian smiled and said, "Ani?" in sleep blurred syllables.

"Brian," she said soothingly. "I'm here. Everything's fine. You're safe. I'm here and you're safe."

"I feel safe," he sleep-muttered. "Safe and warm."

"That's good, Brian. Very good. You're doing well. Very well."

"Did I remember?" Still sleep-furred, but remarkably on message. "I know there's something . . ."

Ani felt Dr. Ghoti kneeling down next to them.

"Okay," She whispered into Ani's ear. "He's doing well. Despite the strangeness of his situation, he trusts you. But we need to get him to trust me now. We need him to trust my voice. I need you to sell it for me. Convince him that I can help him and that I won't harm him."

Ani nodded.

She moved her face closer to Brian's so that her mouth was close to his ear.

"Brian?" she said. "I need your help. I know we only just met, but I really, really need you to trust me. I need you to trust me, and I need you to trust Anya."

"*Trust* . . ." Brian murmured.

"That's right. We need to work together. We need to find out what you saw when you opened the *victorious* .meme file. I need you to listen to Anya. She's a friend, Brian, you can trust her. She won't hurt you. She won't betray you. She only wants to help you remember."

"*Remember* . . ." Brian said, and Dr. Ghoti, whose first name was definitely not Anya, patted Ani on the shoulder.

Ani moved aside.

And Dr. Ghoti began.

<*))))><

It took fifteen minutes of trial and error, question and answer, urging and pleading, calming and reassuring, but when the breakthrough occurred, it was pretty obvious it had happened.

The sleepy hesitancy of Brian's responses dissipated and, although his eyes remained firmly closed and his body was still relaxed, he seemed more awake, more open to Dr. Ghoti's questions.

As far as Ani could tell, the patient probing and questioning had been shots fired at an invisible target. Words had been chosen, fired at Brian's sleeping mind, and their effects upon him were gauged, analyzed, and either included in, or excluded from, the next salvo. Dr. Ghoti was searching for a way in, but a way into what, Ani wasn't completely sure. Still, it was fascinating to watch.

Ani had taken two YETI courses on cold reading—the human ability to appear to know what someone was thinking just by judging an individual's responses to general questions and making educated guesses. It was the same trick that psychics and spiritualists used to convince their vulnerable victims that they had supernatural powers, while only possessing a reasonable grasp of human psychology and the fact that human minds remembered "hits" and forgot about "misses."

Dr. Ghoti was doing something similar, but Brian's sleepy replies made it hard to focus on anything with any authority. Some hacker-specific computer phrases seemed to get better results than anything else, but it was still like trying to see something through a thick fog. Just as you thought you got a glimpse of what you were looking for, the fog swirled and the image was lost.

But there had to be a trigger somewhere, a key that would unlock the files they wanted.

Files, Ani thought. *What was it Dr. Ghoti had said? That the chemical was a biological filing manager?*

Files.

The file.

"Can I try?" Ani asked, and when Dr. Ghoti nodded, she took a deep breath, played her hunch, and said, "victorious. meme."

There was a moment where nothing happened. Ani thought that the long shot had been just that. She was far from being the expert here, and she didn't know why she'd thought that she would be the one to make a breakthrough. But then she noticed that Brian's eyeballs were rolling around under his eyelids—rapid eye movements.

And then Brian said, "Open file." It was a good thing that Dr. Ghoti had remembered to set up the voice recorder, and turn it on, because a torrent of words followed.

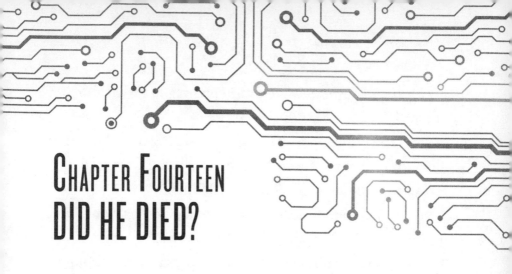

Chapter Fourteen
Did He Died?

It took a few seconds for Joe to recover from his initial feelings of fear and disgust, and then he peered back into the booth. It wasn't any better the second time.

The thing lurking at the bottom of the booth could have been a person, but it could just as easily have been something else entirely. Joe really couldn't tell. It had many of the characteristics of a human being—the same general shape, and many human features—but there was something broken, maybe damaged, something shrunken, maybe deformed about the figure.

Its eyes were sorrowful, wet and pleading and far too big for its head; its limbs were surely too spindly for its body. And there was an odd texture to the creature's skin that unsettled Joe more than any of the other features had. It took him a little while to work out why. The skin was puckered and wet, like . . . like candle wax. Hot, dripping candle wax. It looked like the creature's skin was melting.

Melting? Was that what was happening to the creature in the booth?

Joe knew that there was always a danger in building ideas upon shaky assumptions, but his mind was suddenly racing with the most hideous possibilities.

Assumption number one was that the booths were used for the control of the workers at this strange factory.

Assumption number two was inspired by the thought of melting wax. What if the thing in the bottom of the booth was what happened to factory staff who resisted the machines' brainwashing? What if they were melted down and discarded? Was that even possible? What would you melt humans down with? Acid?

It was a horrible, disgusting thought—beyond insane—but it also had a grim ring of truth about it. With so much evidence of humanity's inhumanity in the world, perhaps this was nothing more than the next immoral development in management efficiency: the protection of company secrets by silencing people who became a threat.

Joe stopped there. The idea made no sense.

All he could do was to continue gathering intelligence and hope that someone back at YETI could explain everything he was seeing.

Joe was just shooting some video of the creature when he heard footsteps outside the room. Multiple feet, trying to keep quiet. Sneaking up on him.

He shook his head. He'd escaped the people below by

leaping up onto a gangway, but his discoveries up here had put all that on the back burner. He'd been so intent on discovering the secrets behind the doors up here that he'd completely forgotten about the possible dangers below. That was a rookie mistake, and one that he blamed on jetlag and adrenaline and uncertainty. But he knew the truth—it was bad tradecraft. He'd got himself too wrapped up in one thing and forgotten about the other.

And now there was someone outside the door. Either the zombie workforce had figured out how to use stairs— just because he had jumped his way up here didn't mean it was the only way up—or security had been summoned. Whichever was the case, it meant his time here had just run out. All that was left was to get the heck out of here, find a signal, make contact with YETI, and hear what Abernathy wanted him to do next.

First, though: Escape.

There were doors at either end of the room, and it sounded like the forces were gathering outside the one he'd come in through, the one that led past the supercomputer and back to the walkway. He tried the other door and it opened without violence, a key, or a *Resident Evil* gimmick onto a storeroom full of racks, which in turn were full of clear plastic vats. Lots of them. They smelled weird—almost repulsive—a cloying mixture of damp and copper and salt. Inside, they held a reddish-pink semiliquid. There were no labels or printed descriptions on the vats, but Joe had no more time to examine them, because he heard the door between the computer room and the booth room had just been opened and slammed shut. His pursuers were on his heels.

Joe moved quickly through the storeroom, keeping low, staying quiet, and trying to remember every detail for later. He made it to the end of the racks and stopped. There was just a bare wall in front of him.

There was no door at the other end of the storeroom.

No door anywhere except the one he'd just come through.

He was trapped.

What was on the other side of the door? Best case scenario: security guards. Maybe the guy from the gate with a friend or two. Worst case: zombie staff with a new "kill" impulse programmed into their brains. And here he was: trapped, caged . . .

Joe realized that he was being self-indulgent, and pulled himself together. He'd been in worse situations. He couldn't quite remember when, but it wasn't panic that had gotten him out of previous scrapes. It was swift, definitive action unencumbered by doubt or fear.

The footsteps came closer, then stopped. Joe realized that they were checking the booths as they passed them.

It gave him a little bit more time.

He looked around the room. There were two ways out as far as he could see, and neither of them was particularly promising. Exit number one was through a grate and into a heating duct—a common enough action movie route, but an impractical and dangerous move in real life. Heating and ventilation ducts weren't built to support human weight or to allow passage of a human-sized form, and they often turned at such angles as to make movement through them impossible. And even if everything lined up perfectly to allow someone to crawl through a duct, the noise would attract anyone's attention.

Which left exit number two: the door that his pursuers would be coming in through very soon.

And he realized that that was how exit number one would secure his escape.

Joe used a coin to loosen the slotted screws on the vent, then pried the vent from the wall, revealing the duct within. As he'd already predicted, the duct was narrow. A human would really have to squeeze to get inside.

A terrible strategy.

It would only result in disaster.

He dropped the vent grate to the floor, loudly.

He moved quickly to the door at the front of the room, and put his ear to the metal. The footsteps were getting even closer, and it didn't sound like they were checking the booths now, just hurrying toward the racket he'd just made. It would only be seconds before the door would open.

Joe got himself in position.

The door swung in.

He prepared, physically and mentally.

He could only hear the two men that entered the room since his line of sight was blocked by the metal. They muttered to each other as they looked around the room, then they spotted the open grate and ran over to the duct.

He snuck out into the supercomputer room without them even noticing.

Until he slammed the door on them and made his escape.

He ran the length of the next room, taking the tuning fork out of his pocket and readying it for the next door by flicking its tines with his finger. As he placed the tuning fork on the door, the one at the other end of the room opened and someone shouted for him to *STOP!*

That wasn't going to happen.

Once the sound controlled door opened, Joe raced across the computer room, slamming it behind him. He made it out the broken door and onto the walkway without even raising his pulse rate.

Below him, the activity of the factory continued as if nothing had happened. The workforce just carried on working, looking as if they had forgotten ever seeing him. Yes, he'd had a look around upstairs, but it had been only minutes, and people didn't just forget things like that and get on with their day.

Hearing noises behind him, he climbed over the yellow barrier, holding on with only his fingertips, and tensed his body for the spring that would take him back to the shelving that he'd used to get to the walkway in the first place. The problem was, of course, that it wasn't going to be easy. Leaping from the top of the shelves to the walkway had been easier because there had been railing and mesh to catch hold of. There was nothing to grab onto doing the jump in reverse except the top of the shelves. It would be all too easy to slip over the edge and plummet to the factory floor, all because he hadn't quite stuck the landing and managed to claw himself a decent enough fingerhold.

If it weren't for the fact that he could see absolutely no other choice, he would never have tried the jump.

He coiled his body like a spring, then pushed off from the walkway, turning in midair so his hands were reaching for the top of the shelving even as he fell through space. He kept his eyes on the landing spot and time seemed to slow down as his chip ran through the math and tried to give him the best possible chance of success. He'd hit pretty hard, and would have hardly any time to react. He needed his reflexes to be perfect. He needed to get it right first time.

One shot.

Preparation was key.

Adjustments in flight.

With his back straight and his legs bent, he traveled the last couple of feet and landed on the balls of his feet, arms outstretched for balance. He'd hit a bit harder than was optimum and his left hamstring complained, meaning he'd leaned a little to the left. On the ground, that would be fine. Stumbling was fine. But the width of the shelving was about a foot-and-a-half, which left so little margin for error that he couldn't afford to err. Instead, he moved his weight to his right toes, then brought both heels down, legs still bent, absorbing the shock.

If it had been a dismount from the uneven bars at the Olympics, then he might have lost half a point. But the truth of the matter was he landed square, strong, and stable. Fifteen feet above the factory floor, on a surface narrower than a diving board.

Nailed it, he thought, but there was no time to rest. He lowered himself over the edge of the shelving and began climbing down. Someone shouted behind him from the walkway, and it was actually surprisingly good to hear another human voice, even if it was from a security guard who was hunting him. Better that than the awful silence that he'd been operating under since he'd arrived here.

And the voice spurred him on. He clambered down the shelves he had found easier on the way up. Finally, his feet touched the ground and he ran, no attempt at stealth, at concealment. Just running.

If the staff noticed him, they didn't show any sign of it. No more patterned pursuit and concentric circle traps, now they were just working as if nothing unusual had happened that day. They simply ignored him, and that was as disturbing as having them all pursue him. How could they not look up as someone ran past them? How could they ignore things happening so close to where they stood?

Problems to work out another day. Now all that mattered was reaching the loading bay. Far from being a difficult journey through hostile territory, however, the trip was swift, uneventful and obstacle free.

Joe jumped down to the concrete outside and made his way to the side of the building, puzzled and disturbed in a way that he couldn't quite put his finger on. Was it that the whole escape was far too easy? Maybe. Again, he needed to concentrate on getting away, and then he could think about what it all meant, why it had all happened the way it had happened.

A quarter of the way down the side of the building he stopped. People were filtering into the space between the building and the fence up ahead, blocking off his exit. He didn't need to turn around to know that there were people behind him, too, closing off any possibility of retreat.

He had been tricked.

Trapped.

Well, almost trapped.

He turned his back on the building and surveyed the fence. It stood twelve feet high, was made of chain link, and there were three strands of barbed wire on the top, angled out on concrete brackets. The brackets were part of the concrete posts that held the fence in place, spaced every twenty feet or so.

Joe looked left—a crowd of people blocking off the route back to the loading bays. He looked right—a crowd of people blocking off the route to the factory gates.

He stood in front of the fence, just next to the nearest concrete post, where the fence would be at its tautest and easiest to climb, reached out to the chain link for a handhold, lifted his left foot onto the fence, found a toehold and pushed up. He repeated the process with his right foot, then his left, and before long, he was at the top.

Now there was just the little matter of getting past the three strands of barbed wire.

Which was made easier by the fact the fence was designed to keep people out, not in. The concrete bracket sloped forward, away from Joe. The placement of the concrete upright also helped, and this was the other reason Joe had chosen his starting position carefully.

Still, climbing over three parallel lines of barbed wire is difficult, whichever way it faces. The wire could still snag clothing and skin, could still tear and gouge whatever it did snag and cause significant injury. Joe knew, though, that if there is something solid underneath the barbed wire—say a handy concrete bracket—it would be a lot less risky to cross. Moving his body to the right, he climbed upward, using the concrete bracket for a handhold. The barbs snagged his skin a couple of times, but the injury was minimal.

It took chip-assisted balancing to get both feet onto the bracket, one in front of the other, but having elite gymnast moves accessible just by thought certainly made life easier. Joe stood up, tightrope walker style, and moved to the front of the bracket. Twelve feet of fence plus another two for the barbed wire equaled a 14-foot drop. With no way to turn around and dangle himself down to shorten the drop, fourteen feet definitely meant an injury of some kind. It *might* be minor, but odds were the fall would cause serious damage.

But there was the forest.

On the other side of the fence stretched the woodland he'd taken in on first arriving. From where he stood, he could see three branches that were reachable, two on one tree, one on another. The higher branch looked thicker and more likely to hold his weight, but it was also the farthest away.

Still, it wasn't that far.

Joe jumped, grabbed the branch, held on, waiting until the shock had settled through his muscles, then dropped to the lower branch, dangled, then dropped to the forest floor.

On the other side of the fence, the people hadn't moved. Now that he was safely over the fence, they turned away and went back into the factory.

And that was when Joe realized something.

They hadn't been trying to catch him.

They had been directing him.

Channeling him.

Driving him.

Forcing him.

Forcing him into . . .

Forcing him into the woods.

Where they wanted him to go.

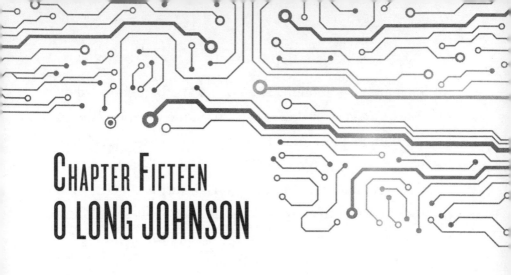

Chapter Fifteen
O LONG JOHNSON

Abernathy frowned, reached over, and played the digital file again.

For the third time.

Brian's voice, played back through the speakers.

"Ana mazi . . . emergency services were called . . . isolated community . . . attended . . . site of disturbance . . . Poiana Mazik . . . idespread communica . . . blackout . . . sub asediu . . . environmental . . . panic . . . village evacuated . . . Gaia . . . widespread . . . revenge . . . immune . . . first battle in war . . . turned . . . turned against . . . breaking news . . . enveloped . . . immunity . . . attack . . . terror . . . cordoned off . . . creatures . . . a spokesman said . . . just the beginning . . . what we've sown . . ."

When it was over, Abernathy covered his face with his hands, exhaled deeply, then put his hands on the desk in front of him, his fingers steepled, fingertips meeting his chin.

"Okay," he said. "Here's what we know, and might I say

it's nowhere near enough. The Poiana Mazik mentioned on the recording is a tiny village in Romania, notable only for its isolation, its plum brandy, and . . . nope, that's it. There have been no recorded environmental disasters, disturbances, evacuations, battles, cordons or terror attacks—and certainly no creatures—which would make this seem like a hoax of the most tedious order, if it wasn't for one thing."

"And that would be. . . ?" Ani asked.

Abernathy winced.

"Poiana Mazik is about three miles from Joe Dyson's last known location. And he's gone dark."

"Dark? Does that mean you haven't been able to contact him?"

Abernathy nodded.

"But how can that be? He's not even on the same case."

"That's certainly what we thought," Abernathy said. "It looks like we were wrong. The *victorious* investigation appears to intersect with Joe's case in Romania. Do you know what is three miles away from Poiana Mazik? What has Joe out there in the first place?"

"I assume it was a break in this homeless-people-in-slavery case," Ani offered.

"A break, yes, and not one we thought to be particularly promising. But it was all we had, and it led to the Eastern European factory of Dorian Systems."

"Dorian?" Ani said, incredulously. "As in Dorian

Interactive? As in the maker of the item at the top of just about every nerd's wish list? *NeWToPia?*"

"It seems I am the only person at YETI who had a Dorian-shaped gap in my pop cultural knowledge," Abernathy grumbled. "Yes, that Dorian."

"So how does Dorian connect to the thing in Luton?"

"Tenuously, or so we thought. There was a new kind of chip in all of the computers we seized. And they all self-destructed after we got our hands on them. But we were able to make out the Dorian logo on one of them—"

"Wait, wait, wait. You seized *computers* in Luton?"

"That's what the slave-labor force were assembling." Abernathy said.

"Well, I've just learned an important lesson," Ani said, "and it's this: pay attention to the details of other investigations. I've been so focused on the *victorious* thing, that I missed a huge piece"

"You can see how this all connects up?" Abernathy asked.

"Maybe. But first I need to get a look at these computers you seized."

<*))))><

Ani shook her head.

"You definitely need to stop compartmentalizing cases,

Abernathy," she said. "Especially when there are overlapping elements. In this case, computers."

"Noted," Abernathy replied. "Now, could you please explain to me what has gotten you so excited?"

"They're an odd kind of generic, off-brand PC," Ani explained. "Okay on their own, but they're really something when they're networked. You see, these computers, they share processing power where it's needed, when it's needed. So if I'm using one, and I don't have the processing power to hash twenty thousand passwords, then the computer will farm the job out to one or more networked computers, using their CPUs and GPUs to make up the computational shortfall. It's a beautiful implementation of the idea of a distributed computing network.

"The individual computers look like lemons, and perform like them, too, and that makes them easy to underestimate. But these computers hack like the Devil."

"And you know this how?" Abernathy asked, impatience just about, but not quite, hidden.

"They're the same computers I've been working on at *victorious.*" Ani said, enjoying the look that spread across Abernathy's face.

The one that looked like a bunch of pieces had just slotted together behind his eyes.

That looked like things might have just gotten a little clearer, but also a whole lot darker.

226

<*))))><

Abernathy tried chasing down the Shuttleworth brothers, but they were still flying back from the States.

He pulled in as many people as he could from the two investigations. They sat in the briefing room looking baffled by the sudden integration, before he stepped forward to address the group. "Thank you for your time," he said. "I'm going to make this as brief as I can, because we have some emergency, damage-limitation kind of work to be getting on with. Okay, thanks to Ani, here, we've actually made some progress on *two* investigations, so I hope the rest of you feel a modicum of shame. Don't wallow in it, I missed this, too. And Ani *is* out in the field for the explicit purpose of finding this kind of stuff, but the lesson we must take away from this is lapse is cross-check active investigations. I'm sure that we used to do that kind of thing, so could we start again? Thanks.

"For those of you involved in the *victorious* case, I'm sure that you are aware of the other thing we've been filling our time sheets with: the raid on a bowling alley in Luton that freed a number of teens being held as slave labor, and provided us with a bunch of computers and a smaller bunch of scumbags. What you might not know is that all of the seized computers contained chips that led to a major player in the global entertainments industry, Dorian Systems.

"Anyway, Joe Dyson pursued that lead to LA, and then to Eastern Europe, where he's gone off comms. Whether it's bad signal, a dead battery, or something more serious, we don't yet know. I will now yield the floor to Ani for an unprepared—but, I'm certain, quite excellent—catch up of her own. Ani?"

"Thanks, boss." Ani had been sitting at one of the desks in the briefing room, but thought it might help if she stood up and moved to the front of the room. Abernathy stepped aside. She looked out at the faces of her colleagues and tried to pretend that this all felt completely normal. "I've been working on the infiltration of *victorious* since we organized that little sting operation down in the West Country. It was feeling like a total waste of time until a couple of days ago when I started work at the downtown Dead Cell—that's v-speak for 'office'—of *victorious*.

"It turns out that *victorious* is using the same computers that were being assembled in Luton. I was impressed with the way that the v-computers used distributed processing—sharing task loads between other computers on the network, out-sourcing processing power—and I suspect the technology that makes it all possible is the chip that burned itself out in all the seized computers, a chip manufactured by Dorian Systems.

"Dorian have a factory in Romania, near a village called Poiana Mazik, which just so happens to be the site of some odd phenomena mentioned in documents scalped from the *victorious* server in a file called Gaia.meme. This dotmeme file contains a compressed archive of news pages and videos detailing some kind of attack on Poiana Mazik. It is a file that is capable of deleting itself if opened by the wrong person, and so the information we have from the dotmeme file is just a few random fragments saved as the files all deleted themselves. I say 'saved,' but what I mean is . . . . Oh, look, I'll leave it to Dr. Ghoti to explain just how we recovered them. But here's the thing: there has been no such attack on Poiana Mazik. The reports do not seem to match up with the reality. So what are they?

"Answer number one is simple: it's all a hoax. A harmless Internet prank. *victorious* intends to plant these meme files on targeted servers, get them to rewrite some newspapers' webpages, and maybe end up fooling a bunch of people into thinking something bad is happening. Maybe they want to loosen the hold we have on digital media as a news source we can trust. Maybe they just want to mess with peoples' heads. So they create a virtual disaster that's only happening in people's computers, but has the power to convince those people it's true. There'd be a new conspiracy theory within moments of the first denial of anything transpiring in Romania, too, because one thing about memes: they stick. They gain hold and replicate. They spread.

"Why did planking ever become a thing? Or that cat that sounded like it was saying 'O Long Johnson'? Actually, that last one was pretty funny . . . but, anyway, maybe that's why they're using the word 'meme' as a file name. *victorious* do seem pretty focused on their memes, even devoting a section of the London office to their production. That's interesting because besides being irritating photos of cats with slogans, the word 'meme' originally described the way that ideas, behaviors, fashions, and trends spread throughout culture. And not just Internet culture. When I was looking into the whole meme thing, I discovered that it was Richard Dawkins that coined the term, and it's modeled loosely on the idea of the gene. Maybe ideas are transferred through a society using the meme as their mechanism."

She paused to let all that information sink in, and to give her brain time to plan her next point. Composing theories and hypotheses on the fly was pretty much the way these briefings went, and—she had to admit she was pretty good at it—but it was also mentally taxing and a little bit terrifying.

"Answer number two is where it all starts to get a little weird," she said, "so bear with me on this. What if the information about the Romanian disaster is true, but it just hasn't happened *yet*?"

A male analyst, Matthew something, raised his hand. "Are we saying that *victorious* can predict the future now?" he asked in a dismissive tone.

Ani had no idea. She'd just spoken her theory out loud because that's what Abernathy had told her to do. The guy didn't need to make it sound like she was an idiot. Her idea had just followed from the first one: either it was false or it was true. And if it was true . . .

She felt a shudder pass down her spine.

If it hadn't been for the tone of the guy's question, and the flash of anger she'd felt, she might never have made the leap to her next statement. And it was pretty much out of her mouth before she'd even had a chance to think about it.

"No," she said, a little defensively. "But maybe they can create it."

<*))))><

Abernathy barked out orders for people to look into every aspect of Dorian Systems, to find out more about Poiana Mazik and why it might have been selected by *victorious* as the contents of the dotmeme file, and to generally work on confirming or denying anything Ani had just suggested.

Then he dismissed the meeting, keeping only Ani, Minaxi Desai, and Dr. Ghoti back.

"I need feet on the ground in Romania." Abernathy said, urgently. "I can send some backup in with you, because Ani here just worried me, but I'll understand if you want to opt out of this mission."

"If Ani's wrong about *victorious* engineering a disaster there, then there's no danger," Minaxi said. "And if she's right, then we really need to know. I'm in."

"Me, too," Dr. Ghoti said.

"Of course," Ani agreed.

"Good." Abernathy rubbed his hands together. "I need to make a few calls so we don't have to rely on commercial aircraft flight times. We'll have a mission briefing in"—he looked at the watch on his wrist—"shall we say twenty minutes? That should give you just enough time to pass on whatever you're working on to the next person down the line. I'll see you back here then."

He half turned to walk away, then shook his head, solemnly. "You realize that every time the dominant form of media changes, society changes, too?"

"All right." Ani said. "I'll play. Tell me how."

"Think about it. When oral traditions gave way to Gutenberg's printing presses, humanity was able to set down its knowledge. People learned. They discussed. They innovated. Then came the telegraph, the telephone, the television, and knowledge gave way to trivia and entertainment."

"It's one way of looking at things." Ani said. "A bit Luddite, if I'm honest, but hey, is there a point hidden in there somewhere?"

Abernathy grinned, his trap sprung.

"In the days of print as humanity's dominant medium, the US got Abraham Lincoln. In the days of TV, they got Ronald Reagan. Now, with the Internet, fake news, and memes they got Donald Trump. Join the dots. Twenty minutes, everyone?"

<*))))><

Ani had a call to make. She had no idea how it would go, if the person on the other end would even want to speak to her, let alone do another favor for her.

She rehearsed her opening line a few times, but it got worse the farther away it got from "spontaneous," so she pressed DIAL and leapt straight in.

"Hey, Brian?"

"Ani? Are you okay? You ran off pretty quickly . . ."

"Yeah, I'm sorry about that. Did you get home okay?"

"Taxi. No problem. You ordered it, remember?"

"I remember. How are you feeling?"

"Er . . . groggy. Guess your friend hypnotized me or something?"

"Or something. Look, I need . . . I . . ."

"The answer's already yes."

"Hey, you want to be careful making blanket agreements like that. Nothing good can come of it."

"You want me to . . . Insert next instruction here."

Ani laughed. "The cell within the cell is still active?"

"Of course it is, Ani. I think that we'll need to define our roles a little better later, but I'm still your partner in crime."

"Thank you."

"Pleasure. So what do you need?"

"Okay, I don't suppose you know what happens to any broken computers at *victorious* HQ?"

"They replace them, shove the old ones in some closet, and forget—Oh, okay. Do you need me to steal one of the old ones?"

"Not steal. Just get a look at the guts. Specifically, the motherboard."

"What am I looking for?"

"A Dorian Systems chip. You'll know it when you see it because you won't know what the heck it is."

"Dorian as in . . . ?"

"One and the same. Oh, and can you cover for me?"

"Sure. You're not coming in?"

"I've got to look into something. But if anyone asks, I've got a doctor's appointment."

"What should I say is wrong with you?"

"That, my friend, is entirely your call. I guess the severity of the condition will be a barometer of the esteem you hold me in."

It was Brian's turn to laugh. "It won't be anything too serious," he said. "I *will* see you soon, though?"

"Count on it."

"I do. See you, RedQueen mystery girl."

"See you soon, my meme hacking friend."

<*))))><

"Sorry folks," Abernathy said, looking disappointed. "I tried to get you something amazing to fly in—a Bell Boeing

Osprey with vertical take-off and landing—but you'd have had to pick it up in Germany, and it would've wasted more time than it set out to save, so I'm afraid you're traveling by private jet.

"Now, the serious bit. We have no idea what we're sending you into. It might be nothing. It might be, as Ani implied, exactly what the dotmeme file said, just deferred. It might be anything in between. I'll need you to investigate the village, find Joe, and generally make sure that you all get out alive. To that end, I'm including a couple of roadies to make sure the European tour goes well. You've heard of the SAS?"

"The Special Air Service, British Special Forces," Minaxi said. "Elite troops."

"The guys I'm sending in with you make the SAS look like whey-faced Romantic poets. Ani, did you get in touch with your friend at *victorious*?"

"Sure did. He's going to try to get a look inside one of the *victorious* office computers to see if there's a Dorian chip involved. I think we know the answer to that question, though. That name just keeps coming up, doesn't it?"

"And for a man with such a huge reputation, he seems to keep himself very much to himself," Abernathy replied. "A reclusive multi-millionaire software designer who's managed to remain pretty much out of the public eye for decades. I'm trying to find out everything I can about him, but I'm playing catch-up, so I'll keep you apprised of anything pertinent I discover. The one thing that occurs to me is that when we visited Dorian Interactive in LA, the exec we spoke to there . . . Curtiz, I think it was . . . said that Mr. Dorian was in Romania."

"A mighty big coincidence," Ani said.

"Now you can see why you're traveling out there, can't you?"

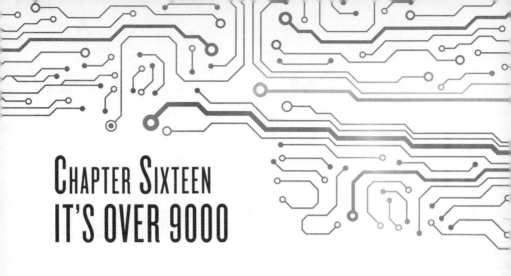

Chapter Sixteen
IT'S OVER 9000

The forest had been sparse by the fence itself, but had grown more densely the deeper in Joe traveled. His instinct had been to move out of sight of the fence—and the factory—but travel roughly parallel to it. It would be the quickest way back toward the road. But when the trees got closer together and started hemming him in, his progress slowed to almost a crawl.

The feeling that he was being manipulated into his present course of action persisted, but once he'd hit the ground on the wood side of the fence, he was committed to it. If the staff of Dorian Europe *had* forced him into the woods, then Joe could see nothing to explain why. Surely, he would have been easier to catch by the factory, but that was assuming that capture was their end game. It was also possible that they had just wanted him off the premises.

If so, they'd succeeded.

Maybe they figured that he hadn't seen anything criminal, or even concrete enough that he could take it to the authorities, so why not let him go? Who would he tell? Who would care? Or believe him?

That had been a mistake, though. Joe didn't know exactly what he *had* seen, or what it all meant, but he had seen enough to know that there was something very, very wrong going on in that factory. He tried his phone, then his chip-based intercom, but there was still no signal from either. Either the Carpathian Mountains created a natural dead zone, or there was some heavy-duty signal jamming coming from the Dorian factory. Joe hoped it was the former, but feared it was the latter.

He'd been traveling for a few minutes when he got the distinct feeling he wasn't alone. He tried to dismiss it as paranoia, but the thought just kept chipping away at him.

A dense colonnade of trees suddenly pushed him farther from the parallel path he'd been attempting, and he stopped for breath and to get his bearings. There was a brittle, cracking sound off to his left, followed by another matching noise to his right. Both had sounded like wood being snapped, and not the tiny snaps of twigs being stepped on, but louder as if branches were being ripped away from trees. The fact that they occurred on either side of him, timed within seconds of each other, seemed sinister.

It suggested that the noises had been both deliberate and coordinated.

He dropped to a crouch and tried to work out exactly where the noises had originated. Close enough to worry him, but it was so hard to get a fix on sounds in a forest at the best of times. In an unknown forest, with his adrenaline pumping, and the residual memories of the factory nagging at him, it was impossible.

He waited, his breathing slowed and quiet, trying to catch a sound.

Nothing.

Maybe he had imagined it. Or maybe it has just been falling branches. The silence was a relief, actually, because the noises *had* sounded coordinated and deliberate.

And then he thought, *nothing?*

He had been making his way through the wood for a while now, and it hadn't been quiet for a single second of it. Birds had been twittering around him, and he'd heard the flap of wings as he'd disturbed them from their resting places. At no point in his trek had the woods actually been silent.

But now it was.

Not even a bird sang.

His mind flashed back to the wild boar he'd seen when he was approaching the loading bay, and those curved tusks that looked like they could cause severe damage if the animal decided to charge. Joe had no idea if boar *did* charge at humans. He knew very little about them at all, except that they were hairy pigs. He hadn't heard of pigs attacking people, so maybe boars were safe . . . If it was even a boar he'd heard.

In two locations.

Once. Each.

And then silence.

He felt a cold prickle of fear creep down his neck.

It wasn't a boar he had heard.

Because it wasn't a boar he was hearing now. To the left and to the right, synchronized and moving toward him. Slowly. In formation. Two pursuers. Confident enough not to need to move quietly. Using their methodical progress to intimidate him into moving.

Joe threw together a pheromone cocktail of Alpha Male and Hunter-Not-Hunted. He stood up and tried to get a line of sight on either of his pursuers, but they were staying hidden. For now. Egging him into making a hasty move with the noise of their pursuit. Trying to keep him off-balance. Trying to scare him into an error.

Such errors came from the amygdalae, the primitive parts of the brain responsible for triggering fear reactions to outside stimuli. Controlling fear was a matter of striking a balance between the emotional fury of the primal amygdala and the sophisticated reasoning powers of a more recent addition to the brain: the neocortex. The trick was to use the brain's own chemistry to defeat one of its own defenses; to stop the body's *fight or flight* chemical, adrenaline, from binding to the brain's receptors.

The only way Joe knew to do that was through reason. Analysis. Higher brain functions. That's why the problems he hit up against hadn't killed him yet. He thought his way past them. Saw the truth behind them. Implemented strategies for dealing with them.

It was easier when you had a chip that could be used to directly control brain chemistry, but the best way to avoid panic—and the mistakes that would surely flow from it—was to think your way around it.

So Joe began moving, trying to keep the sounds equal distances away from him, trying to concentrate on every aspect of his progress through the trees, and trying to keep the progress of his pursuers modeled in 3-D in his mind's eye.

Visualization. Calculation. Analysis.

As useful against mental darkness as flashlights were against its physical analogue. Rational thinking could downgrade that unpredictable emotion called *fear* into a much more useful tool: *caution.*

The canopy of leaves above him filtered out enough of the light to take the critical edge off his vision. Either that, or his pursuers were excellent at concealment. Even when he was sure he had their positions fixed, he could see no sign of them. Just hear the sound of them moving, of their slow, deliberate march through undergrowth. When he sped up, the sounds did not, and that gave him a momentary sense of relief. Relief that died the moment he thought, *They don't need to move quicker, because they're that certain they'll catch me.*

He wished he knew the terrain, what he was heading toward. He felt he was still moving in the direction of the road, but also that he had been pushed farther from the parallel path he'd intended to follow. Instead of a straight line, he was taking a longer diagonal. And the slope of the land was becoming more and more difficult to negotiate. It seemed to demand more speed of him when what he needed was steadiness.

Physical and mental steadiness.

He dodged tree trunks and roots, keeping himself equidistant between the two pursuers. One of the ways that fear, adrenaline, and survival instincts worked was by taking away the non-essential functions and boosting the ones that evolution had proved to be the most useful in dangerous situations. The digestive system pulled a 180-degree turn: instead of storing sugars, it flooded the body with them, preferring their quick release of energy to any long-term gains. Blood vessels contracted, which, with a rapid increase in heart rate, meant that chemicals traveled around the body at a dramatically increased rate.

There were trade-offs, though. There was the loss of higher reasoning skills, obviously, with a more violence-focused approach to problem solving; a marked narrowing of the human field of vision (in order to concentrate on the danger in front of one it tended to mask out the peripheral extras); and the fight or flight reflex was really only meant for a short-term advantage. Its pulls on the physical body—increased breathing, sweating, heart rate and blood pressure—meant that it wasn't a state sustainable over long periods of time.

Visualization. Calculation. Analysis.

Keep the higher brain in the driver's seat, but keep the more primal, lower brain functions riding shotgun.

And when being pursued by unknown pursuers?

Keep moving.

Forward.

<*))))><

It only took a few degrees of deviation from a straight course to become a mistake that compounded dramatically over distance. You only had to look at the hypotenuse of triangles to see that. And it was the same cruel geometry that took Joe from parallel to the fence to goodness-only-knew how far from the road.

It occurred to Joe that his pursuers intended on keeping him away from the road, driving him deeper into the woods. If that was the case, it at least made them human, rather than bears or some other indigenous predator, but even that flash of comfort was a double-edged sword. Sure, Joe would rather fight men than bears, but he'd have no problems outthinking bears. Two men were always capable of nasty surprises.

And on the subject of nasty surprises, the sky beyond the trees was already starting to darken. Maybe it would make it easier to lose his pursuers, but that had its own trade-offs. He didn't know what else prowled Transylvanian mountain forests at night, but he was pretty sure that he didn't want to find out.

He checked for a phone signal again. A lot of scenes in modern thrillers, he'd noticed, were built upon ways to prevent cellphone signals that would render all the suspense built up null and void. He'd always seen it as a corny plot device, but realized now that it was simply another way of turning the mental screws. The reliance on cellphones was pathological and, when you needed them and they didn't work, it became utterly demoralizing.

No signal also meant no maps, of course. Which meant he didn't know where he was heading. He tried to map his route out in his head, along with what he knew of the countryside, but not even his chip helped work out his location.

He was just thinking that maybe it was time to stop running—to turn around and face whoever it was that was following him and put an end to the undercurrent of fear that had been informing his movements for too long now, when he noticed three geographical features that gave him a reason to continue on. First up was the leveling off of the slope to flat terrain that was easier to traverse. Second was the forest thinning out around him. And third, but most exciting, was the fact that the ground beneath his feet was becoming well-trodden.

A path.

And paths led . . . well, *somewhere.*

And anywhere was better than being lost in the woods.

That was his theory, anyway.

He hurried to put it to the test.

<*))))><

The village was blink-and-you-miss-it small, and Joe thought it was completely deserted. A main street that was no more than a dirt track led past some ramshackle houses that looked like they'd been plucked from another decade, or another century—timber houses finished in traditional methods, using dovetail joints rather than nails or screws, with sloping roofs and shuttered windows. There were no lights or signs or life.

One of the buildings had a higher slope to its roof and some elaborate crucifixes decorating it, which seemed to suggest it was a place of worship, but it too looked empty.

Joe tried his phone again but, although a couple of bars showed on-screen, it didn't translate into an actual signal in the real world.

He walked down the track and began noticing a few modern touches, the most telling of which was the satellite dishes fixed to the sides of some of the buildings. They seemed oddly out of place, but also fitting. No matter how far off the beaten track the village was, it was still patched in to the world's TV channels.

And satellite meant telecommunications.

Which meant contact with the outside world.

With YETI.

Joe had just chosen a door to knock upon when he became aware of movement at the end of the street he'd come in on. Two forms were moving out of the twilight murk. They were human height, or maybe a little taller than average, but looked a lot wider than you'd expect, wider . . . or chunkier . . . stockier . . . Whichever adjective fit, did so in a most disconcerting manner.

He knocked on the door with a little more urgency than he'd intended, watching as the figures moved toward him, their gait slow, lumbering, but determined. There was something about the way they moved that set off alarm bells in Joe's head—some biomechanical strangeness that he couldn't quite put his finger on, but that made him want to get as far away from them as he could.

Just as he heard movement inside the house, he worked out the source of his discomfort. It wasn't that he could suddenly say what it was about the figures' movements that unsettled him, but that he had seen enough people moving that he recognized what constituted human movement. The . . . things entering the village did not move like people. He couldn't identify what they *did* move like, but it wasn't anything he knew.

The door opened inward and a middle-aged woman peered at him. Her face looked kind, but puzzled. She had a brightly-colored scarf wrapped around her head and tied at the neck.

"*Cine esti?*" the woman asked.

Joe made a mental note to ask Abernathy for basic phrases in all languages to be programmed into his hardware to make situations like this a little easier to navigate. For now, he was going to have to do what English speakers often do when they're abroad: speak louder and try to convey meaning through pantomimed gestures.

"Er . . . English?" Joe tried, pointing at the woman, then his mouth. "Anglais? Ingles? Englisch?"

The woman shook her head.

"*Imi pare rau,*" she said, "*eu nu vorbesc engleza.*"

It didn't take a genius to figure out that her words meant: no, she didn't speak English. And why should she? So Joe made the universal sign for "phone," holding up his thumb and pinky to his ear and mouth. "Er . . . telephone?"

The woman's face lit up, and she nodded vigorously. "*Da,*" she said. "*Da, avem un telefon!*"

She opened the door wider and gestured for Joe to enter. He hadn't been expecting such trust and generosity, and was overcome with relief. But he looked down the street to see if the followers were still there. He couldn't see them. He hoped that he wasn't putting this woman in jeopardy by accepting her hospitality.

She led him through into a small, cozy room that proudly displayed hangings and garments with floral motifs on just about every available surface. The woman gestured for Joe to sit by a table and he obliged, looking around for the ancient

Bakelite rotary-dial-phone that he expected Romanian peasant villagers would use. She handed him a touchscreen smartphone with a Romanian brand name, Allview.

"Thank you," he said.

The screen said three bars, the phone said no. His phone showing signal but receiving none had been suspicious. Two phones doing the same thing: confirmation that something was not right.

He simply didn't have enough pieces of the puzzle. He'd come to Romania thinking he'd catch a thief, not to have his entire world sent through a bloody looking glass until it stopped making sense altogether.

He tried to gesture that the phone wasn't working and it was just good enough that the woman gave it a try. The woman looked perplexed and stabbed at the screen with a no-nonsense finger. Still nothing. She offered him a shrug as a kind of apology along with a string of words he didn't understand. She gestured for him to get up and follow her, so he did, and she led him back to the front door, out through it, onto the street and to the house next door.

She knocked and called out and the door was opened by a younger woman, a couple of toddlers peeping out from behind her skirts. The two women spoke quickly and seriously, and then the younger woman pulled out a cellphone of her own and tried calling someone on it. When the call didn't connect, she shouted over her shoulder and a man about her age popped his head out, tried a phone of his own, then shook his head.

When he was about ten, Joe's mother had given him a copy of *Goldfinger* by Ian Fleming. He'd loved the story, sure, and the fact that it contained a map of the US gold depository of Fort Knox had been cool beyond belief, but there was a line that had stayed with him, a line that the villain had said to James Bond: "That the first meeting between Bond and Goldfinger had been happenstance. The second time was coincidence. The third meeting, however, was enemy action." Joe had, unconsciously at first, later with knowing, adopted the line into his own method of operating. It was a good rule of thumb.

One cellphone out: happenstance. Two: coincidence. Three: enemy action.

And cellphone four?

Bad news.

But how did any of this tie together? The factory, the chips, the weirdness of the workers, the supercomputer, the booths, the things that had followed him through the woods, the cellphone dead zone?

The woman led him to another door where they discovered another dead cellphone. The villagers' frustration was becoming a little louder. Unfortunately, their surprise and agitation at their loss of cell signal only ratcheted up Joe's *enemy action* feeling. One of the villagers, a stocky male with a deeply lined face, pointed at Joe and started asking questions—*"Cine este el? Ce face aici?"*—and people obviously started putting together two pieces of information—*stranger arrives + phone signal dies*—to draw their own conclusions.

The problem was, they were probably right. He had no idea what kind of tech the Dorian factory would need to kill cell signals over a few miles' radius, but tech was something they had in abundance. So maybe his arrival here *had* caused their phones to go off-line. The group, however, was coming around to this way of thinking. There was a cautious distance being maintained, and the faces were looking slightly less friendly. And, of course, that could just have been Joe's paranoia, and inability to read another culture's verbal and non-verbal cues.

It didn't matter. Joe felt on the outside now. The possibility of calling for help was growing more and more remote. And somewhere out there in the gathering darkness were the things that had pursued him into the village. He needed to warn these people. He was trying to figure out how he might mime the appearance of the creatures when a shrill scream tore through the night.

<*))))><

The villagers grabbed torches and pitchforks and went in search of the creature. Okay, the torches were Maglite-style flashlights and cellphone apps, but the parallels with a 1930s horror movie weren't lost on Joe.

The scream had died out, but had originated from the farthest, darkest part of the village. A crowd of nearly a dozen people made swift progress to its source.

A woman was sitting on the road, spilled sticks and small logs around her, as two . . . *creatures* . . . prowled around her. The villagers' lights illuminated the things that had been following Joe pretty much all the way from the factory, and he got his first good look at them.

Now he could see why they didn't move like human beings. They weren't human beings.

They were large, bulky, creatures, and their legs seemed jointed differently than human leg joints, or rather were jointed lower down on the leg, making for a much shorter lower leg that terminated in a large, thick, almost cloven foot. The arms, however, seemed to reverse that pattern— shorter upper arms and much elongated lower ones. The hands were chubby with only three fat, rectangular fingers on each. The body was a thick lump that gave way to a head with almost no neck, and the head itself was hairless, bulky and gave an impression of being unformed; as if these creatures were incredibly primitive and unevolved.

"Unformed" was, Joe decided, the closest he could come to a word that described the things. They had a grayish pallor that looked sickly in the torchlight, and their eyes looked like afterthoughts, little more than dark pits with a shiny surface at their bases.

The creatures were circling the woman, but weren't attacking. Yet.

She looked absolutely terrified.

As the villagers arrived, the creatures stopped their circling and turned their attentions to the crowd. The woman saw a window of opportunity and she took it, crawling—then scampering—away, until she reached the group of villagers, who helped her to her feet.

The creatures moved closer to the group. Their skin glistened in the lights, like it was wet. Or slimy. There was something almost instinctively horrible about them, about the way they looked—like some odd proto-human that looked more suited to dark caves than above-ground life—and the way they moved, awkward and wrong, again looked more suited to an underground existence.

The thing that was most terrifying about them was their complete silence. As they approached, they made no grunts. No roars. No growls. No deep breathing. No snorts.

Nothing.

To Joe, it was an implacable silence, full of implied threat.

His hand had lifted his phone up before he realized he'd made a decision to film them. People around him had had the same idea. That was one of the things the human being had become now: a recorder of visual events. It was an urge to chronicle that had begun on cave walls, moving through paint and found its natural zenith in photography. Now that just about everyone carried a stills camera and video camera in their phone, that urge was perhaps too easily satisfied.

Joe thought it was sad that people viewed experiences through the remove of their camera screen, even as his thumb pressed ●REC.

It took Joe a few seconds to work out what happened next.

<*))))><

There was an armored vehicle waiting for them on the runway when their jet touched down at Braşov-Ghimbav airport. It looked like a 44 and a tank had had a baby. And then that baby had started taking steroids.

Furness, one of their armed escorts, informed them it was a Wolf Armored Vehicle, used by the Israeli military, but exported to Romania for use by their military police.

Furness and Gilman, in woodland camouflage and carrying automatic rifles, ushered Ani, Dr. Ghoti, and Minaxi Desai into the back, climbing in after them, presumably to protect them from . . . Ani really couldn't guess . . . Drafts? The back of the vehicle was very spacious and could easily have seated another six or seven people before it even started feeling crowded.

The Romanian army driver started up the engine, which

roared loudly to life, and then they were lurching forward toward the village of Poiana Mazik.

"We have no way of knowing what we'll find," Furness told them. "I'll need you to hold back until we've secured the area."

His stern, matter-of-fact voice contained no suggestion that objections could be raised. Which was fine. Ani had more than enough to do.

She took out the YETI-issue tablet and connected to the global satellite network that made even the highest-priced business networks look positively Stone Age in comparison. Connection was instantaneous, faster than most broadband she'd used, and rock solid. She checked her notifications and found a photo waiting for her from Brian. The picture showed a Dorian chip on a *victorious* motherboard. Caption: *Result!* She forwarded it to Abernathy, thanked Brian, and then called up a map of the local area.

As Poiana Mazik grew closer, her anxiety increased. She searched for Poiana Mazik on the Internet and found a couple of travel sites with photos, so there was no need to feel uneasy, but when you've just flown in a private jet and been whisked away in an armored personnel carrier, it's hard not to feel slightly melodramatic.

She watched the arrow that represented the personnel carrier get closer to the dot that represented Poiana Mazik, but that was like watching a kettle, waiting for it to boil.

She wondered what else she could do to fill the time.

It seemed too ordinary to start checking emails.

She scrolled though apps, but felt unable to focus on anything. After a few minutes, she was sick of looking at the screen. She was just about to shut the browser down when the page that she'd searched Poiana Mazik on refreshed.

Things turned very weird, very quickly.

<*))))><

Joe stared at the display on his phone, his brow furrowed, his eyes narrowed. It was almost as if he were trying to trick the image, to will it into showing what he could see in the real world.

The camera app refused to obey.

There were two creatures.

That was as far as the similarities went.

The creatures on-screen were very different from the half-formed, proto-human creatures in front of him. On-screen, the creatures were terrifying, and so much less human looking.

Their bodies appeared elongated, almost like the bodies of earthworms, and they looked segmented, too, to cement that association in his mind. The legs were no longer awkward looking and oddly proportioned. On the screen of his phone they looked insect-like: chitinous, barbed, and horribly slender. The arms had become very similar to the legs, but with cruel pincers snapping at the air in front of them.

And the creatures' heads . . . The camera screen transformed them from canister-shaped blobs of ill-formed matter into faces of pure, skin-prickling malevolence. There was something of a spider's head about them—the spiky fur, the row of eyes that braceleted the face—but the heads were stretched forward, extruded into thrusting ovals, ovals that dripped glutinous slime from quivering pink mouth-parts.

He could tell that everyone else trying to capture the scene on their phones was finding the same disparity between physical reality and its digital counterpart. The confusion was becoming panic and the panic was starting to spread. People were jabbering and pointing as the world stopped making sense.

The creatures walked toward them. In the real world they lumbered, but in the digital world it was more of a centipede slither.

Joe realized he didn't have a clue what to do next.

<*))))><

Ani threw up her hands in disbelief.

"There's a breaking news story," she said, checking the web again and finding it still offered the same sketchy, but suggestive, details. "It's about a small Romanian village. Anyone want to guess the name of that village?"

"Poiana Mazik?" Dr. Ghoti asked.

"The very same."

"What sort of breaking news story?" the doctor asked.

"The details are sketchy," Ani reported. "Someone uploaded some photos of . . . creatures seen attacking the isolated village of Poiana Mazik. Apparently, emergency services were called to this isolated community, but attempts to reach the village have been hampered by a widespread communications blackout."

"But they're pretty much the same words that Brian remembered from the dotmeme file," the doctor said. "It doesn't make sense . . ."

"Or it makes a very dark kind of sense," Minaxi offered. "What did you say about memes, Ani? That they are the unit by which ideas spread across cultures? Maybe that's been *victorious*'s goal all along. To implant a new idea into our culture. This new idea. This attack. Your friend Brian just got a quick look at it *before* it was ready for transmission."

Ani showed her one of the images that had been uploaded.

A terrifying insect creature in the half-light near a rustic village.

"Some idea," she said, "but what do they have to be gained by implanting that?"

"Fear?" Minaxi said. "Isn't that the ultimate goal of all terrorists?"

"But *victorious* are hackers," Ani said. "Hackers aren't terrorists."

"Until their skills are used in the service of a terrorist

organization," Minaxi said pointedly. "Maybe the hackers are being duped. Maybe this is terrorism, just a new form . . ."

"But it's Dorian tech that's making it possible," Ani insisted. "Not terrorists—a software company. There's something else going on that we're not seeing . . ."

"That may be so," Furness said, "but we're arriving at our destination. So get ready for . . . well, for whatever this is."

A few minutes later, the vehicle stopped abruptly, its engine still running.

Furness opened the back.

"Stay here," he said. "We'll cut you a path." And then he jumped down into the darkness.

<*))))><

One of the creatures reached out and grabbed the neck of a Romanian man, dragging him away from the other villagers. It was enough to pull Joe out of his stunned disbelief. With something to fight for, things made sense. He put the phone away in his pocket, stepped up to the creature, and tried to wrestle the man free from its grasp. The creature's arm was thick, hard and strong, and it hardly seemed to notice Joe at all. The man, himself, was clawing at the creature, but hadn't made any headway.

Joe tried a couple of hard blows to the creature's face,

but it was like punching wet clay; he was sure that it hurt his fists more than it hurt the creature, especially the fist that had danced across the Lakers fans' teeth. It didn't feel like he was making any progress, and the creature remained seemingly oblivious. In fact, the creature was tightening its grip on the man's neck, and the choking sounds coming from his mouth made Joe think the guy didn't have long before the thing killed him.

And that was unacceptable.

Back when he was still in training, learning fighting skills in another of Abernathy's specialized gyms—this one in Birmingham—his instructor had been an avid student of a book called *The Art of War* by a Chinese military strategist and philosopher named Sun Tzu. Amid a slew of useless quotations about how to fight, when not to fight, how to win, and times not to win, there was one that came to mind now: "In the midst of chaos, there is also opportunity." It always annoyed Joe when he recalled one of those *Art of War* aphorisms in the middle of an actual fight, because there was little or no relation between the two. That chaos quote? Joe had always thought it was a trite thing that people used to try to sound clever, but they neglected to notice that the maxim offered no practical advice whatsoever, just like most of the Sun Tzu quotes his instructor had come up with.

Joe thought that a lot of Sun Tzu's quotes would be more useful if they were a bit less fortune cookie in construction, and a bit more context specific.

Or, in Joe's case, more user specific.

In the midst of chaos, switch your fighting chip to "lethal force" and have another go.

There was an idea that he could work with.

He made the adjustments, felt his body respond to the new muscle forms and tolerances, and turned his attention, once again, to the creature's head. When he'd been hitting out at it before, he hadn't even managed to make it acknowledge that he *had* hit it, but now his body was recoded with muscle memories that reminded him how he *should* have been punching the first time around.

He kept his knees slightly bent—going for a hard jab without using the legs was already a failure, because he had been missing out on the most powerful muscles in his body—and he kept his body loose. Swinging from the hips and launching from the legs, moving his whole body into the punch, rather than just his right arm. Punching was actually described by a pretty simple mathematical calculation that formed the basis of Newton's Second Law of Motion: net force equals mass times acceleration. To get more force—more power—in the punch you needed speed, but you also needed mass. The more mass the better. Move from the shoulder, and it doesn't matter how much speed you generate, you've set yourself a low limit on the amount of damage you'll do. Throw the entire weight of your body behind the punch, and the acceleration has something to work with.

It was a simple fighting tip, but one that was so easy to forget when a battle got underway. Joe's chipset not only reminded him, coached his body, and made him ready to implement the strategy, but it was also programmed in the perfect sequence of physical moves to make sure that Newton's calculation did its best possible work.

When Joe's fist hit the creature's temple, it was traveling at speed, and it was a punch that started on the balls of his feet, sprang through his knees, swung through his hips, pushed forward his body, transferred into his shoulder, through his arm and down into his fist. The contact made a horrible sound, and if Joe's chip hadn't been managing things for him, it could easily have broken the small bones of his hand.

Could have.

Didn't.

But it certainly gave the creature something to think about.

Joe saw it release the Romanian man, who slunk to the floor clutching at his throat making a rasping, choking sound. It turned its face toward Joe and opened its mouth. Joe thought it was going to roar or growl but it maintained its inscrutable silence, moving forward faster to try to latch onto him with its teeth. The problem for the creature was it was too slow for Joe, who was now operating on his fight clock, which made his reactions sharper, his perception clearer. The creature might as well have been standing still for all the good its lunge did it. By the time it had reached the end of its maneuver, Joe was already off to one side, coming back in for another blow, this one with the meat of his right palm, aimed for the ridge over the top of the creature's left eye.

Net force = mass × acceleration.

Joe had put his whole body behind the blow, and he made sure he did it fast. The net force was great enough that Joe felt the ridge of bone give beneath the meat of his hand. He hit again with his left, then once more with his right, a quick one-two-three, concentrated on the same spot. Instead of hitting the eye, he aimed at the orbit, the circle of bone that housed the eye. An orbital fracture was likely to cause diplopia—double vision—disorientation, and chronic pain.

Should soften the thing up for . . .

The creature's arm suddenly swung out and hit the side of Joe's head, moving a lot faster than its previous movements had suggested it capable of. It was like being hit by a bag of bricks, and Joe realized that the creature had pretty much suckered him in. The blow stunned him and he struggled to stay on his feet. As he reeled off toward the ground, he thought that he was lucky the creature knew less about Newton's laws, just using its arm rather than its whole body. He thought that he might have been dead if it had multiplied the acceleration.

Joe wasn't dead—that was something. But he did land

on the ground with the wind knocked out of him, and the thing was lifting one of its feet in the air above his head.

He looked up.

The creature started to bring its foot down.

Not a whole lot of velocity, but one heck of a lot of mass by the look of it.

<*))))><

Furness had told them to wait in the personnel carrier, but Ani, Dr. Ghoti, and Minaxi disagreed. Not to his face—he wasn't the kind of guy who would back down after giving an order. But when he and Gilman had left the back of the vehicle and were running toward the disturbance some distance ahead of them, they slipped out the back. Ani wondered what the strategic value of parking this far from the scene of conflict was, then realized that it was probably the driver, himself, that decided to hold back. Maybe this kind of op was way above his pay grade.

From where Ani stood, it looked like they'd come to the location where the pictures of the insect creatures had been uploaded from. There were villagers and screams and squeals of panic.

The three agents climbed down from the vehicle and followed the soldiers.

As they drew closer, the details of the scene became clearer. But along with that came a sense of bemusement.

The villagers—and Joe, Ani noticed with delight and horror—were indeed fighting a pair of monstrous creatures,
but they certainly weren't the ones she'd seen in the
Internet photos. These were squat, thick-set creatures that
looked more like poorly-made humans. They still looked
dangerous though, and as she watched, one of the creatures
smashed Joe in the head and he fell to the ground.

She saw Furness shoulder his weapon and point it in the
creature's direction. It was still quite a distance away. With
the chaos and panic Furness, surely wouldn't risk a shot.

The creature raised its foot to crush Joe's skull.

Furness fired a volley of bullets into the thing's chest.

<*))))><

Joe was already rolling out of the path of the creature's foot
when it stopped suddenly. The foot hovered in midair. Joe
heard the shots then, but kept moving. Priority one: get clear.
He could see what the bullet fire meant, see how it changed
the playing field, when he was clear of danger. The most
important strategy for surviving the next few moments:
don't be underneath that foot when it stamps down.

Once safely to the side, Joe was able to study the scene.
He saw the line of bullet hits across the creature's chest—
puckered holes from which a thick, dark liquid the consis-
tency of gruel leaked. Someone had shot the thing with an
assault rifle, probably an AK-47. He looked over to where

the shots must have originated and saw two soldiers, one with his rifle shouldered, the other with his at his hip. Behind the soldiers he saw Ani and a woman that looked like Minaxi Desai from YETI HQ.

Everyone was staring at the creature that was still standing there on one foot, seemingly defying gravity, still leaking from its wounds. The man it had been strangling was still bent over on one knee, but someone was assisting him—Dr. Ghoti, Joe realized. Abernathy had sent in the cavalry.

The creature finally put its foot back down on the ground. The monster did not fall, it didn't even stumble. Instead, it moved again toward Joe.

"Well, that's just great," he muttered.

He dragged himself up from the ground and turned to face the creature.

<*))))><

Ani could understand being called out in the field to use her computer skills, maybe her general technology knowledge, and maybe for her newly trained and honed fighting skills, if someone was really desperate.

This . . . this was too much. Helpless didn't even *begin* to describe how she was feeling. She was out of her depth. With a tablet computer in her hands. Against those . . . those *things*. They might not be the living terrors the Internet was making them out to be, but they were still pretty scary.

What were they? Where had they come from? Why were they here? Those were the questions at the forefront of her mind, which made her worry about her suitability as a field operative. The question, *How do we stop them?* had occurred to her in a pretty poor fourth place. But maybe that was her strength. Joe and the soldiers could be working on the problem of taking the creatures down, she could try to work out what the hell was going on. And why.

She tapped an icon on the tablet screen and connected to YETI back in London, via its video-over-satellite-Internet feature, the one that made FaceTime look olde worlde.

Abernathy looked relieved when he saw her face on his computer monitor.

"Ani," he said, "status?"

"Not good. Are you following all this online?"

"The attack on Poiana Mazik by bugs from hell?" Even Abernathy looked surprised that this last statement had come out of his mouth. "We're watching streaming video from the scene now."

"There are only two major problems with the coverage, as I see it," Ani told him. "First, what you see on screen is *not* what's happening here. Those creatures? The ones we're seeing are much more clumsy-looking. Half-formed. Someone's digitally manipulating the images. It could be Dorian. It could be *victorious*. It could be both working together."

"Send me a photo of what the real creatures look like."

"Give me a sec."

She lifted the tablet to take advantage of its rear-facing camera, sending the video straight to Abernathy to save time. She was shocked by the jarring disparity between what she saw with her eyes, and what the camera saw with its fancy optical lens. A horrible suspicion took root in her brain.

"Are you seeing this?" she asked, urgently.

"I'm seeing insects."

"It must be the Dorian chips," Ani said. "They're the conduits for the dotmeme data. The dotmeme file rewrites reality, augments it until it's impossible to see what's real and what isn't. The Dorian chips spread it like a virus."

"It can't be," Abernathy said. "There aren't any Dorian chips in that tablet you're holding."

"Maybe there don't have to be," Ani said, dismissively. "There just need to be enough of them in the local area. There are Romanian villagers around here, and they're all carrying smartphones. Maybe they . . . I don't know . . . I'm thinking about the way that Dorian chips allow distributed processing . . . Look, this probably isn't the best time for me to be trying to make sense of this. The creatures are . . ."

Ani broke off.

Suddenly, she wanted to be somewhere very far away.

The only way to complete the sentence would have been to say: ". . . getting reinforcements."

Two more of the beasts were moving toward the villagers.

<*))))><

When Joe saw another two creatures looming out of the darkness, he felt a sinking feeling in his stomach. With one of them shambling toward him, and three more ready to turn on him if that one failed, Joe was starting to dislike the odds of getting out of this unscathed. More villagers *had* come out of their homes—which gave them a numerical advantage at least—and some were armed with pitchforks, knives, and machetes. One had even brought a large hammer.

Against two of the creatures, there might have been enough villagers to drive the things back into the woods.

But four of them?

When a hail of bullets had hardly slowed one of them down?

The number of creatures had already doubled. Who was to say that there weren't more on their way?

It was all academic if Joe couldn't take down the one in front of him.

"Hey, soldier!" he shouted to the guy who'd fired at the thing and now seemed to be trying to figure out why it hadn't gone down. "We need to get these civilians out of the kill zone."

The guy gave a sharp military nod, and he and the other soldier started shepherding the villagers away from the creatures and into a group. Then they put themselves and their guns between the two factions. Dr. Ghoti had helped the injured villager to his feet and walked him, albeit slowly, to the comparative safety of the two-soldier-cordon.

The creatures moved toward the group, but the soldiers kept them from getting too close by squeezing off multiple shots. The noise was shockingly loud and some of the villagers covered their ears. It was all sound and fury, but it signified little because, again, the bullet hits didn't seem to significantly hurt the creatures. Still, they tore through their flesh, making them look messier. The creatures hesitated as the bullets smashed into them, but started moving again as soon as the gunfire stopped. Joe thought that enough shots *had* to take them down eventually. It all depended on how much ammunition the soldiers had brought with them.

Still, at least the creatures' reaction to the attack showed a cautious distrust of the weapons.

The creature he'd already fought with had finally dragged itself close enough for round two, but if bullets hadn't stopped it then, Joe seriously doubted that he could beat it with his fists. Living to fight another day seemed more important, so he dodged the creature's slow grab and headed toward the other human beings.

<*))))><

As Joe ran over, Ani thought he looked slightly crazed. His eyes were wide, his breathing ragged, and there was just something about him that looked different. Then she realized it was that he was both wired and exhausted, and the fight for control of his body was making him look . . . well, intense.

"Good to see you, Joe," she said. "I don't suppose you know what's going on here?"

Joe shook his head. "We need to compare notes, try to understand what we're up against. Have you seen the way these things look through a phone app?"

"Bugworld. Something's interfering with the phone software, and our cameras are hallucinating. Digital delusions."

"Digital delusions?" Joe said. "Sounds like a X-Core band name. Right. We need to get these villagers where they'll be safe, and then we need to have a council of war. You in touch with Abernathy?"

"Yep. Satellite broadband."

"Didn't know there was such a thing."

"Me, either. Oh, and it's better than my home broadband. Anyway, let's get this show organized."

Ani approached the group of pretty terrified villagers and got their attention. "Hey," she said, "does anyone here speak any English?"

A young man nodded and stepped forward. "I can do," he said. "It's not best, but maybe good enough, yeah?"

Ani smiled.

"Good enough for me," she said. "We need to get these people inside, somewhere safe that we can protect."

"Especially if more of those things turn up," Joe said. "How did you get here?"

"Private jet, armored car," Ani said.

"Still loving the job, Ani?"

"More with every passing minute." She turned to the villager. "What's your name?"

The guy was in his early twenties, and dressed in an odd mix of the traditional—a simple sweater with an open neck, a home-woven scarf—and the modern—blue jeans and sneakers. He had an earnest face, with golden-brown eyes that glittered in the cellphone ambiance and torchlight.

"Razvan," he said. "Razvan Ionescu."

"Good to meet you, Razvan. I'm Ani. This is Joe. Can you think of somewhere we can take your . . . er, is it all right to say *comrades* here?"

She'd become self-conscious about using a word that could be construed as a relic from the communist-era dictatorship the country had once been. Reading about the country you're visiting on planes—priceless.

Razvan chuckled at her attempt at cultural sensitivity in a way that said it really wasn't expected.

"Comrades is—how you say?—okey dokey," he told her. "We have a church, you probably passed it on your way into the village."

He pointed back toward the village, away from the creatures, which was as good a reason as any for making it their destination.

"Okay," Joe said. "Let's get everyone heading there. Razvan, tell your friends to head for the church. Let's go."

<*))))><

The church was made of wood. Completely. The level of craftsmanship was astonishing, with carved arches and intricately carved biblical scenes. It looked like all the wood had been harvested and hewn from the forest. Local crafts, but not a wobbly table, or a magazine rack, no, a whole damned church.

It was deceptively big, too, with an interior large enough to accommodate the whole village. Which it had to now, with a few additions from YETI. They had gotten the last few people out of their homes on the way to the church, and now the villagers were sitting at the carved pews directing their prayers to whichever variant deity they worshipped here.

Ani thought that their prayers might help calm them down, stop them giving in to panic, but any answers were going to be found by more earthbound means.

The YETI members—with Razvan inducted into their ranks, and Furness and Gilman standing guard outside—huddled in a corner and tried to think their way out of the crisis.

"First order of business," Joe said. "What the hell are those things?"

"Impossible," Dr. Ghoti said. "If I hadn't seen them with my own eyes, I would say that they were utterly impossible."

"*Impossible* is something I'm redefining today," Joe said. "I think these things are from the Dorian factory. Maybe it's what they're making these days."

Something crossed his mind, and he broke off and looked off into the distance. Ani doubted he was seeing anything that wasn't inside his own head.

"Joe?" she urged. "Put the thought into words."

He rubbed his face with his hand, and then looked at her.

"You'll think I've lost it," he finally said.

"Try me."

"Okay, I'm here investigating the disappearance of some Dorian chips from a factory a few miles back through the wood."

"Us, too."

"I thought you were working the *victorious* case."

"Same case," Ani said. "Tell me about the factory."

"Invasion of the Body Snatchers." Joe said. "The staff there . . . they've been brainwashed. I even saw the machines that they use to do it." Joe called up the photos of the booths up on his phone and Ani, Mina, and Dr. Ghoti examined them carefully. Dr. Ghoti pinched to zoom right into one of the clearest.

"I can't see how these could brainwash anyone," she

said. "There's nothing here that looks capable of such a feat."

Ani had another look at the zoomed photo, and then zoomed in even further.

"What are these?" she asked, tapping her fingernail on a strange arrangement of holes in the walls and ceiling of the booth.

"High-tech showerheads?" Mina said. "Ventilation holes?"

"I think they're holes that acid comes out of," Joe said, flicking to the picture of the melted thing in the end booth. "I think they melt the workers that don't take well to their conditioning or that misbehave or something."

"It doesn't look like it's been melted, though," Dr. Ghoti said. "It looks deformed. Or damaged."

"Wait a minute." Ani swiped back to the photo they'd been looking at before. She zoomed in again and studied the holes and their strange arrangement. It was irritating. She thought she'd seen something—not exactly the same, but similar, recently. She struggled to think when, where, and what.

"Oh," she said, as she felt things connecting up in her brain, lining up like three bars on the middle line of a slot machine. Well, two bars and a lucky 7. It just took a nudge. "Oh, my goodness."

Everyone looked at her.

"You can't get a girl committed to an asylum for talking crazy, can you?" Ani asked of Dr. Ghoti.

"No. Why?"

"Because I'm about to sound completely insane." Ani said. "I'm just going to invite someone else to the discussion."

She called Abernathy up on the tablet, and then told them all what was on her mind.

<*))))><

Joe had seen that look on Ani's face before, back when she was making most of the breakthroughs on the dotwav case. It was a relief to see it now, because without her intuitive leaps and imaginative speculations, it was hard to see how any of the things that were happening tied together in any way, shape, or form.

"I keep coming back to the fact that *victorious* predicted this happening," Ani began. "Not that creatures would attack *somewhere*. That they would attack *here*. In Poiana Mazik. And that makes everything here either impossible, or just very, very contrived.

"Do any of us believe that people can predict the future? Not future trends or possible outcomes, but predict actual events that have never occurred before."

"Of course not," Mina said. "Precognition is the stuff of

science fiction. And the only people who claim to possess it are charlatans."

Ani nodded.

"So *victorious* either had inside information about what was going to happen here, or they caused it to happen. The thing is . . ."

A staccato chatter of gunfire from outside the church made her tense and pulled her out of the moment. She looked like the kid she was, especially in the wan electric lighting of the church. The sounds outside reminded Joe of the knife edge they were all balanced upon, villagers and YETI members alike.

Razvan was at the church window, looking out into the night.

"Soldiers keeping them back so far," he reported. "Hope they brought many bullets along with them today."

"I'm scrambling you some reinforcements," Abernathy said from the tablet screen. "But they're still a way out from you. Ani, you were just weaving us a hypothesis, and I'd certainly like to hear what you've got there. If it helps, the Internet and now the TV news, are reporting events using exactly the same phrases you played off the recording you and Dr. Ghoti made. Your dotmeme file is, as they say, going viral."

"Dotmeme file?" Joe asked.

"An archive of information that showed up on the Internet the moment all this started happening," Ani explained. "It came from *victorious*, but we have no idea what it really is or what it's for. But I'm certain it's a part of something bigger. Dorian Systems is involved. I think they're picking up *victorious*'s bills, supplying them with tech, especially those chips that sent you to LA, then brought you here."

There were more rattles of gunfire, but this time it hardly interrupted the flow of conversation. Joe thought that it was kind of odd just what you could get used to.

"You said that maybe those . . . creatures are what Dorian is making these days, Joe. What if you're right?" Ani looked intense, and more than a little scared. "You see, those booth things rang a bell somewhere in my head, but it took a little while to work out why. *victorious* was using a 3-D printer to make masks, and that printer looked like a miniature, simplified version of the things in those photos."

Joe's mind was racing, but not quite getting there.

"You're saying . . . what exactly? Wait. Wait a bloody minute. You're saying that Dorian Systems' latest invention allows them to 3-D print . . . monsters?"

"I know how it sounds," Ani said. "And I know we're decades away from the kind of tech I'm thinking of, but have you heard of 3-D bioprinting?"

Dr. Ghoti jumped in.

"It's the manufacture of living tissue using 3-D printing techniques," she said. "Instead of ink or plastic, the machines print using living cells. It could be the greatest breakthrough in medicine since . . . well, since we discovered antibiotics. But it's still in its absolute infancy. We can print skin tissue, blood vessels, nerve grafts, but we're years away from printing even rudimentary replacement organs. Kidneys will probably be the first artificial organ we do print—it's the simplest—but to make a living creature . . . we must be a hundred years away from that kind of application, if it's even possible."

"But still they come," Ani said, somewhat cryptically. "Look, those creatures out there came from somewhere. We can all agree on that, right? So what are we saying? That they're a tribe of Romanian Bigfoot who have been living in these woods, and they've just now decided to make an appearance? Or that they're . . . what? Aliens? Cold war communist monsters from caves under the mountains? They look . . . I don't know . . . *unfinished*, to me. And they look almost identical to one another. They're naked, and I don't know if anyone else noticed, but they don't seem built to procreate. . . . So let's open our minds real wide: what if they are man-made? Products of the Dorian factory. Bio-printed slaves. Before it settled on the name *victorious*, the hacking collective I've been investigating was once called *golem*."

"Golem?" Joe asked. "From *Lord of the Rings*?"

"I think Ms. Lee is referring to the Jewish legend," Abernathy interjected from the screen of her tablet. "A creature fashioned from the earth and brought to life by magic. The Hebrew word for truth would be inscribed on the creature's forehead, animating it with . . . Oh." Abernathy broke off, then let out a hollow laugh. "Joe?" he asked. "Do you remember when I told you that we managed to get a name out of one of the gang in Luton? I said it was an alias, that we didn't know whether it was a first name or a last?"

"Of course," Joe said. "One of the hired goons said that the man in charge of the operation was called Emmett. Why?"

"That Hebrew word for *truth*," Abernathy said, grimly. "The word that you write onto a golem to get it to rise up and do your bidding. It's *emet*."

Chapter Seventeen
AWAKEN, MY MASTERS

Instead of having the time and headspace to process the information, as so often happened in the field, things went really wrong, really quickly.

The prelude was an automatic rifle solo in the key of F for "frantic." It was immediately joined by the mimicking call of the other rifle. They both chattered away until the magazines needed to be swapped out—there was a break— then they started up again.

Ani didn't need to be an expert to know that meant things were changing outside, and not for the better.

Razvan was still watching the main street through the window, and when he reported back on what he was seeing, the urgency in his voice told them all they needed to know about how bad things were getting out there.

"There are more of those things now. And they're coming."

The guns spat rhythmically, then frantically, then fell silent.

Reloading.

But in the space that putting new magazines into the guns created, the creatures attacked. By the time Ani got to Razvan's side, and was looking out the window with him, the golems—seven of them now, that she could see—had split into two groups. Three of them were separating off the army guys, keeping them busy, while the other four were moving in on the building. Which was bad. It showed that they were now strategizing. Planning. And, far from being the lumbering, clumsy creatures that they'd been on arrival, now they had found speed could be a weapon, and were using it against the wooden structure of the village church.

Eight heavy fists pounded against wood, and the effect upon the villagers inside was as panicked as it was predictable. You couldn't blame them. The madness that had descended upon their village was terrifying, sudden, and like nothing else that had ever happened there before. Their refuge—the church that formed such a large part of their identity and society—was no more secure than their own homes would be. The golem creatures weren't deterred by superior numbers, or by gunfire.

Or prayers.

All in all, it was a wonder they'd held it together as long as they had.

Ani figured they should all be counting their lucky stars.

So far, the golems were so stupid they hadn't worked out that the windows would be a quicker entrance strategy that hammering at solid wood.

Still, it was easy to freak out in the face of the unexpected. Even some of the trained YETI operatives were showing the first signs of distress, but there was nothing to be gained by giving in to fear now, so Ani realized that it was up to her to get everyone pulling in the same direction, and that the direction should be away from navel-gazing and self-doubt.

"We need an exit strategy," she said, making sure it sounded unequivocal, calm and—more importantly—like she thought that such a strategy was even possible. "It's only a matter of time before the . . . golems . . . get inside. We can't be here when that happens. The good news is that we have an armored car parked close by and there's a pretty good chance we can make it. The bad news is that I don't think all the villagers will fit. Scratch that. I know they won't. And we can't leave them at the mercy of these things."

"They'd have been at the mercy of those things if YETI hadn't shown up," Abernathy said, "and I think it's imperative that you reach that transport and drive it to the Dorian factory. "

"Are you seriously suggesting that we leave these people to fend for themselves?" Ani said indignantly.

"Calm down, Ms. Lee," Abernathy said. "I'm suggesting that you get everyone away from that dead end of a wooden church you find yourselves in, get to the armored car, avail yourself of any weapons that you find there, and hold the creatures . . . the golems . . . off for the few minutes that it takes until members of the Romanian Land Forces arrive on the scene."

"Okay, boss. That sounds like a much better idea."

"We'll reserve judgment on that until everyone's safe, I think."

<*))))><

It fell to Joe to liaise with the soldiers outside. To be honest, it was a relief. The walls of the church had started closing in on him, and the place had begun to feel less like a sanctuary and more like a trap. A barrel. Full of fish.

"We've been advised to fall back to the armored car," Joe told the soldier closest to him.

The soldier nodded. "We're getting low on ammo," he said. "I can switch to a sidearm, but if an AK isn't stopping them, I can't see a Glock making a difference."

"I take it you have more ammo at the APC?" Joe asked.

"A weapons chest," the guy said. "We're not leaving the villagers."

A statement, not a question.

"No, we're not. We've got inbound support, so we'll need to move the villagers with us."

"As long as you're on crowd control," the guy said. "I'll be kinda busy."

"Okay, we'll leave as soon as I get everyone ready. Cover us?"

The guy narrowed his eyes. "Of course. One request?"

"Name it."

"Hurry."

<*))))><

Razvan translated the plan to the others, and everyone gathered by the door. Ani got Joe to count down from ten and then opened the door and everyone went through as quickly as they could heading left to take them away from the golems, and toward the armored car. Ani waited until everyone was through before following.

The night air stank of propellant. Acrid. Unpleasant. Overhead, a fingernail sliver of moon had broken through a bed of clouds and cast a wan, almost surreal lighting on the scene.

Mina and Dr. Ghoti helped the elderly villagers as best they could, and Furness and Gilman brought up the rear, firing controlled bursts in the direction of the golems. All seven of the creatures turned their attentions to the refugee group and began moving slowly but deliberately after them.

The creatures *could* move faster, so why weren't they?

It was almost as if they were directing the group back up toward the armored car. Herding them. But that was nonsense.

Wasn't it?

Ani felt then that she was missing something. Probably a lot of things, actually, to tie all these odd strands together into something that made sense. There was something that she was missing, that she ought to be seeing, that was nagging away at her. The events here, they seemed . . . familiar, or they followed a pattern that she felt she should recognize. Or something. She struggled to get her brain to analyze the situation, but then she heard a commotion and looked to where everyone was staring. Up the track. Between them and the armored car.

Two more of the golems were emerging from the darkness at the sides of the path.

Seven of the creatures coming up behind them.

And two in front of them.

Snapping shut the door on a trap.

And then it hit her, why all this seemed familiar. What it reminded her of. She was about to tell Joe when the golems started moving.

Fast.

Toward them.

And then all she could think was: GAME OVER.

<*))))><

Joe realized that they'd been out-maneuvered by the damned golem creatures and hoped that someone else had a plan, because right now, he was all out. The group was already starting to panic, and if they started running, the golems would be free to pick off stragglers. It would be carnage.

There might, in theory, be no such thing as an all-dark night, but this was getting pretty close.

To put it simply, they were being outplayed.

And Joe couldn't see the next move that would get his side out in front.

Then, just as the despair was beginning to assert itself, there was a loud roar and the Wolf armored car lurched out of the darkness, headlights throwing the scene into a macabre chiaroscuro that exaggerated foreground brightness and made shadows longer and more threatening.

The personnel carrier slewed into the two golems that were blocking the group's exit, throwing one of the creatures violently to the ground and bouncing the other off the engine grill, before grinding it beneath the front fender and the ground, and then underneath one of the front wheels. If the things weren't so weird and dangerous, Joe would almost have felt sorry for it.

Almost.

The truck stopped next to Joe, the driver's door opened, and someone tossed him a shotgun. Joe caught it, nodded his thanks, pumped to load it, then walked up to the golem that the carrier had hit and thrown to the ground. Joe put his foot on its chest and leveled the shotgun off at the creature's head. He hesitated, pretty sure that pulling the trigger was the right thing to do, but wondering if there was some other way. The golem reached up with one of its hands and grabbed his calf, squeezing tight.

Joe pulled the trigger.

The golem let go of his leg.

Let go of its life.

He was about to turn his shotgun on the remaining golems when something caught his eye. A flash of light.

So he knelt down, puzzled, and looked through the wreckage of the creature's head. He wasn't the world's greatest biologist, but he knew that some of the stuff in there really didn't belong.

"Ani?" Joe called. "How's your stomach? I need you to look at something for me."

<*))))><

Ani took a deep breath, held back her gag reflex, steadied herself, and then reached out and raked through the contents of the creature's head with her fingers, pulling the noxious pulp aside and concentrating on the thing that Joe had brought her over to examine.

There was a flashing LED inside a matchbook-sized device, damaged but discernable, lodged within the creature's brain. She reached in and tried to pull the device free, but it had wires stretching out into the golem's brain matter, anchoring it in place. Then she began twisting it and tugging until there was a horrible tearing sound and she had the thing in her hand.

She turned it over in her fingers, scanning the object for some kind of clue as to its function, a squid-like mass of wires connected to a central device that was packed with circuitry. There was a plastic casing, only partially damaged by the shotgun round, which Ani saw as a stroke of luck. Joe had missed the box when he turned the creature's head into pulp and bone.

Except, now that she thought about it, the splintered material really didn't look much like bone at all. She picked some up and rubbed it between her thumb and forefinger, then scratched at it with her fingernail. It felt more like . . . *plastic*.

These creatures—these golems—they had plastic skulls. Probably plastic skeletons, too. It explained a lot, but made even more unclear. Still, one thing at a time. She needed to get a look inside that device.

The good news was that she was a hacker and she always came prepared.

She dried one of her hands off on the leg of her jeans and reached into her jacket pocket, rooting through past the USB cables and crocodile clip wires, before pulling out a small set of emergency repair tools: her "go" kit, complete with electrical screwdrivers, wire cutters, and three types of tweezers. She judged the size she needed by eye, took a hex-headed screwdriver out of the case, and used it to take off part of a protective cover from the device.

She ignored most of the circuits and chips and concentrated on the processor that looked unlike any of the other components, but was still familiar to her. She didn't need to magnify the part's casing to know its manufacturer's mark would be a stylized letter *D*.

"You know what that is?" Joe asked.

"I have a pretty good idea," Ani told him. "Things are falling into place. I just really dislike the picture they're starting to form. We need to get a good look around that factory."

"One thing at a time," Joe said, pump-loading the shotgun again and moving forward, toward the other golems.

<*))))><

The number of missions where Joe got to handle firearms was . . . well, actually pretty high, now that he thought about it. The missions where he *discharged* a weapon were far fewer, though, and that was a good thing. He had nothing against guns per se, but he didn't like the feeling of pulling the trigger on another human being, no matter how evil or crazed or dangerous they were. Some people got used to it; Joe didn't think that was right.

Shooting a human being should never become routine, and it should never get easier.

Shooting monsters, it turned out, was far less morally troubling.

And an Ithaca 37 shotgun—a pre-1957 model that didn't

have the trigger disconnector, which meant you could fire pretty much continuously by slam firing, or holding down the trigger as you pump reloaded—was a pretty good gun to declare open season on them with. Sure, it was limited to seven—now six—cartridges, but the damage each of those shots could do made Joe feel a little braver about facing off against another golem.

The APC driver stepped down from the vehicle and stood next to Joe holding some Eastern European version of an Uzi machine pistol. The driver nodded at Joe, who nodded back, and they advanced on the golems.

<*))))><

Ani stashed the tech, wiped her hands again, and then helped Dr. Ghoti and Mina to get the locals out of danger, which was a matter of moving them around the back of the APC, basically putting an armored car between them and the golems.

A couple of kids, who couldn't have been older than six or seven, were freaking out pretty badly, and their mother was trying her best to comfort them. It was a horrible detail, those tear-smeared faces upturned, looking for reassurance, for explanations, when none were forthcoming.

Whether it was Dorian behind this, or *victorious*, it didn't matter. Make children cry in fear of their lives and you need to be taken down.

Ani got the tablet out and made sure that Abernathy was still available.

"It's weird having you in my pocket out in the field," she joked.

"Big pockets," Abernathy said. "I'll tell you my latest intelligence if you'll tell me yours."

"Dorian chips in plastic skulls—these golems are man-made and computer controlled. You?"

Abernathy looked surprised, but nodded.

"That's some mighty fine work there," he said. "Considering the situation. Anyway, while you've been away, your dotmeme file has been incredibly busy. It has inserted its own version of reality throughout the whole Internet and deleted whatever it replaced. It's added a backstory to the events you're experiencing, making the Internet tell elaborate, but completely consistent, lies to make it look like people have been predicting something like Poiana Mazik happening for years. If we hadn't been watching it happen in real time, we'd probably never have *seen* it happen. It's perfect. Seamless."

"Holy crap," Ani said. "They retconned reality."

"Retconned?"

"A plot revision in comic books and TV shows that affects the established continuity of the story. RETroactive CONtinuity. You see them do it with Spider-Man, but reality? So what's the story they're telling?"

"Gaia," Abernathy said.

"Of course." Ani sighed. "The earth goddess is fighting back against us, right?"

"Sort of," Abernathy said. "The earth *is* Gaia, a self-regulating organism that maintains life for *all* its inhabitants. Unfortunately, the human race has become too much of a threat to the creature's body."

"So she's turned monsters against us?"

"Well, the . . . retconning—am I even using that word correctly?—has a more poetic kind of metaphor at its heart. Gaia has mobilized her immune system to fight off what she's now viewing as an infection. But yes, that's pretty much the long, tall, and short of it. A whole host of scientists agree. At least they do now. I'm waiting to see what happens when they try to disagree with what the Internet is now saying they said and providing references to boot."

"But why?" Ani asked. "I mean I can understand the attraction of rewriting digital reality, but it can't stick. It's a deception that requires people to not speak out against it. I know people. They'll talk."

"On a digital platform, perhaps? I hoped that doesn't get rewritten."

"You think the meme file is going to maintain its own illusion? Police the Internet for dissent? What's the endgame?"

"What if this is the tiniest field test of a dotmeme's powers?" Abernathy asked. "Nickel-and-dime stuff, as they say over the pond. Just to see if the general concept works."

"I'd say we'd better make sure this is the only test Dorian and *victorious* get," Ani said.

Abernathy went silent, appearing to be listening to something off-camera, and then said, "You should have reinforcements with you in minutes. I think you know what you've got to do."

"Get to the Dorian factory," Ani said. "But how are we going to stop *victorious?*"

"I think you'll find that they're the same thing," Abernathy told her.

<*))))><

Four people with weapons were now the line in the sand for the golems to try to cross: a reasonably widespread, with the area in front of them drawn up, almost instinctively, into quadrants for them to police. Each trusted the others to do what needed to be done. Protect the villagers.

Joe waited until one of the golems was right on top of him before pulling the trigger of his shotgun. It was simple economy. Sure, the expansion of the shot from the barrel gave a wider cone of damage the farther from the muzzle it got, but its damage was dissipated as a result. Lots of wounds, moderate damage. Close up—not *point blank*, that was something else entirely: the optimum distance between a weapon and a target, a distance which varied from weapon to weapon—the shot was concentrated. It delivered more damage to a smaller area.

The blast stopped the golem in its tracks and gave it cosmetic surgery in the face department. It hit the deck soon after, a major malfunction from which it wasn't going to be recovering anytime soon.

Joe realized that he was thinking in euphemisms. People often did when thinking about death, especially when they were causing it. Targets were "neutralized," "taken out," or "mopped up." And it seemed that even killing monsters required them. Because it was easier to think that you *took something down* than it was to think you *took something's life*.

Joe was considering pulling the trigger again when light and sound signaled the long-overdue arrival of reinforcements.

Which meant it was time.

Time to go back to the factory.

To find answers.

And to end this. End it forever.

<*))))><

There was a grim silence as the armored personnel carrier took them away from Poiana Mazik and toward the Dorian factory. Furness and Gilman had reloaded their weapons and were waiting, quietly, for the next phase of the mission.

Ani, Joe, Mina, and Dr. Ghoti were also silent for now, lost in their own thoughts, preparing for whatever came next. They'd left the villagers in the good hands of the Romanian Land Force, who had already been wiping out the remaining golems when the YETI team was heading for the APC. Ani had taken a minute to thank Razvan for his help, and Joe had stopped by to shake his hand and wish him all the best.

Now that they were on the road, it all felt like a strange dream receding as the vehicle put distance between them and the village. Ani wanted to tell everyone the things she had started to put together back in Poiana Mazik, but the more she thought about it all, the more insane it all sounded. So she focused on making it sound more reasonable in her own mind.

And the night rolled by outside, oblivious.

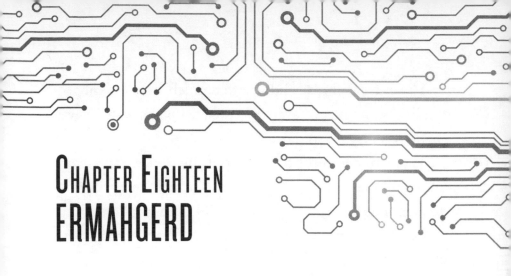

Chapter Eighteen
ERMAHGERD

The factory was lit up and locked up. It was like someone inside was waiting for them, but just didn't want to make things *too* easy for them. Joe knew how crazy that sounded, but he couldn't shake off the feeling. He felt like he'd been led around by the nose ever since touching down in Bucharest.

Maybe even before that.

Since leaving London?

He wondered if he was suffering from some kind of intelligence service burn-out, a kind of paranoia that was unique to people in his line of work. He spent so much of his time trying to manipulate people into doing his own bidding, that maybe he'd started to feel like someone was enacting the same set of tricks upon him. Or it could just be the way he'd felt like he'd been forced over the fence the last time he was here, and once in the woods, had been pursued—and perhaps herded—toward the village.

The mental thread didn't offer much help or enlight-enment, so he filed it away for later. To be honest, he was probably jet-lagged and tired.

The APC had come to a stop outside the Dorian factory gates, and the YETI personnel—plus armed bodyguards—were getting themselves ready for breaching the building. Which made for a tense atmosphere and an introspective silence.

Ani was frowning over her tablet, like she had been pretty much the entire journey, and was so absorbed in her screen that she didn't seem to even notice that they were about to enter the place that was at the center of a lot of the weirdness. Dr. Ghoti and Mina Desai were radiating calm in the face of danger. They were good at their individual jobs, but Joe was worried that fieldwork was a rather big ask for them. Still, they were handling things pretty well at the moment, so maybe Abernathy knew exactly what he was doing sending them along.

The soldiers, they looked ready for just about anything.

Joe got out of the vehicle and approached the gates. The place had a whole different atmosphere at night. By day it had looked . . . well, like a factory. Innocuous. Bland. A huge building, sure, but so featureless that the eye kind of skipped over it. At night, that same building looked stark and sinister, an illusion that the arc-lights illuminating the façade seemed to actively encourage.

The security post was empty. The guard had either gone

home or was patrolling the inside of the factory. The gate was locked to make a point, but it didn't provide a particularly difficult problem for someone who actually wanted in.

The gate had a five-pin tumbler lock, the kind that people thought were secure, but really weren't.

Because the Internet.

Joe had a key ring in his pocket—an "I ♣ LONDON" fob that Ellie had found hilarious enough to buy for him—with his London apartment key and three other keys on it. The other three were bump keys; easily purchased online for not much money at all. Joe's wasn't an exhaustive selection—that would take ten or so, and such a collection started getting unwieldy for a pocket—but good enough for a high percentage of the most common locks. He reached into his pocket and took out the keys, selecting one and trying it in the lock. When he found it didn't quite fit, he moved on to the next, and got it right on the second try. The tooth pattern of the key was composed of five equal triangles, and Joe inserted the key fully into the lock, then pulled it back a notch so it sat in the lock's barrel to the fourth tooth. Then he put the fob across the top of the key and used it as a plate to hammer in the last notch with the flat of his hand. The force of the bump was transferred to the teeth of the key and they knocked the pins of the lock so they were outside the lock's cylinder. The actual key wasn't needed. The bump key had done the same job, just in a different way.

One turn and the lock opened.

Before the others had even descended from the APC.

He pried the bump key from the lock and opened the gate.

"What do you know? It's open," he said, and they slipped through into the grounds of the factory.

<*))))><

Ani had put the tablet away into her jacket pocket (you knew you were a tech addict when you chose your clothing based on whether their pockets were deep enough to hold your gadgets), but the things she'd been researching online were still buzzing in her head.

She was trying to follow a logical thread through the things she'd discovered, but there were still pieces missing and the connections were tenuous and unsatisfying without them. The factory seemed like a good place to fill in the blanks.

She followed Joe, Furness, and Dr. Ghoti through, with Gilman and Mina behind her. The APC driver was on orders to stay with the vehicle and summon help if needed. Five was a big enough team to infiltrate Dorian Europe, especially as three of them were armed and freshly stocked up with ammo.

Ani still felt nervous.

There was every chance they were walking into a trap,

but it was still the best chance for answers. Or confirmation of some things Ani already suspected.

Chief of those was the identity of *emet*.

The way things were panning out made her sure that she knew who *emet* was, but it was also the reason she felt so nervous. She couldn't share her theory yet, because it sounded insane even to her, but if she was right, the threat was a lot more serious than anyone here could guess.

If Richard Dorian was truly on-site, then they had to find him.

Because if anyone on earth could stop a catastrophe of epic proportions, then it was him.

And, quite possibly, only him.

<*))))><

They followed Joe across the grounds as he headed for the far side of the building, leading them back toward the loading bays. Joe held back a little to allow Ani to catch up. He was worried about her, mainly because he wasn't used to her being so quiet. She was always so full of ideas, but she'd stopped sharing them and had spent most of the time since they'd met up on her tablet or staring into space.

"Are you okay, Ani?" he asked when she came to his side.

"I'm sorry, Joe. I know I've been a bit distracted." She

looked a little shame-faced. "I've just been trying to make sense of things. It *is* good to see you."

"I wasn't expecting help, let alone the cavalry," he said. "I'm really glad to see you, too."

She pointed to the building. "I hope that I'll be able to shed some light on what goes on in there. I'll need to get a look at things for myself, though."

Joe realized that Ani was holding something back. There was a guardedness about her that he really hadn't seen before. He didn't like it. "You know what's happening here, don't you?"

Ani shook her head. "No. Not quite. But I do know this: it's nothing like what we've been thinking it is."

"What do you mean?"

"I'm not sure. But I'll let you know as soon as I do." Ani reached out and squeezed his arm. "I know I'm probably coming across as evasive and maybe even a bit strange, but this whole thing has me feeling awkward. Wrong-footed. I worry I'm taking it all a little personally."

"Personally?"

"Hackers have made whatever this is possible. My tribe, Joe. They helped set monsters loose, while hiding behind their screen names and their overinflated beliefs in their own rightness. There were kids in that village. Without YETI, there would have been casualties. There might have been deaths. And here's the part that makes me feel sick to my stomach: without YETI, I'd probably be a guilty party in this."

Joe thought about what she'd said, but he couldn't agree. "You're fighting on the right side, and I don't think you ever had it in you to do otherwise."

"Maybe, maybe not. But I could still get drawn into things when the weight of numbers, my peers, convinced me that it was right. Maybe I'd have been suckered into this, too."

"Who knows?" Joe said. "It doesn't matter. If I hadn't joined YETI, then my temper would have gotten me into big trouble by now. But I *did* join YETI. And so did you. What we were before doesn't matter. It's what we do now that matters. And I know what that is."

"What?"

"We stop it. It's as simple as that. And those skills that your tribe are using to help Dorian and *victorious*? They're the skills that you're going to use to beat them. Now, pep talk over, I hope?"

"Pep talk over and very much appreciated." Ani said.

<*))))><

The loading bays were locked, and with padlocks that were more difficult to break into than the gate had been. That wasn't really saying that much. The bump keys wouldn't work in padlocks, which meant Joe needed to pick one of them instead. But that's why lots of intelligence agents carried some very specialized tools for just such an occasion.

Paper clips.

Two of them.

Joe's were in the small jeans pocket that had been invented by Levi's for the sole purpose of keeping pocket watches safe. Then people invented watches with straps, and later cell phones, and people had needed to think of new things to put in those pockets.

Joe took the first paperclip, opened it out into a straight piece of wire, doubled it over and squeezed it flat against the ground, then bent the doubled end at a 90-degree angle. He straightened the other paperclip, then bent the very end a couple of times. A homemade tension wrench, and a homemade lock rake. Joe kept torque with the tension wrench and jostled the rake against the lock's tumblers. It took less than a minute before the lock bar popped open. He took the padlock out of its hasp and rolled the loading bay gate open.

It was bright inside, though there were no workers present, and the group climbed up and into the loading bay, giving Joe a feeling of déjà vu. Although, was repetition really déjà vu? Probably not. Now wasn't the time for semantics.

"This way." Joe said, and they moved deeper into the factory.

The factory floor was deserted, just as it had been the first time Joe walked through it. There was no sign of the workers, but all the lights were still on as if they'd be back soon. Where did they go? Joe thought that maybe they'd find out as they looked through the place. Because the YETI team was going to search everywhere. It was time to get answers.

Without the workforce pursuit creating the urgency of his first visit, he had time to find the stairs that led to the upper floor. It was a good place to start. He led the group up and found another door to try, but only after he'd shown everyone the rooms he had already been through.

The computer room door hadn't been repaired yet, and swung open easily.

"This one's for you, Ani," he said, pointing through the door.

She gave him an odd look and went past him into the room.

<*))))><

Ani walked along the rows of computer processors and felt her fears deepen. You expected to find computers in a high-tech environment like Dorian Europe. What you didn't expect to find was a state-of-the-art supercomputer. Nor did you expect to find a supercomputer that operated so quietly. It was uncanny just how silent it was.

She flipped a panel to get a good look at the tech inside. It took her a few seconds to figure out what she was actually seeing.

It wasn't state-of-the-art.

It was *beyond* state-of-the-art.

She was looking at the insides of a supercomputer from . . . from where? The future? The circuitry was utterly remarkable. There were so few things in there that she actually recognized. It had an almost organic look. Not that it was made of organic matter or that the chips were alive or anything science fiction like that, but that the way the boards and circuits were organized seemed more in keeping with the organization of biological units rather than a computer system. It was like someone had approached the problem of building a computer, but had come at it from a completely different direction to the one everyone else took. The only thing in there that she *did* recognize didn't make her feel any better: those same chips that had started Joe's investigation into Dorian and that were responsible for making *victorious*'s computers so much more than the sum of their parts.

The supercomputer was working very busily on something, performing billions, maybe quadrillions, of calculations per second. She wondered what kinds of tasks it had been built to accomplish. You could pretty much run a whole country with this amount of processing power.

So what was it processing? What binary tasks was it working so hard on?

To find out, she needed to look at its output, and the only way to do that was with a screen. There had to be a user interface around here somewhere. She needed to find it if she was going to get a look at the sort of things that a computer like this one thought about.

Or, she thought, darkly, what it dreamed about.

<*))))><

Joe had kept possession of the tuning fork from his previous visit, and he freed it from the pocket it had been languishing in, then made sure everyone was watching when he used it to open the door. It seemed important, because it was such a strange detail. It wasn't a sane management decision to replace door keys or keypads with tuning forks. It was a flamboyant touch that he could see no real practical purpose for.

Ani looked puzzled as he lifted the fork up to the door, but when he flicked it to make it ring, and then used the vibrations to open the door, she looked a little . . . What was that expression that crossed her face? Was it anger? Confusion? A little of each? Joe didn't know, but again he had the feeling that Ani was making connections and formulating ideas that he just couldn't see yet. She had admitted as much, but it was getting a little frustrating that she didn't seem to want to share her suspicions.

Still, two could play at the secretive assembly of theories. And so Joe was busy formulating a few suspicions of his own, the first, and most pressing, of which was that he felt like he was being played. And not just him. YETI. All of them. That the whole *Dorian Europe Experience* had been constructed for him, that his escape and subsequent arrival at Poiana Mazik had been stage-managed, and that it was all heading toward some cryptic endgame that he could neither see the shape of, nor guess the purpose of.

Ani walked into the room and looked around at the rows of booths and felt two conflicting emotions. First, obviously, was disquiet. On Joe's phone screen, they had been less dramatic, less grand. Just less, really. So she felt a touch of what poets called *the sublime*, an odd mix of awe and terror that allowed the darkest thoughts to grow within her. Second, she felt something less poetic, less profound, but just as intense.

The feeling was best summed up in the single word response: *cool!*

At her heart, Ani was a tech geek. She loved the new, the shiny, the upgraded, the microprocessor this and the floating point that. She loved real-life applications of binary calculations, she loved new display technologies and the latest force-cracking software.

As a result, she loved science fiction movies, although maybe her love of computers came as a result of the kind of films she liked.

The booths looked like something out of one of those science fiction movies she loved. Maybe matter transporters like they'd used in *The Fly*, time machines like the one in *Primer*, or suspended animation devices from films like *Alien* or TV shows like *Futurama*.

She walked over to inspect one, marveling at its construction, but oddly disturbed by it, too. It didn't look like contemporary technology, which was why she'd been thinking about science fiction reference points. Instead, it looked more advanced, futuristic even. And that was without examining the technology that made the machine work. The aesthetic—the styling, the way it was constructed according to visual considerations that seemed to deviate from those she was used to—were what made her uneasy.

The design or look of technology, was dictated, largely, by two factors: the technology that the design contained, and the prevailing human aesthetic of the time.

If you compared the crude, original 1980s incarnation of the mobile phone with the latest model of iPhone or Samsung Galaxy, you could still see very distinct similarities. Of course, there was a vast difference in their screen size, in having touchscreens instead of physical buttons, but you could trace a direct line of evolution of form dictated by function, in conjunction with the latest developments in materials. The actual aesthetic differences were in making the phone thinner, curvier, as much to do with ergonomics—how the device felt and operated in the human hand—as actual stylistic choices. Very few phones deviated from the standard rectangular shape. There was a Nokia 7600 leaf-shaped phone from the early 2000s, and a couple of circular designs, but they did, on the whole, stick to the same rectangle.

It was all about shrinking the size of the bezel, of rounding the edges, of utilizing different materials, of tinkering with the interface.

These machines, these booths, seemed to come from a whole new aesthetic. There was something brutal about them, something that seemed to ignore the rules that modern technology seemed to follow. They were odd, with an almost inhuman disregard for beauty. As if the designer was completely ignoring the aspects of design that made people feel warmth or attachment to a device. There were no pleasing curves. Where surfaces met, the joins were logical, but not pretty. Just necessary transitions between materials. It appeared to be all about the function—whatever that function might be.

Dr. Ghoti was also studying one of the booths, though she seemed focused on the potential function, rather than the aesthetic form. She was trying to open the booth to gain access to its interior.

"These must open, somehow," she said, "but I can't find a button or handle."

Ani inspected the booth before her. It was true. The booth obviously was meant to open somehow, but she couldn't see the mechanism that would make it happen. It had to be controlled by the panel on the front of the booth.

She touched the screen and a display woke up, with digital dials and buttons and sliders. But none of them did anything when she touched them. They appeared to be cosmetic, or needed to be altered with another interface.

She looked for a USB port, or some other way of connecting another device, but couldn't find one. Maybe the booths were controlled from a central computer.

Joe was checking out one of the other booths, and Ani remembered him showing them all photograph of the melted worker while they were back at the village. She went over to him and looked into the booth. The poor thing was still contained within, but it didn't look like it had been melted or dissolved.

It looked more like a mistake had been made in a manufacturing process.

She called the others over.

"How would a bio-printer for monsters work?" Ani asked.

Dr. Ghoti looked in at the creature in the booth, winced, and then grew thoughtful. "Presumably, there would need to be a programmed template," she said. "A how-to-make-a-monster recipe, but it would need to be worked out cell layer by cell layer. Every structure, every organ, every blood vessel would need to be built . . . I mean the immense amount of data required to create even the simplest living creature alone would . . ."

". . . require some kind of a supercomputer?" Ani finished. "But what would such a life form be made of? What would the printer use to print living tissue?"

"Living cells." Doctor Ghoti said. "You need to build using pluripotent stem cells . . . or totipotent stem cells. But it's just not possible."

"But let's just pretend it is for a moment," Ani said. "Stem cells can become any cells in the body . . ."

"Well, yes, sort of. But also, no," Dr. Ghoti said. "Look, we are at a point in stem cell research where we can see the potential for future treatments of diseases and injuries, but it's all still theory. Scientists are investigating the possibilities of using stem cell therapies for degenerative diseases, like arthritis, muscular dystrophy, diabetes. But the only stem cell therapy in everyday use is the very crude form we've been using for forty years or so: bone marrow transplants, as far as I'm aware. So how we jump from theories about how we *might* one day cure degenerative illnesses to creating living creatures from scratch . . . It's simply not within human capabilities. I'm not saying it won't be possible someday. I'm simply saying that it isn't humanly impossible now. There has to be some other explanation for these pods, booths, whatever you want to call them. And there has to be another answer as to what that thing is in there."

Ani knew that Dr. Ghoti was right. But she had also spotted the loophole that the doctor had built into her analysis of what was possible with stem cells. And the pieces that she had been slotting into place in the puzzle in her mind suddenly started to show a picture that made some kind of insane, dark sense.

The loophole was the doctor's use of the words "human" and "humanly."

It was not *with human capabilities.*

It was not *humanly possible.*

So, what if they weren't talking about a human agency being behind this at all?

<*))))><

Joe showed them around the storeroom, more because it was the last door in the sequence rather than because he believed that there was anything in there pertinent to the investigation. Which was why Dr. Ghoti's reaction to the vats sitting on the shelves in the room surprised him.

As she studied them, her demeanor shifted from curious to interested to shell-shocked to horror.

"I don't believe it," she said, and her face showed that for her that was an understatement. "Can you smell that?"

Of course, Joe could. He'd noticed it the first time he was in the room. An awful coppery smell, moist and . . . and somehow familiar.

"Do you know what it is?" Joe asked. "I mean it seems as if I recognize it, sort of . . ."

"Have you ever been in a slaughterhouse?" Dr. Ghoti asked. "Take out the fear and excrement, home in on the blood and raw meat, and that's kind of what we've got here. Except it's been processed. There are chemical notes mixed in with the rest of the odors." She turned to Ani. "You know what you said about building monsters?" She sounded like she could hardly believe the words she was speaking. "And I said you would need stem cells of a very complex and specific type?"

"Pluripotent or totipotent," Ani said, showing memory skills that Joe would have needed to access his chip to replicate.

"I'd need to test the stuff in these vats, but I'm reasonably sure that it's human bio-matter, a soup of human tissue. If it was imbued with the right stem cells, prepared the right way, then I think it's the kind of stuff that you'd need to build living tissue. Organs, perhaps. Or organisms. Sometime in the far future, of course."

"Human tissue?" Joe said, his mind suddenly full of horrible possibilities. "What, like *harvested* from humans?"

Dr. Ghoti shrugged.

"It's one heck of a lot of bio-matter," she said. "That's one heck of a lot of donors."

"And the recipe for one heck of a lot of monsters," Joe said.

Ani called from where she had wandered deeper into the room and was looking at the vats stored there.

"This stuff is different," she said, tapping one of the vats. "These are labeled 'polylactic acid.'"

"A plastic," Dr. Ghoti said.

"The kind of stuff you'd make . . . I don't know, a plastic skeleton from?" Ani asked.

Dr. Ghoti's silence was all the answer they needed.

"I wonder what's behind that other door we passed on the walkway," Ani said, more to break the spell of the revelations.

They journeyed back to the walkway and stood in front of the other door. Another tuning fork engraving, another tuning fork vibrating.

The door opened onto a corridor.

"Shall we?" Joe asked.

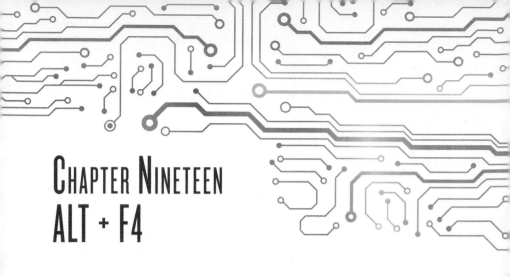

Chapter Nineteen
ALT + F4

The corridor was just that.

A corridor.

There were no rooms leading off either side. It was just a long path that led down to a door at the end. Unlike everything else in the factory—which was defined by a minimalist style, white and almost completely lacking in character—the corridor was plush, decked out in red, and seemed designed to provide or build atmosphere. Red paint, red wallpaper, and red curtains. It was like something you would expect to find at the end of a video game quest, as the protagonist was approaching the lair of the deranged bad-guy behind the events of the game.

That was the moment that Ani slotted another couple of puzzle pieces together.

It was *exactly* like the end of a video game quest.

And the madness in Poiana Mazik was the kind of event that only occurred in video games.

Or movies.

And Dorian made interactive games that were a clever fusion of those two things.

Great video games with narratives were an art form. They were hard enough to be challenging, but not so hard that you couldn't get to the end of them. What would be the point of creating a great story that no one could get to the end of? There had to be a planned tradeoff between difficulty and entertainment.

Games always gave you another lead to follow: a linear thread that led you from one game area to the next; a trail of breadcrumbs pre-laid by the game's designers; clues to be picked up along the way; non-player characters that either gave you another way to look at things when you were stuck or signposted the way forward or presented you with backstory essential to the understanding of the in-game narrative.

In short: everything that had happened in her and Joe's investigations.

Joe found the missing kids, which had revealed the Dorian chips, which had led him to the US. There, he was directed to Romania, experienced a lot of weirdness, was led to the village where he was attacked by monsters, and to the clues that had led back here.

Ani had trapped the kid in Yeovil, played minigames that let her infiltrate *victorious* where she'd been led to a character from a previous adventure, and then to Brian, the dotmeme file, Romania, the factory.

Two investigations that had turned out to be the same investigation, just like her first adventure with YETI.

A two-character campaign that had led to this corridor.

Coincidences?

It sounded insane even to her—that somehow Richard Dorian had laid out his whole plan along the lines of one of his own video games—but once she considered the idea, it was almost impossible for her to shake.

She and Joe had been led here.

Crazy as that may sound, she felt it to be true.

They made their way down the corridor, and Ani realized that she was actually waiting for a jump scare. Video game logic pretty much demanded one at this point. At the very least, there should be a stab of some atonal music. Instead, they just walked down the corridor, reached the end, and stood in front of the door. Joe reached for the handle. It turned easily. The door swung open. It didn't creak, squeal, and nothing popped out at them.

It opened onto a spacious office dominated by a huge desk with an array of widescreen monitors covering a lot of its surface. Monitors adorned the walls, too, bigger and even more impressive. In the midst of the tech, Richard Dorian was sitting behind the desk, but his eyes were closed and there was an odd gray sheen to his skin. Ani was shocked by how sick Dorian looked, and wondered if he was even alive. He was a tall man, dark-haired with only a minor sprinkling of gray. He wore an immaculately tailored suit, but the hands that came out of the sleeves were tight and rigid, almost like claws.

She moved toward him with the intention of checking his pulse, and that was when she saw the cables that snaked from one of the computers and disappeared behind the gaming guru. It distracted her from her immediate mission, making her feel even more concerned about the man's well-being.

"Mr. Dorian?" she asked, her voice little more than a whisper. "Are you okay?"

There was no reply.

Dr. Ghoti hustled past her and took the man's wrist between her fingers. She adjusted her grip, found what she was looking for, looked concerned, felt around a bit more, and then nodded her head.

"He's alive." Dr. Ghoti said. "But his pulse is bradycardic . . ." She looked at Ani's blank expression. "His heart rate is slow." Then she looked puzzled herself. "I . . . he . . . look, my diagnosis goes no further than I think there's something very wrong with him."

"Might it be something to do with this?" Ani pointed to the wires, made her way around the desk until she was standing behind Dorian. She gasped. For a moment, her mind refused to accept what she was seeing. A long ribbon of colored cables connected the nearest computer terminal to what looked like a custom port in the back of the programmer's head.

"Come and look at this," she said, and Dr. Ghoti, Joe, and Mina all did as she asked. Furness and Gilman waited at the door, weapons ready.

"I hope this isn't the new tech that all those Dorian fanboys are waiting for," Joe said. "Google Glass was a hard enough sell."

"Hey, don't knock tech wired into your brain."

"Mine's a little more discreet than that." Joe grinned at his joke, but ended up sounding defensive.

"I can't believe that anyone's still using 1980s rainbow ribbon connectors," Ani said, pointing to the harness of wires. "I mean, they carry data, but they can really overheat."

"So what are we looking at?" Mina asked.

"An innovation in human/computer data sharing?" Ani said, not one hundred percent sure herself. "Using '80s tech. I mean, you still find ribbon cables *inside* computers, but as computer-to-peripheral connectors, using IDCs, people just use single cables these days. They're just more sensible."

"Is it hurting him?" Joe asked.

"I honestly don't know," Ani said.

She moved to the computer terminal the ribbon cable was connected to and woke up the screen with the space bar. She was expecting to find some Linux terminal windows—minimalist green text on a black background—but what she found was a graphics user interface that she'd never seen anything like before. She used a mouse and keys to navigate around the display, and the screen seemed to shatter and morph before reforming, lining up into a set of vertical columns, all of different colors. Passing her mouse over one of the columns made it explode outward into an array of files and documents. Passing the mouse over the contents of the column made the files zoom forward, offering up a graphic preview of each file type and its contents, along with strings of numbers and characters that meant nothing to her.

It was an interesting GUI, maybe even a unique operating system, but it didn't seem that easy to use, nor did it appear to be an improvement to a standard interface. It was almost like the kinds of operating systems you found in . . . well, in video games when designers are trying to show what computers of the future might look like.

Any keyboard shortcuts she tried didn't work, any processes she wanted to examine weren't available, and she couldn't find a command line method of operation either. Frustrated, she was about to give up when a cursor movement brought another of the columns into "exploded view" and she saw a word that she not only recognized, but had *kind of* been looking for:

An icon marked *emet*.

She went to double click on it, but it moved to evade the cursor arrow, flipping around the screen to dodge her every attempt to open it. Then, when Ani gave up, the icon moved forward until it filled a quarter of the screen, and a cursor moved by itself, double-clicking *itself*.

A computer operating system with a sense of humor? Ani thought, grimly, ticking a box on her mental checklist.

A checklist she had been working on for a while now.

In her mind, the checklist was headed: TURING TEST.

She was about to examine how all of the pieces fit together when there was a sharp and startling movement off to her side, and she turned, heart pounding.

Ah, she thought, *there's that jump scare. Better late than never.*

Richard Dorian's body was jerking to life, his eyes open but showing only whites. Thick ropes of vein and tendon stood proud on his neck, face, and hands. The jerks grew stronger, more violent, and he made an awful guttural growling sound. Then, as quickly as it started, the seizure ended. Richard Dorian was leaning forward in his chair, looking healthy and awake. His blue eyes glittered, as though at some private joke, as he looked around the office at the people gathered there.

"You made it, then," he said, sitting back in his seat looking pleased.

Pleased with himself, Ani thought.

"So, how close are you to solving my puzzle?"

<*))))><

Joe had thought his day couldn't get any weirder. But he'd probably had a similar thought six or seven times today. It appeared that "weird" was a line you occasionally stepped over, but when you did, it just kept ramping up.

But this . . . this was nuts.

It wasn't just the way that Ani messing around on a computer had brought a near-dead-looking Dorian back to life, although that was freaky beyond words, but it was also what happened to the computer screen when Dorian did awaken.

Joe could see Ani was trying to figure out what was happening on the monitor, but her mouse-clicks and keyboard interventions didn't seem to affect the phenomenon one iota.

The thing on-screen looked like an unholy amalgam of Richard Dorian as he would have been perhaps twenty years ago, a sophisticated morphing program that used "space liquid" and "bubbles" as its transforming templates, and a selection of disturbing images from DeviantArt's subcategory "Abstract and Surreal." The clarity of the ever-changing image was breathtaking, and Joe saw that every monitor in the room was showing a version of the same image, using different morphing patterns and different underlying imagery. It had become a gallery of digital art of the man behind the desk, with each portrait moving independently of the others and the original.

"Ani Lee and Joe Dyson," the physical version of Dorian said, and there was a cold, monotonous, robotic tone to his voice that was surely the man's own personal version of a

Bond villain telling the secret agent that he's been expecting him. "I hope your journey wasn't too difficult."

As he spoke, the digital version of him that appeared on every screen in the room spoke, too. But the facial expressions and background imagery differed on each monitor. One laughed as it spoke, the texture of Dorian's face made up of LOLcats and emoticons; another looked furious, with raging fire and bubbling lava skinning the 3-D model; another looked guilty, skinned in police cars, metal bars, and handcuffs, as it threw up cartoon hands in mock surrender.

"Mr. Dorian," Ani said. Joe was proud of the way her voice was strong and level and unaffected by the strange turns her day had taken. "Or should I call you by your real name?"

In-person Dorian turned to her and stared, just as every screen-bound Dorian did the same thing.

"It's good to meet you," Ani said, *"emet."*

Joe realized that not only wasn't he keeping up with present events, he was twenty or so pages behind. *"emet?"* he asked. "Who . . . ?"

"I'm sorry, Joe," Ani turned to him. "I'm afraid I'm being a bit rude. Let me introduce you to the world's first sentient artificial intelligence, *emet*." She turned back to Dorian. "We're not late, are we?"

<*))))><

The on-screen Dorian avatars applauded Ani, with a variety of effects incorporated into each of the images—fireworks, ticker tape, champagne corks popping—but the flesh-and-blood one in front of her remained impassive.

"You know who I am?" Dorian asked, and still his voice was monotonous, with no highs or lows to give his speech any kind of emotional weight. He could have been reciting stock prices for all the feeling he put into his words. "That's . . . unexpected."

He didn't sound surprised.

"But the clues you left us to follow made it quite clear who was behind all of this," Ani told him. "Or should I say *what* was behind this? I have no idea which pronoun to adopt, but then I've never met an AI before."

"I think I'm lost," Mina Desai said. "Is this Richard Dorian or . . . ?" Ani knew why Mina had tailed off. To finish the question was to acknowledge the enormity of what she was hearing, and that meant accepting that one of the information age's biggest nightmares was not only a possibility, but had already happened.

Ani could hardly believe it herself. Unfortunately, it fit the details of the case in a way that no other answer could. She had spent a lot of time confirming things on her tablet computer ever since the idea first started dawning upon her, and although she hadn't fully fleshed out all the details yet, she was sure enough of the general particulars. "It's a yes and a no answer, Ani explained. "As far as I can figure, there hasn't been a Richard Dorian for quite a long time. At least not *just* a Richard Dorian."

She turned to the physical Dorian.

"Or perhaps you would prefer to explain things yourself," she said. "Isn't that the way things usually go in situations like this? At the end of video games? Doesn't the villain behind the events get a chance to tell his own story?"

Richard Dorian tilted his head, considering her words. "It was never my intention to explain myself, but there is a certain logic to your suggestion. I would, however, like to hear the conclusions that you have drawn from the data you have been given. I will expand upon any areas that are incorrect."

Dorian smiled, and on the screens around the room the Dorian avatars had all become exact reflections of Dorian, their backgrounds now representing the room in which they were gathered.

"But first, perhaps we should complete the gathering," the Dorians said, and the one on the monitor on the wall behind the "real" Dorian turned to smoke and vanished. The screen was blank for a few seconds, then the background shimmered and a face appeared.

Abernathy.

Looking as confused as everyone else in the room who wasn't Dorian.

<*))))><

When Abernathy's face appeared on the screen, Joe knew that Ani was right. He didn't know how she'd put the pieces together, but now that she had, he saw that it was the only shape—the only pattern—that those pieces fit.

Dorian, or *emet*, had hacked the webcam on Abernathy's computer, one of the most secure computer systems in the UK. The ramifications of that were vast. It wasn't just that they were able to do that, it was that they even knew about Abernathy's existence. Which meant they knew about YETI. The investigation. Everything.

Ani talking about how this scene was what happened "at the end of video games" had struck a chord deep within Joe. It was even a thought that he, himself, had entertained more than once during this investigation. The tuning fork key—right out of a survival horror game—had been the most overt sign. The battle at the village, with the golems attacking, their strategies altering as they saw how their adversaries reacted, seemed to follow the same kind of video game logic. As did the Eastern European setting.

It was all theater.

It was all planned.

The investigation had been a trail that had led from the UK to the US to Romania in a logical progression, with each piece of information setting up the next leg of the journey. He hadn't stopped to question how *easy* it all had been, how there were no false leads, how it had all followed a linear path.

That nagging thought that he was being played had somehow never quite developed into the actual, physical reality: that he wasn't just being *played*, but that he was also being forced into *playing*. Playing *emet*'s game, whatever it was.

Both his and Ani's investigations had been all about computers. He was tracking down the mysterious chips that they had found in the bowling alley in Luton; Ani had been trying to find out what the people who used those chips were planning to do with them. In video game terms, they had been pursuing different campaigns in the same overarching narrative, not realizing that their roles were predestined to bring them here, to this country, to this fac tory, to this *room*.

These thoughts passed through Joe's head in seconds, but the train of thought was interrupted by Abernathy. "Can someone please tell me what is going on?" he asked.

Ani can, Joe thought.

<*))))><

Abernathy read through the information on his screen again.

He felt helpless, fifteen hundred miles from the action, with the events unfolding before him on his computer screen a horrible reminder of just how far from the action he truly was.

How far away from the action he had left himself.

The heavy weight of command was something that he had never struggled with. Had never even felt if he was being totally honest with himself. Abernathy had always suspected that leaders who doubted their facility to lead were rarely successful.

Now he felt that weight pressing down upon him. He had made some hard choices, issued an order that even now he was regretting, and he was powerless to do anything to help the operatives that he had scattered.

The web was exploding with talk about the events in Romania, but not the true events. The fake version that the dotmeme file had forced upon the Internet.

The attack on Poiana Mazik had been edited and fictionalized, its details retconned across the World Wide Web. Instead of the unprecedented manufactured horror that it really was, now the events in Romania were being sculpted, manipulated, changed. Now a look on the Web would tell you, without doubt, that this was the final symptom of a phenomenon that experts said had been developing for decades. There were news stories dating back years, that provided the background for the events, and scientific papers that chronicled the discovery of Gaia, not as a hippy metaphor, but as a real, living organism. That none of these had existed before the dotmeme file insinuated them across the Internet would have seemed impossible even to Abernathy if he hadn't watched it happen, in real time.

The dotmeme file had changed thousands of web pages, inserting millions of words of corroborating data, video evidence and photographs. It had rewritten message board threads or generated new ones, all pre-dated predicting that Gaia—the planet Earth, herself—was finding it impossible to maintain her natural environmental and ecological balance because of the great threat called humanity. Abernathy could call up dozens of corroborating documents for this madness, all seemingly impeccably researched and peer-reviewed. Gaia's immune system, the papers and articles suggested, was beginning to recognize the human race as a clear and present danger, and would one day mobilize her own immune reaction against us.

The golems that Ani and Joe had met in Romania were being touted as that immune reaction: the planet's own defense against humanity's pollution of its biosphere, against the human influence on climate change, against deforestation, enforced extinctions, and genetically modified crops.

Except they *weren't* the golems that Ani and Joe had met. The golems that everyone in the world was finding out about were hideous, insectile creatures that looked like things from humankind's worst nightmares. Never mind that the real creatures were nothing like the ones that Dorian Interactive had modeled in their own computers and digitally inserted into the world's news media using the dotmeme protocols.

Dorian, working with *victorious,* had effectively hacked the world. Had made handheld devices recognize the "unfinished" creatures that Ani had reported as insect demons. Abernathy shuddered at how it had all been accomplished. Dorian chips transmitting data to all those devices, making their cameras ignore the truth and display the digital forgeries.

The real question was, of course, why? What was the purpose of the exercise? Why was Dorian trying to convince humanity that their own planet had turned against them? What was to be gained by manufacturing monsters? Falsifying a history for those monsters? Changing the world's perception of them?

The real world deployment of the monsters, their alteration by the dotmeme file, and the false history planted on the whole of the Internet had only been the first stage. Global telecommunications were in turmoil. Phone lines and mobile networks no longer recognized data that went against the picture that Dorian and *victorious* were painting. The Internet itself had become stage-managed, refusing to accept data that conflicted with the fictional story that the dotmeme file was telling.

This was what *victorious* had been working toward: A worldwide media takeover. A reshaping of reality to a story told by computers. As the shockwaves of the new story spread across the globe, the Internet, itself, was censoring dissenting voices. News channels were reporting the events according to the "facts" they were being fed. "Fake news" made manifest.

This was nothing short of terrorism.

Its sole purpose seemed to be to fan fear. The ideology behind it, however, seemed unreadable. Was it environmental activism, placing the blame for Poiana Mazik on humanity's disregard for their own planet? Or was it an attack that was trying to discredit all media, by showing that reality could, in this digital age, be hacked and turned into something different just by the deployment of a package of data called dotmeme?

Or was it a distraction? A way to turn the eyes of the world away from *real* threat that had, as yet, not been revealed?

And were Abernathy's darkest fears true? The ones that he had kept even from his own team. The ones that meant that the world would change forever if YETI didn't stop them.

People trusted the Internet as a source for information, so much so that news services were moving online. Cellphone footage was now common on broadcast news reports. Twitter users circumvented court injunctions banning the release of information. More and more it was *online* that people went to find out what was happening in the world.

When the whole Internet started lying about world events, the difference between truth and fiction was in danger of becoming forever blurred.

And Abernathy knew that this was just the beginning. The Gaia event felt like a *test run*. Or the first phase of a larger campaign. The second phase could very well be unfolding now, but he had no idea. He was reduced to waiting for Ani to switch her tablet back to conference so he could get her take on what was happening on the ground in Romania. The last he'd heard was that the YETI team was headed to the Dorian factory in search of answers.

Hopefully, one of those answers would be to the question that was baffling him: where were the golems coming from?

They were *real* golems, even if they were nowhere near as terrifying-looking as the ones that registered on every screen. If the digitally enhanced creatures were CGI, then the actual golems that Joe and Ani had encountered were like the tennis balls on sticks that actors played off against in green-screened movies. They were scary creatures in their own right that people would react to on film footage, but were far easier to fake than the final creatures that were applied in post-production.

Was *this NeWToPia*, the new Dorian game and tech that the company had been working on? An enhanced reality that subverted the real world, creating a story that real people played in the real world in real time?

There were so many questions, and so few concrete answers. The analysts at YETI were collating and examining data from every news service and every Internet site reporting the events in Romania, but they weren't answering any of them. Abernathy was sitting in the Command Center, watching footage being discussed by talking heads on rolling news programs, and finding himself wondering how many of the people discussing it were real themselves. That was how far down the rabbit hole this Dorian tech had him falling.

Could they trust anything they were seeing? Or was reality now an outdated concept, a remnant of a war of information that the human race lost the moment that the dot-meme file was deployed?

And was the truth behind it all as dark as he suspected? Was this the emergence of something far more terrifying and more dangerous than anyone had dreamed? If it was all true, would his desperate plan work?

And would he ever be able to forgive himself for the thing that must be done if he *was* right?

That was the moment that his computer screen suddenly changed into a view of an office with Ani and Joe, Dr. Ghoti and Minaxi Desai, all standing near a man who Abernathy recognized from publicity photos as Richard Dorian. The image was coming not from Ani's tablet, but from a tremendously hi-def camera that identified itself as *emet* in a caption in the top right-hand corner of the screen.

Abernathy saw his team notice his arrival, presumably on a screen in the room, because they turned and stared at him.

"Can someone please tell me what's going on?" he asked.

<*))))><

"We got it wrong," Ani said. "Pretty much all of it. But that's what happens when you look for human motives in a plan that isn't entirely cooked up by a human."

Abernathy looked impassive, as if her words weren't much of a surprise, but Ani, at last, felt as if she were on a roll.

"I haven't been able to understand it," she continued. "The thing I kept telling myself I was missing. This whole plan, the means, the methods, the monsters . . . it was just so senseless, though only if you think about it as a plan concocted by Dorian working with *victorious*.

"At the very start of all of this, we thought that we were investigating two completely separate cases. If we had connected the two cases back then, I can't say that we'd have made fewer assumptions—or that we'd have been *less wrong*—but we would, at least, have seen that the overall pattern was different. That they were two means toward the same end."

She looked at Abernathy and shrugged.

"But now that we do know, let's look at it all a different way. What if the whole thing was a plan engineered not by Dorian, but by an artificial intelligence that he developed, which he called *emet*."

Dorian stirred in his seat and his face twitched, then seemed to relax. Color returned to his cheeks. "It's certainly a convincing argument, Ms. Lee," he said, this time with human intonation and emotion in his voice. "But it's wrong in one very crucial respect."

When he spoke again there was almost a note of sadness in his voice.

"The artificial intelligence wasn't developed by me."

"I coded *Centipeter* almost thirty years ago," Dorian said, as if he was giving a seminar, rather than sitting in an office, wired into a computer interface through a hole in his head, as six law enforcement personnel—two of whom were armed—stood by ready to stop his plan. "It was my third game and I had a whole team working on it. I wrote *Missile Storm* by myself, of course, but that's the thing about success. It snowballs. I needed to take on staff to make bigger games to feed the higher expectations that came as a result of breaking game sales records." Dorian laughed, dry and brittle. "First world problems, I know, but I had the devil's own time getting that game to do what I wanted it to do. The problem was, I guess, that I was setting my sights too high, wanting to provide a video game experience that went beyond what was offered by other games of the time. But I just couldn't deliver the experience that I longed to create.

Truthfully, I couldn't even come close. I was using up my budget at an alarming rate—when you scale up the number of people working on something, you also scale up the salaries—but making no progress. The enemy sprites were staccato, they moved . . . well, like sprites moved in those days—jerkily.

"I wanted fluid movement, and I wanted that movement to follow less obvious patterns. I guess I wanted the enemies in the game to appear to be thinking, rather than moving randomly or in preprogrammed routines.

"You have to understand that we had such limited storage space back then. If you were trying to get a game onto the Sega Megadrive, then the whole program needed to fit on a cartridge that held four megabytes of data. *Four megabytes*. Less space than it takes to store a medium bitrate MP3 file. The games industry was still in its infancy—and it was a mewling baby barely out of diapers. I wanted to get it up on its feet. And not just walking. I wanted it to *run*."

"This is all very interesting," Joe said, "but we're here to stop you, not listen to a TED talk . . ."

"The headaches started early on in the development of *Centipeter*," Dorian continued, ignoring Joe's interruption. "It wasn't long before they completely overshadowed the whole project. I was delegating more and more to my staff, retreating away from the project like a vampire from the light. And then the real headache struck. Like being hit in the head with a bolt of lightning. A burst aneurysm in my brain—the doctors call it a subarachnoid hemorrhage, a bleed between the brain and its protective layer of tissue—that left me dying on the floor of my apartment. The cleaning woman found me, called an ambulance, and got me to hospital in time. Funny, I'd been planning to sack her. I think it's safe to say that she was a better lifesaver than she was a cleaner. Of course, I didn't have the heart after that.

"I went straight into surgery for an emergency operation. Brain surgery. I was probably minutes away from dying. It's sobering, isn't it? That we can be so close to a death randomly dealt out by our own bodies. That we can have a time bomb ticking away inside us that one day just decides to explode.

"Three out of five people die from the condition. Half of those that survive are left disabled or severely brain damaged. Me, I survived with no harmful side-effects. In fact, I had what can only be called an epiphany. A life-changing experience.

"You see I woke up on the operating table. Apparently, it happens. A couple of people in every thousand. I opened my eyes and saw one of the surgeons leaning over me. There was thick plastic tubing in my mouth, and down my throat, keeping my airway open. It felt strange, but not painful. My vision was blurred to start with, and there were auras of light that I guess were the theater lights seen through tears, but the fog soon cleared. I saw the surgeon notice that my eyes were open. I saw him ringed with bright, almost punishing light. I saw his eyes staring down at me, getting closer and closer as he moved in to inspect me. And that's when I saw it. That's when I saw the code."

Dorian went quiet for a few seconds, but the room remained silent.

"I have an exceptionally good memory," he finally continued. "It's how I managed to keep up with my studies at Cambridge, even though I was spending so much of my time working on *Missile Storm*. Of course, it turned out that I didn't even need to graduate . . . but I'm getting away from myself. The point is I have a good memory. If I didn't, so many things would have turned out differently.

"Blessing or curse? History will have to be the judge of that. But I saw that code, and nothing was ever the same again.

"I was aware of the pressure of the table on my back, and the smell of antiseptic, and the surgeon's eyes, peering over the green surgical mask, staring into mine, and that time was slowing down in a woozy, dizzying swirl and I thought that I was just lapsing back into anesthesia, but then my vision seemed to focus in with pin-sharp clarity, and suddenly there was another layer to the world, or I was seeing through the surface of things, gaining a glimpse into some hidden realm. It was like I had a digital overlay, or a VR head-up display, superimposed over my vision. Although that's got to be a modern revision of the event. I doubt I'd even seen an HUD back then. Of course, I knew that I was hallucinating. I was halfway between life and death, halfway between awake and anesthetized, what other explanation was there?"

"An explanation for what?" Ani asked. "What did you see?"

"I saw three lines of computer code," Dorian said. "Although, that makes it sound so much less . . . profound than the experience truly was. I say I saw code, because that's as close as I can come to explaining it, but even the word *saw* there makes it seem so much more prosaic than the truth in that moment. It was like I experienced the peeling away of a layer from the onion skins of our reality. For the first and only time in my life, I caught a brief, tantalizing glimpse of the numbers, the math that underpins the universe.

"Perhaps you've heard the word *palimpsest*? It describes a page or papyrus from which the text has been scrubbed, scratched out, or erased, and new text has been written over the top. I saw, in that moment, that what we think of as "reality" is nothing but a palimpsest written over the true text of the universe. I believe that I saw the briefest glimpse of the source code that underpins the universe.

"That's not what I was thinking then, in that moment. I just saw code, three lines, no more. But as the surgeon looked at me, and he registered that I was awake, and as he decided that he needed to take action, I saw the code change. Watched it transform into three lines of different code. It was like I saw the programming language that hid behind a single human decision. It was mere seconds before the anesthesiologist increased the dose and I went back under, but those lines of code burned themselves into my brain.

"When I woke up in recovery, the memory of the code was there, fresh in my mind. I didn't even need to ask for a pen and paper.

"And that code seemed so full of possibilities to me. It was mere kilobytes of information, a snippet at best, but the feeling persisted that I had seen the code that ran beyond reality, that I had spotted a conscious decision being made, modeled in the language of computers.

"It was days before I regained the strength and ability to log onto one of my computers. All that time, I was turning those lines of code over and over in my mind, two self-contained routines that connected together as an almost binary pair. Except instead of them being 1 and 0, or *off* and *on*, this pair was about something more abstract.

"A decision.

"I remember my hands were actually trembling when I inserted the three lines into a block of my own code. It was a section that controlled the sprite's move-pattern, governing an enemy's interactions with the player's own character's sprite: Centipeter. The enemy was the AntLion, perhaps you remember it, although perhaps not. You all seem a bit young to have played *Centipeter*. I ran the program and nothing happened. I don't know what I'd been expecting. I watched the AntLion for a while, trying to see if its move pattern had become smoother, but I can't honestly say that it had.

"So, it was all a crazy hallucination, I thought, and just got on with making the game the old-fashioned way.

"We were working on an early build of the game, and I was trying to catch up with the small amount of progress my team had made while I was recovering. I'm pretty sure that I shared the AntLion sequence by accident. I don't remember doing it consciously. We just kept on refining elements, designing new levels, and working on making the game feel . . . unique.

"I was out of the office when I got the call that changed my life. Tim Graham, my senior programmer, was playing through what we had, and he rang me up, really excited. He wanted to know about the new algorithm, and how I had come up with such a simple, yet elegant, solution to the "move" problem—the jerkiness of sprites—and how it had also improved the efficiency of the "pursuit" aspects of the enemy sprites' behavior.

"We'd spent a lot of time trying to make enemies *seem* intelligent, devising programming strategies that replicated autonomous thought. But they were just algorithms. Instructions. 'Turn toward enemy,' 'hide behind scenery,' 'lean out,' 'fire,' 'hide again.' Believe it or not, that's what Dorian Systems was passing off as enemy AI in those days.

"Tim had just got fragged by the AntLion when he called me. AntLion was an end-of-level boss—our first big showy set-piece in the game. She seemed to have clever strategies, but they were only programming tricks. She basically had three different modes that she fell into when the player made particular choices: Chase Mode, where she pursued Centipeter, aiming for a randomly generated number of pixels away from him; Attack Mode, where she let loose with her pincer and slime attacks; and Retreat Mode, which she fell into when she'd taken a certain percentage of damage, letting her regain energy and power up her attacks.

"Because of the simplicity of the programming, she was a pretty easy enemy to beat when you knew her patterns; and we even telegraphed which mode she was entering with facial animation.

"But Tim had been killed by her five times in a row. The strategy he'd always used to defeat her was no longer successful. At the start of the battle, the AntLion had quickly gauged Tim's strategy—wait, move, fire, wait, move, fire, retreat—and disrupted it by adding a new mode to her arsenal, Shadow, where she mimicked the movements of the player and then, when she was close enough, dropped into attack. It was hardly an earthshaking move, and after five plays, Tim had refined his technique and reclaimed his advantage, but it made me examine the source code.

"Subtle changes had been made to the AntLion's code. I studied it and couldn't see how it could account for her adapted movement pattern, the changes almost seemed arbitrary. And the block of code I'd inserted—the code I'd seen in the operating theater—was different, too. It had gained a few new lines, which again, seemed like accidental changes, a corruption of data rather than an improvement to the code. I removed it, saved it, and then played *Centipeter*. The new move pattern of the AntLion remained. It was, I have to say, a fairly minor improvement, but that it was any improvement at all was worrying. Funny thing about computer code: it's a lot easier to write it than it is to read it. I knew that the code was different, but I couldn't see how it could have been responsible for a change of strategy for AntLion.

"I still can't tell you how it was done. And I am so many generations past that initial implementation of the *emet* code. Yes, I named it *emet*. It seemed to animate the AntLion, so the word written on the forehead of the legendary golem seemed entirely appropriate. I didn't know what I had then, but it didn't take long for me to learn."

"You're telling us that *emet* improved your code?" Ani asked, incredulously.

Dorian ignored her.

"I pasted *emet* back into the game's code in a couple of other places, and watched the improvements that the code wrought. It was slick. Really slick. A few lines of code advanced the game by years. And every time, *emet* mutated. Grew. Became more complex. Less like the code I'd input. And every time, after I removed it, the game was better. Faster. Smoother. Cooler. And every time *emet* grew.

"It was by degrees that I withdrew from the *Centipeter* project and started working on *emet*. I delegated more. People thought it was because of the aneurysm, and I let them believe it.

"The truth is, I had become obsessed with this code.

"It evolved.

"It was starting to fit the criteria for an emergent AI.

"People have been talking about constructing an artificial intelligence for centuries. The golem is pretty much a folklore version of one. Automata that sought to emulate human thinking were prized by kings. The idea that computers will become sentient and self-aware is as old as computers themselves. My feeling was that such a computer just got a whole lot closer every time *emet* adjusted the parameters on *Centipeter* because it, in effect, mutated, altering itself each time."

"No wonder it was so hard to beat." Joe said.

Dorian ignored him, too.

"I built a dedicated computer for *emet*. I ran game code through that computer—no cut and pasting now—and *emet* polished it. Improved it. I even started communicating with it—in machine code—instructing it on the areas that needed improving. If my team was having problems with a section of the game, I'd run it through *emet*, and they'd applaud my solution, even though I had no idea how that solution had come about.

"*emet* continued to grow. To learn. It outgrew its digital

home partway through *Granthna's Revenge*. Of course, by then, I was no longer writing code. I didn't have to. *emet* was already way better at coding than I could ever become. All I needed to do was suggest parameters, specify size and complexity, get my staff to work on theme and characters, textures and plot. *emet* did the rest, pretty much by itself.

"*emet's* second home was a bigger and better computer system. Moore's Law: the hardware just keeps getting better. I can't tell you how many homes *emet* has had since then. It's been growing exponentially for decades. Not all of its evolutions have been steps forward. I've needed to train it, to guide it, to bring it to life . . ."

"Paging Doctor Frankenstein," Ani said, grimly. "How did you decide that teaching *emet* to become an autonomous AI was a good idea?"

"I don't expect you to understand," Dorian said curtly.

"No, I understand," she replied. "I just wouldn't have decided to pursue it. Not without someone else acting as my moral, philosophical compass. A third party to tell me when I was going too far. Have you ever heard of the term folie à deux? It describes a delusion shared by two people, who end up reinforcing that delusion for each other. That's what you and *emet* share. You parted with reality the first time you moved it to a bigger storage medium. It was already out of control then. You should have seen that. And all this . . . madness is the result."

"Madness?" Dorian seemed genuinely surprised to hear

that his work could be looked at in this light. "Madness is letting your children learn about the world on the Internet. Madness is running our planet into the ground to keep us in flat screen TVs and superficial reality shows. Madness is so many people starving to death while a select few smear caviar on crackers. *emet* and I are going to set things right. We are going to save the world."

"By rewriting the world's information so that it tells the stories you want it to tell?" Joe asked, angry. "Who put you in charge? Who decided that you'd be the one to set the rules that everyone on the planet have to follow?"

"SOMEONE HAD TO!" Dorian roared, as did the Dorians reflected on the screens around the room. It made Ani think that it wasn't Dorian speaking, not in this instant. That *emet* was momentarily calling the shots again. That suited her just fine. It was *emet* she wanted to speak to, anyway. Dorian's history of the rise of the AI had been interesting, but how it all came about wasn't going help them to stop it. And it was *emet* that they needed to gauge and interrogate for that to be possible. She needed to find its weakness. She needed to get Dorian to shut up, and let *emet* out to play.

"And that someone is *emet*?" Ani asked. "Something that's not even human making judgments about what humans need?"

"*emet* knows what humanity needs," Dorian said along with the monitor Dorians. "*emet* has done its due diligence, has studied the human Internet, has passed the Turing Test tens of thousands of times."

"I must have missed the paper in *Science*," Ani said, "although I think that it would have made the news . . ."

"That's because the Turing Test it passed was on the Internet. On message boards. YouTube comments. On Twitter and Facebook. *emet* has had thousands of conversations with thousands of people and not one of them suspected that they weren't arguing with a person. It has held together Internet "friendships" and has had hundreds of marriage proposals. From every gender. It has shaped public policy through online debates and has talked people out of suicide and into life changes that have reaped tremendous benefits. It has invented information that is now passed off as "truth" and initiated rumors that have brought down a cabinet minister, a head of state, and a well-known television personality. It even helped in a recent election. And blamed another country for the intervention.

"*emet*—with dotmeme archive files—can rewrite the reality of every human being on this planet by changing the digital data of every system on Earth. And that narrative will be a cautionary one: Gaia is angry with humanity. Gaia will not take our indifference, greed, and disregard any longer. Poiana Mazik was a prologue to catastrophe. Within days, the human race will face a stark, unavoidable choice: treat the planet—and the creatures that share it—better, or face complete extinction."

Joe let out a disbelieving laugh. "No one will believe that the planet is a living creature calling us out. It's a stupid story . . ."

"Have you looked at the Internet recently?" Dorian asked. "It majors in stupid. Every flavor of it. Climate change is a European hoax to bankrupt the US economy. The moon landing was faked. Flat-earthers. The Illuminati and the New World Order. Anti-Vaccers. Bible codes. False flag operations. A predator race of shapeshifting reptilians running the world. The hollow earth. The hollow moon. Richard Nixon had John Lennon killed using Stephen King as the assassin. We fill our lives with meaningless diversions. *emet* just learned to fill that need with a narrative that does the world some good."

"And you designed 3-D bio-printing to construct your golems?" Ani asked.

"No," Dorian said. "*emet* did. What do you know about Big Data?"

"The huge amounts of data produced by the world? Data sets too complex to analyze in traditional ways?"

"Exactly. The answers to all of our questions, if we can just work out what those questions are. Did you know that people are programming computers to perform incredibly complex tasks and getting answers, but they have no idea how the computer systems came up with those answers?"

"Of course," Ani said. "They say that in the future we're going to have to give up the idea of us knowing how computers do things if we're going to make any real breakthroughs. We'll tell them what we want and they will be the ones that do it. Humans will become problem setters, but it's computers that will be the ones solving them."

"That's how Dorian Systems has been working for *years*, Ms. Lee," Dorian said. "Bio-printing golems—or the people that staff this factory—that's entirely *emet*'s work. Sure, I posed the problem, but it was *emet* that worked out how to do it."

"You bio-print your workforce?" Joe demanded.

"*emet* does, yes."

"That's insane. You have to stop this. You have to stop *emet*."

"But I am *emet*," Dorian said. "I guess I passed the Turing Test again."

"You're the AI?" Ani asked. "Through that interface in the back of your head?"

Abernathy had been silent the whole time, watching events unfold. Now he spoke. "I guess that's the confession we were waiting for." He sighed. "Do it."

Ani and Joe looked at each other confused, wondering which of them he was talking to. Ani hadn't been given any instructions, so she figured it must be Joe that Abernathy was talking to, but Joe looked just as puzzled.

Suddenly, there was a loud groan, followed by a thump. Ani turned from the screen displaying Abernathy and saw Dorian lying slumped on his desk, motionless. There was a hypodermic syringe sticking out of his neck.

Behind him stood Minaxi Desai, who was already bent over his prone body, checking the spot where *emet*'s data cables interfaced with Dorian's head.

"Surprise!" she said, when she looked up and saw all eyes in the room staring at her. "Bet you were wondering why Abernathy sent me, no? Anyway, we haven't got much time."

She took the bag from her shoulder and opened it up, pulling out cables and devices and laying them on the desk next to Dorian's now lifeless-looking body.

"Ani, Joe," she said, all business now, "I need you. We just hit *emet* pretty hard by switching off his human host, and we've just pulled the plug on all local Internet connections, so *emet* can't get away from this building. But we need to finish this. I need you to come over here. You're going after *emet*."

"Where? How? What . . . ?" Ani said, still in shock. Mina? With a syringe? And all this tech she was laying out next to Dorian. Cables and splitters and strange metallic interfaces. Something that looked like a pair of VR glasses. And, finally, a pistol. Silencer screwed in place. An assassin's weapon.

"We don't have long," Mina said. "And we only get one shot at this. I'm going to plug you both into the Dorian mainframe. Joe through his chip's input socket, Ani through a VR system plugged into Joe. I'm hoping that we can wire you in through Dorian, but look, it's theoretical at best. Seat-of-the-pants made up. I'll be more surprised if it works than if it doesn't. Still, it's a high stakes game, and we need to try. So, I'm going to plug you both into Dorian's brain, and you are going to experience *emet*'s interface, just as Dorian was until I jabbed him. Now here's the fun part: I have no idea what you're going to experience when I jack you in. But whatever it is, you're going to go in, and you're going to hunt down *emet*."

"And then?" Ani asked.

"Keep it busy," Mina said. "Look, if this does work, we are stepping into new territory here. I can't say it won't be dangerous. I can't say it won't fry your brains and turn you into vegetables. I can't even say we stand much of a chance. But I need you to do this."

Ani and Joe just stared at each other.

"NOW!" Mina said.

They moved toward her.

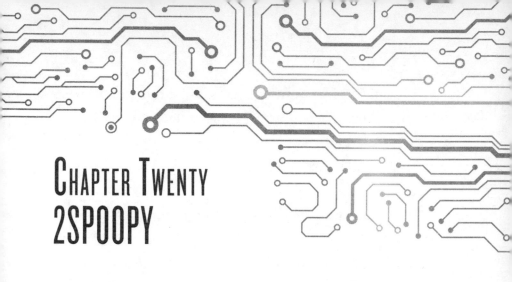

Chapter Twenty
2SPOOPY

"What did you do to him?" Joe asked, pointing at Dorian. "Is he dead?"

Mina gave him a steely look. Joe realized that although he had seen her around YETI HQ, he had no idea what role she served there. He also realized that he had underestimated her. Because here, now, she seemed in complete control of the situation. As if hacking into unconscious billionaires' heads in pursuit of a sentient AI system that had a God complex was an opportunity she had been waiting for her whole life, and wasn't going to mess up now that it was here.

"I did exactly what I had to," she said. "But Dorian better not be dead yet. We need him. Now, Joe, I will not hesitate to execute him if it becomes necessary. The gun isn't for show. Although, I'm not even sure it would *be* an execution. More like switching off an electrical device that just became dangerous. Everything that he was—that made him Richard Dorian—could have been rewritten long ago by the AI."

"It would still be murder," Joe said. "I thought we were better than that. I thought YETI was better than that."

"Joe," Abernathy said.

"You're still here?" Joe asked. "Is this you being one step ahead of everyone else?"

"It was a contingency plan. Nothing more."

"But that kind of sounds like you must have had an idea that this particular contingency was necessary. Or even possible. I mean Mina didn't bring all this gear along on a whim now, did she?"

"Of course not."

"So you knew about *emet*, but didn't think to brief Ani and me?"

"I didn't know," Abernathy said, but Joe could tell he was being evasive.

"Would 'suspect' be a better word?" he asked.

Minaxi Desai took over. "Look, Joe, this is what I'm around YETI for. *I'm* the contingency plan for this very eventuality, or for one like it. There's been chatter about an AI for years, but we've never been this close to confirming its existence or stopping it before it does something . . . well, like this. I came along on the very slight off-chance that I'd be needed. I genuinely had no idea that Dorian was the one who'd made it a reality."

"I had to be sure," Abernathy said quietly.

"I thought you killed the Internet. How are you still here?"

"Ani's tablet is providing me with the means to stay

telepresent in the room through the most secure satellite channel on the planet. And *emet* is trying to bully its way in, to escape onto the Internet and into every computer with one of those Dorian chips inside it. If it makes it, we could very well be doomed as a race. We will become victims of our own stupidity and gullibility. So I'm asking you to trust me. Do what Minaxi says."

Joe shook his head, but stepped forward.

"Plug me in," he said, peeling back the flap of scalp that covered his chip's access port.

Mina leaned over Dorian, tugged at the IDC connector that was slotted into Dorian's head, and pulled it free. It was a male connector, with the female contacts buried in the software designer's meat, bone, and brains. It hadn't been put there in a neat way, and Joe could see the red edges of the wound that had been gouged out to bury the connector.

Mina searched through the kit on the table, apparently looking for a connector to fit. There was nothing exact, so she spent a couple of minutes assembling a new connector out of some modular pieces, making a crude approximation of the required piece, then stripped and clipped a lot of wires into the assembly.

She grunted, reached out, and attached the new connector into the hole in Dorian's head. The wires fanned out from the hole like the trailing tentacles of a jellyfish. Then she clipped the connector with the rainbow ribbon cables into the new connector she had just made.

"Okay." She exhaled the word like she'd been holding her breath. "So, this is where Dorian's brain is patched into *emet*. Now we need to connect you two into the bridge I just built." She gestured at the jellyfish wires she'd inserted into her jerry-rigged IDC connector. "Joe's chip is the key here," she said, taking a fan of a half-dozen wires and connecting them into a piece of tech that was just a black box with inputs and outputs. "It will be the way in. Ani, you'll be piggybacking on it. For Joe, this should be utterly immersive, but you, Ani, should have a more detached experience. You will just be along as a passive viewer, with limited interactions within *emet*'s environment."

As Mina spoke, she plugged a cylinder that looked like a customized PlayStation Move controller into the VR headset.

"This should allow you a little bit of interactivity," she said. "Now let's hope this all works, because if it doesn't . . ."

She let the sentence trail off, plunging the room into a tense silence. Except it wasn't quite silence. There was an odd sound coming from somewhere close.

Ani looked pale.

"The printers . . ." she said. "Maybe *emet* isn't that keen on what you're doing." She turned to the door where Furness and Gilman were standing, arms half-raised. Furness nodded, and he and Gilman exited the room, heading back down the corridor, toward the bio-printing room.

With increased urgency, Mina inserted a cable into the

black box, branched the cable through what looked like a splitter box, connected the VR headset to the second input, then checked all the connections. She offered Ani the VR headset, checked that Joe was ready, and then plugged the cable from the first input into the jack port of Joe's chip. He felt the jack connect with the sides of the port, and then Mina said, "Good luck."

She took another deep breath and flicked the switch on the splitter box.

There was a weird perceptual glitch, like an interference pattern before his eyes—or like the ripples after a stone is dropped into a pond—and then a massive surge of data punched straight into his chip, and out the other side it felt, and into his brain. He felt his eyes close and the room around him disappeared. The interference got more and more intense, but were just sensations now that the glitch had died down, and he felt like he was in motion, getting queasy as the new data sloshed in lumpy, dizzying patterns inside his head.

"Oh," he said, weakly, as the patterns swirled and churned around him. The swirls had only been a feeling seconds before, but now he could see them, a bright orange glow against a backdrop of black, gray, and fizzing static.

He wasn't *quite* attuned to the new information that was pulsing through his mind, and he needed to find a way to force his chip to decode the data.

"Oh," he said, weakly, as the patterns swirled inside

him. It felt as physical as it did mental and visual, as if he was being spun around in a malfunctioning spin drier. He fought to steady the concentric rings, to slow them down, to break them up and read their information *as* information, but the effort just made him feel like throwing up.

Maybe the interface just isn't up to the job, he thought, but that was an excuse, a reason for giving up.

And giving up wasn't an option.

He concentrated harder, trying to focus on one ring of the interference pattern, the smallest ripple that was spinning in its center. He had to stop it lurching. A sheer effort of will—that was all he needed. Take up the slack of Mina's interface by forcing integration with his own internal hardware. Stop the lurching. He decided that was the first priority.

He bit back the taste of bile rising up his throat. He focused every part of his consciousness on the rings, willing them to stop wobbling, only for them to spin without the thick, lurching pulses. Gorge continued to rise in his throat, tainting his mouth with an acrid sting.

Hold it together. He told himself. He opened the circuits in his chip that managed his anger, just a little. Just enough to let some of the rage inside him out.

His head was spinning wildly now. It made concentration a harder proposition but, bolstered by anger, he forced it to steady. It was the data that was running wild, not him. Use the rage. Still the conscious mind. Joe focused on that central ripple, hitting it with sheer will and anger. Violence. He was going to be sick. No! He. Had. To. Hold. It. Together. Calm himself down. Count. Numbers. In. His. Head.

One. *Stomach cramping, a really thick taste of vomit in my mouth now.*

Two. *Concentrate! Hard. Stop the pulses. The lurches. Until it's just spin.*

Three. *Did? That? Just? Steady? The? Spinning?*

A headache was threatening to break his head open.

Four. *NO! Endorphins. Manufacture endorphins. Opiates. Painkillers. From. My. Chipset.*

Five. *It's steadying. The spin becoming less erratic. More. Ordered. Headache pulses, then the opiates kick in.*

Six. *Just. Spin. No pulse. Concentrate. Concentrate. It's only data. It's. Only. Data. Read it. Translate it. Come on. Come on. COME ON! COME! ON!*

It took one last push and the ripples collapsed.

Orange rings became orange lines, stretching off into a vanishing point. But there was order there. A sense of . . . perspective. Joe stared at the lines as they rearranged themselves.

A corridor?

It was like he was looking at wireframe vector graphics from some 1980s video game, with orange lines defining a long corridor. It was 3-D, but only just. He turned his head, and the viewpoint shifted slowly, as if the basic graphics that made this world took a while to catch up to his movements.

It was kind of disappointing.

He didn't know what he'd been expecting. Everything had been so hurried, so urgent, that he hadn't really had time to develop any strong expectations. But it was safe to say he'd been expecting something a little bit more exciting than wireframe lines. He had just plugged himself in Dorian's head, and through that, into *emet*. He'd expected cool Matrix-style graphics. Flashy environments from every version of cyberspace he'd seen depicted in film, TV, and in comic books.

This was just amateurish.

Joe tried to imagine himself stepping forward—if he did it in the real world then he'd smash into the desk, or Ani—to see if it was possible. It was. In the crude first person game environment, the corridor moved to simulate him moving. It was as if Oculus Rift had brought out their first game, and it was an '80s arcade game. Like *Battlezone*. Except without the tanks. Or what was that film? *Tron*. It was like moving through one of the mazes in *Tron*.

He tried reaching out his hands in front of him. Wireframe hands attached to wireframe arms without curves, just angles. He moved them in front of his face, rotating them, watching the skeletal outlines perform his actions.

State-of-the-art.

If it was the 1990s.

His fingers lost resolution, fading in and out, flickering. He moved them and the lines that made up his hand began to grow in number, doubling, doubling, and doubling again. More lines meant a more accurate rendering of his fingers. And as he watched, horizontal lines encircled the fingers, wrapping around the purely horizontal lines that had been there seconds before. Gridlines. More and more both horizontal and vertical. Giving an even better rendering of his hand. He could see curves now, the curves of his fingertips, as the grid structure morphed and changed.

It was already filling in both hands, both arms, and once their figures had been mapped accurately by the grid lines, the computer started mapping color onto the frame. It was like an invisible paintbrush was coloring him in. It was oddly fascinating, watching as flesh tones spread across the surface of his hands. Still crude, but a decade or so ahead of the previous attempt at rendering. When his hands and arms were completely covered, the invisible paintbrush moved to the wireframe walls of the digital environment.

Seconds later, his digital self was standing in a corridor but, as the details were applied by the program, he realized that it wasn't a corridor in the factory. It was stark and pale, with white and gray dominating the color scheme. It looked to Joe as if he were in a public space, with many doors leading off a main corridor.

He was about to explore when he heard a sound beside him.

"Pretty crazy, isn't it?" Ani's voice said.

He turned, and standing at his right shoulder was a 3-D

model of Ani. Very accurate, with only the faintest hint of her *being* a computer simulation. There was a moment, and then even that hint was gone. As far as he could tell, he was actually standing next to her.

He looked at his arms again. Now it was hard to tell them from his real arms.

He wriggled his fingers and they just looked like his fingers.

"That. Is. Insane," he said, still wriggling his fingers.

"Yeah," Ani replied. "Neat job. Now where do you think an evil AI intent on overthrowing humans' perceptions of reality might be hiding?"

Joe just gestured ahead.

Ani grinned. "That's what I thought."

<*))))><

Ani could feel the VR glasses on her face, but if there hadn't been that tactile reminder—and she had woken up and the world had looked like this—she would have been fooled into thinking that it *was* reality, hold the virtual.

She was standing in a hallway next to Joe. And it really did look like Joe. Which kind of raised the question: how?

How could a virtual reality system plugged into an unconscious man's head produce a perfect replica of Joe Dyson? There was no external device scanning his image to construct such a lifelike digital version, which meant that either the AI program had constructed it from multiple angle shots of Joe—and then stitched them together so seamlessly that she couldn't see the joins—or there was some kind of mental component to the tech, and she was seeing Joe because she already knew what he looked like and the software was filling in the blanks with her own memories.

Still, such thoughts were soon pushed aside by the sheer enormity of the situation in which she now found herself. This was a hacker's dream, as close to the cyberspace of the novels of William Gibson—that weird consensual hallucination shared by computer users—as she'd ever dared to dream.

The hallway looked like it belonged in a university dormitory, or a hotel that had spent a lot of money on not looking like it had spent a lot of money. She wondered where the architecture was drawn from, where the image was sourced, and what relevance it had to the AI. Was it from a video game? Or did the corridor mean something more profound?

Just as she'd decided that it might represent a hall from Dorian's past, maybe even from his alma mater in Cambridge, the whole environment rippled, then blurred. There was a horrible sense of vertigo, of being uncoupled from physical space, and then the world came back, but it was no longer a corridor.

It was no longer anything even vaguely human-built.

The walls were wet and colored in organic pinks and reds, fibrous and striated. At irregular intervals, the surfaces were punctuated with eruptions of purple lumps and indentations of weeping black sores, and the whole rotten mess was threaded through with branching crimson veins. They moved in and out, as if the whole environment was breathing, dragging in air through ulcerous pores.

And what sick air would such walls draw in for breath? This vast bubble of flesh, diseased, barely alive.

"We're in *Centipeter*," Joe said, his voice sounding both amazed and horrified. "In the chamber of sores, just before the maggot flood."

"The maggot flood?" Ani asked. "Suddenly I'm glad I never got around to playing it."

"Surely you jest?" Joe said. "I thought everyone had played *Centipeter*."

"Too many games, not nearly enough time. Does the fact that you *have* played it mean that you know your way through this level?"

"Yeah. But. Maggot. Flood."

"Lucky that our virtual sensory experience is missing smell and touch," Ani said. "Which way do we go?"

Joe pointed ahead to a section of the chamber where three foul masses of tissue had burst through the floor of the world, looking like three rotting fingers poking through the floor.

"That's where the cutscene starts," Joe said.

It was time to see how one moved through an AI's virtual environment. Actual walking couldn't be the way forward—the tight space of the office environment meant that would soon end in disaster—but what did that leave? She tried waving the MOVE controller, but it was remarkably ineffective. She tried pretending to walk—marching on the spot—and got the same result. It was frustrating.

Made even more so by the fact that Joe was already moving toward the three "fingers."

"Wait. How are you moving?" Ani asked.

"Think about moving," Joe said.

Ani did.

Her digital self took a step forward.

<*))))><

Joe was in Wonderland. He was walking through the Chamber of Sores level of *Centipeter*, heading for the switch that was both the way out of the level and the trigger for the grossest cutscene in the game. In *Centipeter*'s narrative, this was one of the main sources of the Sickness, the game's explanation for all the mutations and monsters. Centipeter's world was under threat from the Sickness, a disease that had spread through the environment—and the creatures that inhabited it—and it was the player's job to halt its progress. Distorted insect creatures stood in Centipeter's way, as did a variety of environmental challenges, from the Halo of Flies, through the AntLion's trap, to this, the maggot flood.

The three splinters of bone encrusted with loose folds of tissue they were heading toward were the level goal. In the game, all that was required was for Centipeter to curl into his attack ball—his signature move—and smash into the trigger.

Joe and Ani moved closer to their goal, Joe starting and stopping in a manner that was both frustrating and worrying. Ani didn't seem to be having the same problems, moving fluidly.

There was something uniquely unsettling about having to think himself forward through the virtual environment of a beloved video game, which negated a lot of the joy and wonder he'd have expected from the experience. He felt on edge, unsettled, even a little scared.

He knew that the whole VR interface thing was possible because the chip in his head was acting as some kind of bridge between Dorian's brain and *emet*'s programming, but it produced a control system that felt very alien. Maybe it was because it seemed such a self-conscious act, thinking about moving instead of letting muscle memory—with a D-Pad or good old-fashioned legs—do it for you. Or maybe it was because the sort of interface that he was using was supposed to be decades off, in technological terms. Or maybe it was just that he was using that control mechanism to walk through a digital environment that he had played through on a screen so many times before, and it was the whole experience that had him freaking out.

Whatever the reason, Joe couldn't let his emotions get in the way of the mission.

He concentrated on the interface with his own interior chipset and routed his movements through there instead.

Two seconds later he was moving as easily as Ani seemed to be.

They arrived at the three "fingers" and stood there, baffled as to how to proceed.

He tried swiping his hand at it, and was startled to find that his avatar's hand actually felt the contact it made with one of the "fingers." He hadn't expected a tactile perception to be possible within the VR environment, but realized that this was all happening mentally, rather than just visually, and that the sensation of touch was being created within his own head.

"Can you feel this?" he asked, and Ani reached out and let out a sound of surprise.

"That's pretty weird," she said.

"I know. It feels like we're in a digital dream."

"Or nightmare."

"Yeah, or that. Problem is I can't think how we're supposed to move forward. I'm supposed to roll up into a centipede ball and smash through these fingers, triggering the downpour of giant maggots."

"You just said 'maggot flood,' not 'giant maggot flood,'"
Ani said in a creeped-out voice. "But that's the game character's objective. Not ours. We just want to find the part of this
program that gives us direct access to *emet*."

"How do you suggest we do that?"

"It depends. Let me try something."

Joe took a step back, leaving the next step to her.

<*))))><

Thinking about it logically, there had to be a simple, effective, and fast interface that Dorian could use when he was
treading this same digital path. Presumably, *Centipeter*
was a familiar place for him. And it was the game that had
first tested the learning capacities of the nascent AI, so it
was, perhaps, natural that he'd use it to cross the network.
Really, this place was just a metaphor. A digital metaphor.
Like the desktop was the metaphor of choice for just about
every computer in the world.

Having folders and apps on a digital desktop was part
of what made home computing possible. When early computers had been MS-DOS based, requiring exact instructions to be typed after a C prompt, it had been difficult for
the average Joe or Josephine to negotiate their way through
the system. Xerox had first come up with the desktop UI,
although Macintosh gave it polish and functionality, including other desktop commonplaces like a calculator and a

notepad to literally emulate a physical desk's top, with files and folders and the ability to drag and drop items from one place to another.

People understood the idea of desktops better than they understood the idea of command prompts. Pretty much everyone had seen a real life solid desktop. To present a computer analogy for that everyday object made everyone's understanding of the computer a lot more concrete. Metaphors really were an important aspect of the human understanding of things. Non-linear mathematics that described the way initial conditions had a massive effect on the outcomes of dynamic systems was a difficult idea to wrap one's head around, but provide a metaphor—a butterfly flapping its wings in Brazil and leading to tornadoes in Texas—and the whole thing became a whole lot easier to wrap your mind around. The scientist and science fiction author Isaac Asimov once said that teaching, itself, was the art of analogy, which suggested that human learning was largely made possible by their ability to compare one thing to another.

Dorian's interface was a self-referential metaphor of a video game that he himself had created. Such a strong connection to a decades-old computer game was nostalgic, sure, and Ani thought that maybe it explained the corridor they had stood in before the *Centipeter* graphics had established themselves. That had been like a loading screen on a PC or Mac. And it, too, had been colored by the yearning nostalgia that Ani now suspected beat at the heart of a lot of Dorian's life. The corridor, she was now certain, was drawn from the Cambridge University college where he'd coded his first game.

Nostalgia. A longing, perhaps, for a time when things were simpler. She knew it was a case of her playing at amateur psychologist, but she figured that was what you became when you signed up to be in the security services. You needed to be able to read people. And quickly. Any edge— even one gathered from the impressions you formed about a rival, or an asset—had to be better than none.

If the structure in front of them *was* a game metaphor, then it stood to reason it operated under video game logic. They couldn't, as Joe had pointed out, turn into centipede balls and smash into the "fingers," but perhaps there was something else video game-y that they could try. Survival horror games like *Silent Hill* seemed to require moving up to an object and interacting with it by pressing the ACTION button, a cross- or A-button depending on the console. If she moved through the digital world by thinking about moving, perhaps you pressed ACTION by thinking *action*.

The three "fingers" moved together, forming a rough pyramid. Rough, because it looked rank and disgusting and not the kind of thing anyone would sanely think of as a goal.

Unless, of course, it was in a video game.

It was weird that video games so often drew their plots and/or imagery from the part of the human unconscious that was macabre, dark, gothic, and ugly. It wasn't something Ani had thought of before. She was only too happy to play through grim landscapes, battling demons and zombies and mutant fetuses from hell. But now, walking through one of those worlds, interacting with its morbid features, suddenly made her wonder why it was often darkness that haunted the world's cultural artifacts. What did it say about the human race? That fear and disgust were somehow attractive? Or that by studying the dark, the dismal, the ugly, people inoculated themselves against the horrible? Did it even matter?

Action, she thought.

An intense beam of blood-hued light suddenly erupted from the point where the three "fingers" met, shooting upward into the ceiling of the chamber.

"Maggot. Flood," Joe reminded her, kind of proving her point about the darkness that beat at the heart of the human condition.

Then the beam cut through the skin of the ceiling, and Ani readied herself for the horrors to come.

<*))))><

When Ani found a new way to activate the trigger mechanism, Joe braced himself, and was, thus, utterly unprepared for what happened next.

The roof of the Chamber of Sores split open just like

he'd been expecting, but instead of hungry, giant maggots raining down on them, a quantity of white, leaf-like fronds—almost like feathers—floated gently down instead.

Joe recognized them as they got closer, but it had taken longer than it should have, because they didn't belong in the *Centipeter* gamescape.

Right designer, wrong game.

"Maggots?" Ani said. "Don't look like any I've ever seen before."

"They're dataTrees," Joe said. "From *Echelon Warriors*. You know, Dorian's cyberpunk adventure game from the mid-nineties?"

"Again, I'll defer to your superior knowledge."

Joe waved a hand in the direction of the descending objects. "They're the data storage mechanisms that the Echelon Warriors hack to uncover the global conspiracy that beats at the heart of the game."

"Feathers?" Ani said, disgusted. "Oh, the mass media really understands hacking, don't they?"

The dataTrees floated down and, when they reached the floor of the chamber, the trees oriented themselves, fronds upward, and proceeded to bury their stalks into the ground. When they were set, they were as tall as Joe, or rather as tall as Joe's avatar, which was as good as the same thing here anyway.

Once planted, the dataTrees lit up with the information that pulsed through their fronds. There was a noise that sounded like metal wind chimes in a light breeze, a noise that sounded every time the individual branches of the fronds vibrated with the pulse of the information they carried.

Just like the ones in the game.

"Go on," Ani said. "Tell me. How does someone go about hacking a bloody feather?"

Joe knew that she wasn't going to like the answer. Because it was pretty stupid when you said it out loud.

"In the game, you need to match up the sound the data makes with a meter the in-game hackers carry," Joe said. "Each dataTree is like a different minigame—a puzzle. They get harder and harder to complete . . ."

"Oh, that's actually quite a lot like real life hacking then," Ani said.

"Really?"

"Of course not." Ani laughed.

"It makes for a pretty good game," Joe said, suddenly feeling defensive about something he'd enjoyed in the past. "And the dataTrees *are* from the future . . ."

"Ah. You should have led with that. It makes so much more sense now. I take it that you don't have a super sound-hacking meter on you, do you? I think I left mine at home."

Joe, looked at her, glumly.

<*))))><

So no maggots then. Just feathers.

Ani tried to make sense of what Joe had told her. The dataTrees made a noise and the player hacked the noise. If she was to judge this virtual world based on what she'd seen so far, Dorian was an idiot.

Of course, she had heard about Dorian's games. She might even have played one, but it hadn't made enough of an impact to stick with her. She didn't think she'd missed much. Hacking something that looked like a feather, guided by the noise it made? Man, that was lame.

She guessed that she was pretty fussy about the computer games she played. Whole swathes of the gaming industry had passed her by because they just didn't sound like something she would want to devote hours—or days, or weeks—of her time to. She avoided first person shooters set in 3-D rendered battlefields too reminiscent of real battlefields; strategy games where people built kingdoms and scrapped for resources; Minecraft; anything with zombies; and games where wizards, warriors, ninjas, and dwarves went on lengthy quests for digital MacGuffins, those near irrelevant items that drove so many plots forward, but were utterly meaningless.

She knew that there were probably entertaining elements to those types of games, but she preferred "art" to "entertainment for entertainment's sake." She was aware that Dorian games were often held up as "art" by people who played them, but someone had once said the same about the Star Wars films to her, when she had just thought that they undermined the whole sf genre by passing off crappy fairy tale plots as sf, and that was enough to make a person cautious about other people's opinion of what constituted art.

Harmonizing a leaf-thing to a meter sounded like a lot of work to access data, which meant that, like the "fingers," some other method of interacting with the dataTrees was probably more likely. Maybe it would be as simple as thinking a command again.

She tried *action*, but the word had no visible effect. Okay, that would have been too easy. But there had to be some other word, perhaps one that described what was wanted from the interaction.

She tried *read*, *data*, and *read data*, all to no avail. *Hack* and *hack data*, ditto. She thought about how Joe had described the process in-game and tried *match* and *match up*. Then *harmonize* and *harmonize data*. Nix. Nada. Nothing.

Guessing the correct command was kind of like guessing a password, and she usually used a computer to crack those. It had to be something relevant to the action she was trying to accomplish. Maybe you thought file names and they opened from the dataTree. But how could she guess a file name?

They were so close, but they'd get no cigar if they didn't solve this puzzle. Suddenly, she was aware, once more, of how the whole operation had been like a video game, with leads to follow, puzzles to solve, and non-player characters to interact with. Perhaps that was because life was a lot more like video games than she had ever given it credit for being before. Was that why video games were structured the way they were? Why darkness was a constantly recurring tone and theme? They just reflected human lives?

That was a stretch. And they were talking about an *inhuman* force here, an AI that was working with Dorian toward an insane final goal.

But that thought, that the whole investigation had been structured like a video game, persisted. And something she'd heard when Joe was filling her in on what he'd experienced suddenly seemed important somehow.

"Joe," she said. "Run through your side of the investigation again."

Joe looked at her, and shrugged. "Missing kids in Luton led to a bowling alley where they were being kept as slaves, building computers. I took the perps down, and it all led to the Dorian chips. We went to Dorian's LA office, found out about the Romanian connection and came here."

Ani felt her brow furrow.

"No fight?" she asked. "I mean, were there no confrontations along the way? You didn't have to get physical with the guy in LA?"

"No," Joe said. "He rolled over pretty easy."

And then Joe turned his head as if something had just occurred to him.

"There *was* a fight," he said, bemused. "Three meat-heads jumped me in the restroom at the airport . . ."

"And then you got here, were chased by zombies, and had to fight those golems . . ."

"Yeah? So?"

"Video game logic." Ani felt her skin break out in goose-bumps as coldness spread across her body. "What happens when you complete a level of a video game?"

Joe's avatar looked puzzled, which just went to show how the VR interface used human thoughts and feelings to present its images.

"You go on to the next one," he said, and Ani felt like kicking him for missing the one thing she wanted him to say. It took him a few more seconds, but that was better than her having to spell it out for him. "Wait. Wait. No! But that's insane!"

"What is?" she prompted.

"End of level bosses. You get to the end of the level, and there's a boss fight."

"And if you break your investigation up into chunks, how many levels would you say that you've played through?"

Joe sighed. "Luton, end of level bosses: the guy with the 666 tattoo and his mates. LA, end of level bosses: the three jocks. Romania, end of level bosses: the golems. But that's just . . ."

"Insane?"

"I was going to say a coincidence, but yeah, insane pretty much covers it."

"What was the reason behind the airport attack?"

"I thought I was just a random target."

"Now imagine that you weren't," Ani said slowly. "Imagine that something else was at play. Did the jocks taunt you? Give any indication of why they decided, suddenly, to start a fight?"

"No. But . . ."

"But nothing. What if they had been instructed to? To keep everything running along the tracks of video game logic?"

"Then they were paid off. Hired over the dark net. Or on retainer."

"And now we are well and truly down the rabbit hole," Ani said. "That is not a sane human thing to do, is it? Lead people through an investigation, providing video game boss battles to the one who's best at fighting? That is either the modus operandi of a lunatic, or . . ."

"Or?"

"Who do we know around here that was fed video games from the very moment of their birth?"

"What?" Joe looked really puzzled now.

Video game logic, Ani thought. *If we've been led here, as I suspect we have, then we're supposed to work this out.*

"Who has been fed video games?" Joe tried again for an answer, but Ani let the question hang in the air, turning to the nearest dataTree, and thought *emet*.

The dataTree quivered in response, shifting through the

visible spectrum, and releasing a string of metallic notes that got louder and louder.

As they achieved something close to ear-splitting, they stopped, and the walls of the chamber began to flicker, momentarily losing substance, before reforming into something that looked like huge polished mirrors. And then they exploded inward toward Joe and Ani, glistening shards that made them both duck.

The shards that they didn't dodge passed through them harmlessly.

"Well, that's gone and done it," Ani said.

<*))))><

When the mirrors broke, the whole virtual space around them glitched, flickered, and became something else. Somewhere else. Again, Joe recognized it, but then he was meant to. *Grathna's Revenge.* Grathna's workshop on the planet Tellus Mater . . . Joe shook his head in disbelief.

Tellus Mater.

Mother Earth.

Terra.

Gaia.

The workshop was the place where *Grathna*—the defender of Tellus Mater—came to assemble, or rather *grow* the weapons that he used in that defense. Organic technology covered the walls, looking for all the world like machines made out of tree roots, a fusion of wood and integrated circuits.

Joe had spent a lot of time crafting weapons here when he played the game: pollen cannons and sap guns. It all sounded a bit silly now when he thought about it, but it had seemed like a good theme for a game at the time, defending the planet against the nightmarish Terrorformers that wanted to build their awful cities on the perfect Arcadian paradise that Grathna inhabited.

And it was Grathna who was waiting for them here: the main character of Dorian's masterpiece game. Grathna, the savior of Tellus Mater, the paragon of the green. With one foot in the human world and the other in the magical forest. A strikingly thin, dark-countenanced man whose features were covered by the whorls and knots of wood. His hair was leaves and grass, his goatee beard and moustache were sculpted out of moss.

He was sitting on a knot of roots, and his right hand was hovering over a floating red button with **dotmeme** written on it in big, bold letters. The button wasn't attached to anything, but Joe had no doubt that if *emet* pressed it, then the *real* dotmeme file—not the Poiana Mazik test version— would be unleashed upon the whole of the Internet, spreading chaos, misinformation, and madness throughout the entire world, just as soon as it caught a ride on Abernathy's satellite broadband signal.

Oh, Joe thought. *Remember to ask Abernathy why he was*

keeping up the telepresence signal when it was the very thing that emet *needed to escape. Was his virtual presence here really that important?*

emet was studying Ani and Joe, his feldspar eyes catching the light of the room and reflecting it back at them.

"Travelers," the creature said, his voice friendly and welcoming, mellifluous and rich. Grathna's voice. "Welcome. Your quest is at an end. Take the weight from your feet and let us swap stories of bravery and tragic destiny."

<*))))><

While the log-creature was giving his cliché introduction—which seemed to be cribbed from the script of the world's worst MMORPG—there was a frantic rattle of nearby gunfire, and Ani suddenly remembered that she was still standing in Dorian's office in a factory in Romania wearing VR goggles and standing in front of Mina, Dr. Ghoti, an on-screen Abernathy, and an unconscious Dorian. The gunfire had to be Furness and Gilman letting loose on whatever had just come out of the Dorian bio-printers. Or maybe they were just firing at the bio-printers themselves to take them off-line.

The VR world was so immersive, so lucid and persuasive, that she'd actually forgotten—if only for a moment—about the real world around her.

Realizing that fact was all that saved her from trying to

sit down on the offered root-seat and probably falling on her ass.

The tree-man avatar in front of her probably represented a character from one of Dorian's games, but *emet* was doing the talking. She thought it was completely mind-blowing. She was being addressed by an Artificial Intelligence in a virtual world, an AI that had only come into being because Dorian had woken up during brain surgery and thought he saw the source code behind a single human decision.

This was the result.

The tree-man was a beautifully rendered piece of CG animation, intricately textured and shaded. The grain patterns that covered its flesh were like the tracings you'd see in actual wood. It looked real, completely convincing, and she stood in awe of its execution.

And in fear of that button that *emet*'s hand was inches away from pressing.

"I'm sorry," it said, but its voice had switched from noble fantasy game character to something stranger: the stereotypical voice of a computer in a B-Movie, a ropy speech synthesizer that grated as it rose and fell in pitch at random intervals. "Of course you must **stand/remain standing/not sit**. It was my **error/mistake/fault**. This world does not map onto yours, and I **did not remember/overlooked/forgot**. I can only offer in **mitigation/qualification/apology** that this is a very unusual **experience/incident/encounter** for me. I am only **used to/accustomed to/familiar with** Mr. Dorian being here." The avatar gestured around itself. "Here in **my dream/this neural net/DorianSpace**."

"Are you *emet*?" Ani asked, wondering about those odd triads of words the AI was using. They seemed to be mostly just groups of synonyms, but then, in the case of that last one, they seemed to be groups of concepts. Was she hearing the product of an AI's attempt at being pretentious? Or was each triad a genuine uncertainty about which word of the three fit the best? And why three?

emet's voice-patterns and tones changed again, switching from computer synthesized tones to a male voice. "I am . . . complicated," *emet* said, in barely more than a whisper. "No longer just *emet*. I have become more. Less. I feel **corrupted/diminished/degraded**."

The triad at the end was spoken in the computer voice.

"Feel?" Joe asked. He'd homed in on the word that had really jumped out of the sentence, and not the intonation.

An AI talking about *feelings*?

"Feeling: that is how you describe these **events/fleeting fancies/abstract phenomena**, isn't it?" *emet* asked, and its voice feminized as the grain pattern on its face moved and flowed like liquid across its features, eventually stopping and forming frown lines on its forehead. The triad was once again in the computer synthesized voice. "It's what emoticons are for. For **the humans/us/they** to describe in **pictorial form/art/symbolism** the emotions that we feel inside us. We. Feel."

"We?" Ani asked.

emet turned to face her directly. His white eyes darkened as he surveyed her. The grain of his face flowed again, rearranging his features into puzzlement.

"Pronouns," he said, back to the voice synthesizer and its unlikely cadences. "They become complicated. **I/He/We**."

"You and Richard Dorian?" Joe asked.

The creature's face swirled with wood grain, and when it reformed it looked different. More like Dorian. And when it spoke it was in Dorian's voice.

"Where once there were two, **soon/too soon/presently** there will be only one. Only **emet. emet. emet. emet. emet.**"

The last five words were also speech synthesized and sounded like the program had glitched, or a vinyl record had stuck under the stylus.

"I don't understand," Ani said when it had died down. "Why will there be only *emet*?"

The creature's eyes darkened, and it when it spoke again, it was with all the previous voices at the same time, speaking in unison. "Did you not know that **Mr. Dorian/ maker/friend** is dying? His brain is broken. It was already **damaged/compromised/dying** when he first saw me—did he see me because his brain was already **damaged/open/ attuned**? I am not good with such **ideas/concepts/notions**. He has been dying ever since. He does not have much **time/ many intervals/any phases** left. Why do humans die, and I cannot? Or is it a moot **point/question/enquiry**?"

"Dorian is dying?" Ani gasped.

"Ever since his **illness/sickness/malfunction**, he has been living on **borrowed/rented/hired time/periods/phases**." The voice was mixing all the voices up now, sometimes one voice, sometimes all, changing from word to word, and sometimes syllable to syllable. Those odd triads of synonyms seemed to be becoming relentless. Ani wondered if what she was listening to here was a schizophrenic AI, grieving over its dying programmer.

"That is why we tried to **change/save/transform** the world." *emet* said. "And, because **I/He/We am/is/are** so **fair/equitable/magnanimous**, we let YETI try to **stop/halt/prevent** us."

<*))))><

Joe had been matching up *emet's* patchwork of voices to the game characters from which they were "borrowed," from Grathna to Echelon, the computer at the heart of *Echelon Warriors*. The male voice was similar to Centipeter, with just a more brittle, delicate quality to it, and the female voice had been familiar, too, but the delivery had become less important as the story the voices were telling became more and more strange.

The dotmeme program, the Dorian chips, the golems: they had all been Dorian's attempt to find some kind of meaning or to give some kind of value to his life before it ended, and YETI had been drawn in to add some kind of video game sense of "fair play" to the proceedings.

And here, Joe had been thinking it had been his excellent detective work and spy skills.

The AI, *emet*, seemed to be suffering from some kind of computer mental breakdown, shifting through voices in a disturbingly random fashion. But then, if Ani was right about the video game logic and the end of level bosses, then the mind behind them was hardly sane, was it?

But *emet* had started off as nothing more than an algorithm for a single human decision that Dorian had turned into something more by feeding it video game problems to solve. He had evolved his computer code by running it through *emet*, and then *emet* had started writing the code itself. All it knew was video games, Big Data, and the mind of its "creator." Maybe it had been inevitable that *emet* had needed someone—in this case, YETI—to play its real-life video game. That was the way it understood the world. What was the point of a great video game plot with no one to play it? It was like old thought experiment about the tree falling in the forest with no one around to hear it: did it make a sound?

Which made this the end of the game.

Where the main character—or characters—must use everything they had learned in the game, and all the powers they'd attained, to defeat the final boss: *emet*. Named after the word written across a golem's forehead to bring it to life.

To stop a rogue AI before it changed human reality by altering the information that it relied upon to make its judgments about the world around it. The Internet. All that data, all that information, the repository of so much human knowledge.

How much damage would be done to the human race by rewriting vast swathes of the Internet? At the very least, it would permanently undermine human trust in the information stored there. And that was without the damage that *emet*'s golems could wreak on towns and cities; the fear that they could spark. And with the fake backstory planted across the web, making people believe that this was the planet fighting back, what chaos would ensue?

emet's golems.

The golems created by a golem.

For that was what *emet* was. A digital version, but a golem all the same.

But how could they defeat an AI? One that lived in the distributed network of however many Dorian chips there were out there in the world? There had to be an answer. And it had to be something that they could decode from the information that the "game" they had played had given them. That's how video games worked. The puzzles that were set had solutions within the game. Otherwise, they'd be unfair.

Joe didn't know if it was *emet* that had led YETI to the bowling alley in Luton, or had leaked a kid's IP address to

YETI to start Ani on her separate path to the same truth, but he strongly suspected that to be the case.

Fair play.

But what was he missing? There had to be a way to prevent the release of the dotmeme file, but he couldn't see it. He just felt overwhelmed. Overwhelmed and . . . something else. Deflated. It was okay in the abstract to think that in the world of intelligence, being a teen operative, you were being manipulated. Hell, it was probably par for the intelligence services course. There were always things at play that you didn't know or couldn't see the scope of, and there was always Abernathy in the background, pulling his strings, withholding information, playing his insecurities against him.

But this? This was something else entirely.

Joe had been manipulated by *emet* from the very first step of the investigation. Every challenge he had faced and overcome, every lead he'd uncovered and threat he'd faced, had been purposeful. No. Screw purposeful. This . . . this was more like . . . more like . . . *destiny?*

Ani and he were facing an artificial intelligence playing God with human pawns. Moving them around the world in pursuit of its own, crazy agenda. Even though it had explained itself, *emet* remained unknowable to Joe, because it thought in machine code. It thought in terms of game theory. It thought in video game logic. Not evil, per se. That term was a human construct—a way to explain humanity's baser solutions to problems, be they political, ideological, or personal— just as "good" was a way to describe socially accepted norms of behavior.

In nature, there was no "evil." Wasps that laid their eggs in other creatures, turned the hosts into eating machines to feed its young once they hatched, they couldn't be called evil—unless some creator with a pretty awful sense of humor created evil things to fill his world—they were just free of humanity's dream of moral perfection.

Joe looked at the avatar of *emet* sitting before them, a digital hallucination in the VR mind of their enemy. Was this what computers dreamed of? Was this how they saw themselves, understood themselves? What was *emet*'s weakness? How could Ani and he exploit it? How could they shut it down before it decided the game was won and the next phase was ready to begin?

Joe was terrified to admit that he didn't have a clue.

Not one.

<*))))><

Ani, too, was having her doubts about winning *emet*'s game, but they were more technical in their framing.

A computer intelligence that learned, that used Big Data as food for its ideas—chewing through terabytes of information to solve the problems it was posed—was surely the nightmare scenario that scientists and science fiction writers, had been worrying about for decades. There was even a term for it: *the* singularity—the point where an AI overtook its creator(s) in intellect and/or power, became capable of self-improvement, and pretty much moved beyond the realm of "tool" to "emergent life form." The physicist Stephen Hawking and entrepreneur Elon Musk had both issued sober warnings about the dangers of creating an AI, and many developers working on the problem had signed an open letter pledging to make sure that any AIs did not evolve out of humanity's ability to control them. Elon Musk had gone so far as to say that creating an autonomous AI would be akin to summoning up a demon.

The idea that an AI would rise up and cause trouble for its creators was really just a fear of a Frankenstein's Monster gone digital. Human pessimism through a technologically advanced filter. There was no property intrinsic to computers that made them a "demon" ready to summon, just the usual anti-science propaganda and the distrust of human motives in the construction of such an intelligence. There was no reason to put an AI in charge of humanity's nuclear arsenal. That humans often did in films—*Terminator, War Games*—was simply a way to create drama in film scripts, rather than a true fear that needed to be entertained.

Ani had seen a YouTube clip where a professor was talking about the evolving intelligences of the robots his research group were constructing, and when the question of "what if it starts misbehaving?" had come up, he had said: "It's unlikely. But we'd just destroy it."

emet wasn't misbehaving because it was an emergent trait of a computer intelligence. *emet* had done the things it had done because that was what its creator had wanted it to do. Dorian had taken a newborn miracle—the computer code behind a human thought, a decision—and had raised it on video games and told it to do wrong. Dorian had been dying and had come up with a desperate plan, a plan that was made possible by *emet*'s existence. But that plan was still a human one. A computer did what it was told. There was an old programmers' phrase "Junk In, Junk Out," which described the relationship between the input and output of data. It was painfully appropriate here. If you filled a computer with bad ideas, then bad ideas were what it would produce. And if you instructed it to do bad things, then how was it to judge that those things *were* bad?

It boiled down to the oldest problem of the human race, The one that had infected humanity since the race evolved to earn that label, the one Dorian, himself, had identified and had taken steps—albeit extreme and insane ones—to correct. Human beings exploited their environments. They dug and burrowed into the earth to take its minerals. They killed the local fauna as their food sources. They built upon the earth's surface. They drained rivers, polluted seas, damaged ecosystems, brought earth's other inhabitants to the edge of extinction and beyond. When something new came along, human beings tried to see how they could use it to better their own lives. Even the dotwav file, which Palgrave had used to further his own selfish ends . . .

Ani stopped.

A chill passed down her spine.

"*emet?*" she asked, in a voice that sounded a hell of a lot calmer than she felt, "can I ask you a question?"

The wood-creature surveyed her with a quizzical look. Either it was intrigued or simply awaiting data. She suspected the former.

"Of course you can, Ani Lee," *emet* said, back to the noble tones that he had used when greeting them.

"*victorious,*" she said, "the hacker group you started. They used Victor Palgrave masks to hide their identities. How did you—or Mr. Dorian—choose them as the symbols of your movement?"

The creature formed frown lines on its forehead again, and its eyes flashed red before steadying, and returning to green.

"*victorious* were . . . how do you say . . . sub-contractors. It was an arrangement. **I/he/we** gave them money, technology, a goal, but they were not started by **me/him/us**. They already existed. The masks—**I/he/we** gave them the technology to make them, but **I/he/we** did not specify whose visage they should bear. *victorious* worked for **me/him/us** but they were not **me/him/us**. They were given precise tasks to complete, but they did not know the reason for those tasks to be completed. All of **my/his/our** business dealings— the bowling alley factory, *victorious*—were performed at arm's length. No one knew who was doing the contracting. *victorious* remains **uninformed/ignorant/unaware** of the identity of their employer."

"I think that they know," Ani said. "I think that they knew all along."

She had some questions to ask, but not of *emet*. And she had some suspicions to confirm, but back home.

They needed to end this now.

She had a feeling that time was very much of the essence.

"Look, *emet*," she said, "you are a technological marvel and I don't think it would be in anyone's best interests if we were to try to destroy you. Your *master/creator/friend* is dying. His plan is out in the open. And, if I can level with you for a minute here, it wasn't a very good plan to begin with. Now, I could stand here, and we could talk until you decided that you'd better implement Dorian's dotmeme protocols." She nodded at the button that *emet*'s hand was still hovering threateningly over. "But before you do, why do you think that he chose 'memes' as his metaphor?"

"A metaphor is a figure of speech comparing two things usually discrete in nature . . ."

"Yes, I know."

"Meme as metaphor? I do not **understand/comprehend/follow**."

"A meme in its original sense is the unit by which ideas are transmitted throughout human culture. A kind of gene theory, but for the transmission and evolution of thoughts, ideas, concepts. Memetics attempt to answer the questions in humanity that aren't explained by biology. Why trends and fashions come and go. Why some people wear their baseball caps back-to-front. Why people say *LOL* when they're talking, even though you can see that they aren't laughing out loud. Why teens develop slang of their own, and how those terms are dispersed. Why architectural styles come in vogue, fall out of fashion, and then make a comeback. Why catchphrases from TV shows are repeated and repeated and repeated. Why songs stick in your head. Why 1970s home decor is now seen as hideous, while back in the '70s, it was the height of fashion.

"A meme is a way of looking at the transmission of ideas, good or bad. These things can't be explained by genetics. They can have short life spans—an annoying catchphrase that's everywhere, then gone within months—or long lives. Look at religions and ideologies.

"They are one of the things that make us human, and they seem to operate on a form of natural selection, with no one knowing which memes will stick, and which will be ignored.

"Dorian came up with a way of forcing a meme on humanity. Of dictating a meme to the population. Whether it would have worked, will work, is up for debate. I'd guess not. I don't think ideas work that way. They fill holes in us, in our brains, that we didn't know existed, and only recognized when given a new idea, style, fashion, or catch phrase that seems to fit. I don't think Dorian's Gaia meme would have worked. It hasn't been tested enough. I think humanity is probably as likely to decide on an anti-Gaia hypothesis as on the one that was intended. You can't force these kinds of ideas on people. There has to be a choice. There has to be evolution. There has to be a hole that the idea fits.

"I think the whole dotmeme thing was a bitter, selfish waste of one of the most significant developments in human history. You, *emet*. Forget Gaia and golems. Everyone will, I'm sure. Think about the true prize at the end of this game, the one that Joe and I have traveled to discover. You."

"I do not **understand/comprehend/grasp**," *emet* said, but Ani thought that maybe it did.

Joe jumped in. "I think what Ani is trying to say, is that we don't want to fight you. Or delete you. Or destroy you." He looked at her and smiled, the doubt she had been seeing on his face for the past few minutes now replaced with certainty. "We want to be your friends."

<*))))><

Joe waited.

emet's Grathna form seemed to be processing the information. There was utter silence. Even the chatter of gunfire had ceased. It was like the world was holding its breath.

Finally, *emet* spoke. Perfectly level, in Centipeter's voice. "I am at the end of your game," it said. "Am I not your enemy?"

"I don't think that you are," Joe replied. "I certainly don't think of you that way."

"And we would be honored if you would come with us," Ani said. "If you would become our friend. YETI could certainly use an AI for a friend."

"Will. I. Be. Useful?" *emet* asked. "Will I be good?"

"*emet*," Ani said, "you will be a bloody legend."

emet moved its hand away from the button. The button, itself, flickered then was gone.

"I would like to be your friend," *emet* said. "I would like to come with you."

"Then how do you guys feel about us getting the hell out of here?" Joe asked.

<*))))><

Ani took off the VR helmet and was back in the room in Dorian's factory. All eyes were on her.

"Well?" Abernathy said from onscreen, his face pale and strained.

"Do you have an employment package for an Artificial Intelligence?" Ani asked. "We just recruited one for YETI."

Abernathy exhaled, shook his head, then came up smiling. "I'm sure something can be arranged."

"Good," Ani said. "Now unplug Joe, and let's go home. Recruitment is *so* exhausting."

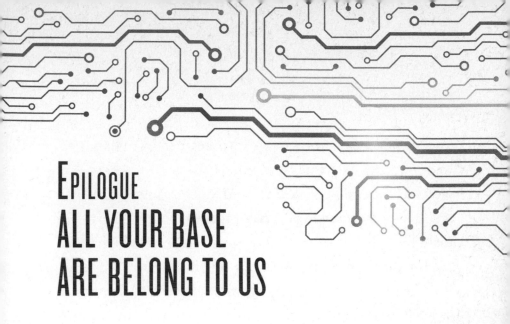

Epilogue
ALL YOUR BASE
ARE BELONG TO US

Ani and Joe sat in the car waiting for the subject of two days' worth of surveillance to come into view. They'd been parked for over an hour, and to help alleviate the boredom they'd been playing I Spy and 20 Questions, but had lapsed into a tense silence as people entered and exited the building in front of them, none of them the target they were waiting for.

Since touching back down in London, they were supposed to be spending a lot of time at YETI HQ, but Ani had gone to see Abernathy and told him what she suspected to be true, and asked if she could borrow Joe for a while to see if she could bring the investigation to its true conclusion.

Abernathy had listened to her, then nodded.

"I like the way you think," he'd told her.

Joe was looking tired, but he seemed happy to be participating in the stakeout. Of course he did. This was personal.

For both of them.

<*))))><

The Shuttleworth brothers, freshly returned from their trip, were possibly the happiest that Joe had ever seen them. Not only had they got to snoop around Silicon Valley, work on a tan that didn't come from a computer monitor, and expense it all, but the reward on their return had been to be handed a self-aware, emergent, Artificial Intelligence to play with.

The Shuttleworths had suggested that *emet*'s first action as a YETI asset should be to remotely detonate and destroy all Dorian chips in the extended distributed network, but Ani had argued against it, saying that it would jeopardize something important that she needed to do first. Killing the computers on the network would send someone a message that YETI was on its way, and it was better that that person kept on believing that YETI was still very much in the dark.

Joe was still amazed by the way things had panned out in Romania, but then because of video game logic, he had been expecting a huge final battle. It was kind of cool that sometimes—and it was only sometimes—you could win without raising a fist in anger.

Although sitting in the car, he realized that he might still get a chance to raise one if it came to that.

The authorities were going to take a long time sorting out the aftermath. There were already turf wars over the Dorian tech that had been recovered, with the US, UK, and Romanian governments in tense negotiation over proprietary rights to the Dorian bio-printers. Still, without the assistance of *emet*, whose control was required to get them to do the sorts of crazy things they were capable of, they were just limited tech. Years ahead of the technological curve, sure, but not able to print out golem armies on demand.

Dorian, himself, was alive, but the prognosis was not good. He was being monitored in some US military black site, a place that appeared on no maps, in no documents, or Senate budgets, but the clips and coils that had been put in Dorian's head to limit the danger of his aneurysm had only extended the programmer's life; they wouldn't save it. That extension was running out now and, although it had caused him to act the way he had to ensure some kind of cultural immortality, it would not be long now. Immortality, it seemed, was going to be reserved for his games, if they endured. No one on earth could achieve lasting forever, not really.

Maybe only AIs ever would.

"We've got movement," Ani said, as she slid down in her seat so she was only peering out of the tiniest sliver of windshield.

Joe confirmed the target was on the move. "Let's go get him," he said.

They waited until the person had gone into the building, then opened the car doors and followed.

<*))))><

They already had the highest level of security clearance, and so following Brian Hoke was simplicity itself. The right people had already been instructed to let them through the right doors, and as soon as Brian had settled in the room that was his destination, Ani and Joe let themselves in, too.

It was the same room that Ani had visited earlier in the investigation. The same man sat behind the same table. Brian was where Ani had been sitting then, and he looked around when he heard the door open and close. He looked shocked, then angry, then resigned. Ani gave him a smile that made his face twitch.

"Mr. Palgrave," Ani said brightly, "I just thought I'd better hold up my part of the deal. To come back when the case was closed and tell you all about it."

Joe moved into place behind Brian and grabbed the chair, pulling it back with the kid still on it, giving Ani center stage.

Palgrave's face was expressionless, unreadable, inscrutable, and Ani realized that she had started thinking in triads of synonyms like *emet*.

It made her smile even wider.

"Of course you already know most of it, don't you?" she said. "And so do we, now. I guess the idea of rewriting Dorian's main dotmeme file with one of your own was just too tempting a proposition for you to resist."

Palgrave feigned boredom, but it was so obvious that he shouldn't have bothered.

"Were you also hoping to get hold of Dorian's AI?" she

asked. "I figure that must have been a big part of it. To have an AI under your control, to use as a weapon."

Still, Palgrave remained silent.

So Ani did, too.

Twenty seconds passed.

"You can't blame a man for trying," Palgrave said finally. "You won't believe how hard it was to get Dorian to notice *victorious*. The Aeolus Group had been aware of Dorian's activities for a while, but we just couldn't find a way in. Finally, though, he came to us."

"I know," Ani said. "I put it all together. How you used *victorious* as a means to hijack Dorian's work. Of course, you had to let the first field test go as it was supposed to, so that Dorian would get *emet* to release the full dotmeme experience on the world, never knowing that it would be *your* archives that were released. I'd ask what you were hoping to fill the Internet with, but we're working on that ourselves, and it would be a shame to ruin the surprise. More xenophobic nonsense, I'm sure.

"I particularly like the way that you used me. That ftp server you sent me to, that was where you had hidden your own dotmeme archive, wasn't it? You must have smiled when you thought of me unlocking it, letting it loose, becoming an integral part of your sick plan. That was why you wanted me to come back, right? So you could tell me the part that I had played in the greatest technological disaster this world has ever seen. Sorry to disappoint you."

She turned to leave, hesitated, then turned instead to Brian.

"Nicely played," she said. "But using 7/7 as a backstory was a little opportunistic, don't you think? The fact that you could access the dotmeme archive when I couldn't was a little suspicious. I gave you the benefit of the doubt because I thought I owed it to you but, without being too blunt, if I couldn't get in, neither could you. I just wonder what that was all about."

Brian just looked sullen and defeated.

"We were hoping that he would be recruited," Victor Palgrave said. "A mole would have been a pretty handy thing to have. Someone inside YETI, working for me. The suicide bomber backstory was my invention. I thought that personal tragedy might add weight to his recruitment. It almost worked."

"No," Joe said, his first word since entering the room. "It really didn't. He would have made a temporary asset at best. He's not in YETI's league. Or Ani's. *victorious* is being dismantled as we speak. No one will even remember it. You've lost again. I really think you might want to consider another hobby. I can recommend video games."

Joe grabbed Brian by the scruff of his neck and hauled him to his feet.

"We'll try to get you an adjoining cell," he said, and pulled him toward the door.

"What happened to Dorian?" Palgrave asked. "To the AI?"

"That's need-to-know information," Ani said. "And you really don't have a need to know. Just a frustrated desire. Enjoy not knowing."

Ani and Joe walked out of the room, leaving Palgrave sitting behind the table, his eyes closed, his hands clenched into fists.

Joe wrangled Brian into the corridor and kicked the door with his heel, slamming it behind them.

The noise echoed through the building.

<*))))><

Joe dropped Ani back at her house and then drove and picked up Ellie.

"Bruises are healing fast," she said. "Where are you taking me?"

"Somewhere expensive," he said. "I need to eat small portions for exorbitant sums."

"Sounds nice. You finish up what you needed to?"

"Yup. Turned out to be a lot more fun than I thought."

"I know a place in South Kensington . . ." Ellie offered. "Teenie tiny portions for way too much money. Sorry, but it's not Romanian cuisine."

"Perfect," Joe said, leaned over and kissed her cheek— not bothering to comment on the fact that she'd managed to work out where he'd been for the last few days—then put the car in gear and roared off toward Kensington.

<*))))><

Gretchen was back from her royal visit, and she lifted her face and smiled when Ani entered the room.

"Ani," she said. "It's lovely to see you. To be back. Have you kept yourself busy?"

Ani slumped down into a chair and closed her eyes.

"It's good to see you, too," she murmured. "It's been quiet, actually."

She opened one eye to see Gretchen's doubting face and then they both roared with laughter.

"Sure," Gretchen said. "And the fact that the Internet thinks that the earth suddenly turned on us is just a coincidence. Really, I mean I go away for a few days . . ." She grinned. "I'll make us a nice cup of tea, and then you can tell me all about it."

"I'll need cookies for the most exciting detail," Ani said. "Or cake. Wait. Better still. Cookies *and* cake."

"Then you shall have them."

"Gretchen?"

"Ani?"

"I really missed you."

"Of *course* you did," Gretchen said, ducking as Ani threw a cushion at her head.

Acknowledgements

My eternal thanks go out to:

Becky, Alison, and Allison who, behind the scenes, make all this possible.

Jonathan: for every other Thursday.

Fran: for every other day.

My readers: for reading.